Selected
A Thriller

by

J. Allen Wolfrum

ISBN: 1981498974
ISBN-13: 978-1981498970

For my beautiful bride

SELECTED

1

Susan Turner looked up through a haze of white dust and saw a group of men in black suits huddled around her body. The muffled ringing in her ears overpowered their voices. The men helped her to her feet and they ran as a group toward the entrance to the underground tunnel. Her hearing slowly returned, screams of panic in the hallway replacing the ringing. As they ran, she recognized the men surrounding her were Secret Service agents.

Four agents surrounded Susan as they jogged through the underground tunnel together. Ten yards into the tunnel, she slowed down. In mid-stride, she took off one heel at a time and returned to the pace of the group. There were no words exchanged; they moved together in focused silence. Four hundred yards down the tunnel, the group stopped at two large steel doors. The lead agent opened the doors and light from the helicopter pad above burst into the tunnel.

Before moving toward the helicopter, the agent standing behind Susan shouted into his headset, "Checkpoint Bravo. Waiting for clearance." He nodded as the response came through and relayed the message to the group: "Let's move." They ran from the tunnel into the daylight and across the tarmac to the open doors of the helicopter.

The agent sitting across from Susan handed her a communications headset. "Ma'am, are you okay? Any injuries?"

Susan wiped the sweat and dust from her face. "No, I'm fine. My family?"

"They're safe. Your children were brought to a safe location under the Pentagon, and your parents are there with them."

She nodded. "Is it over?"

He pursed his lips before responding, "I don't know. I only heard snippets of radio chatter while we were on the way to the helipad."

Susan leaned back in her seat, cupping her hands over her face and replaying the events in her mind. The group stayed in radio silence for the remainder of the brief flight. The helicopter landed at Andrews Air Force Base and the doors

SELECTED

immediately opened. Susan and her security detail rushed across the tarmac and boarded the Boeing 747. She walked onto the plane in her bare feet. Jogging on concrete caused the pinky toe on her left foot to bleed. She left a trail of blood down the center aisle of Air Force One.

2

Eight Months Prior

Susan Turner looked over the helicopter instrument panel at the lush green tree line of the Sawtooth Mountain Range in northern Idaho.

The radio crackled in her headset. "Turner this is HQ. Jacobs is on his way out to finish up your shift. We need you back at HQ."

"Roger that." Susan Turner focused her attention back to the flight gauges and the timber hanging from cables attached to the fuselage of her helicopter. Just outside the drop site, she brought the CH-47 to a steady hover and contacted the ground crew foreman. "Emerson, this is Turner. Waiting for clearance to unload."

The ground crew foreman replied, "This is Emerson. You're clear."

SELECTED

"Roger. After this turn I'm heading back to the airstrip. Jacobs is coming out to finish up the shift."

"Tommy and Greg causing trouble again?"

Nobody could ever accuse her boys of being dull. Susan smiled and half-chuckled to herself before responding, "I think so. Nothing I can't handle."

Susan gently lowered the last log from the hook to the ground. After the all-clear signal from the ground crew, she pulled back on the stick and began the fifteen-minute flight back to company headquarters.

She finished her postflight checklist and walked from her helicopter toward the Bighorn Logging corporate offices. Susan kept her shoulder-length brunette hair in a ponytail and wore jeans with a long-sleeved flannel shirt. Her attempts to avoid unwanted attention from the other pilots and loggers were only moderately successful.

She headed to Mr. Frederick's office to turn in her flight book. In the hallway outside his office, she saw two men in tailored black suits with freshly starched white shirts guarding the door. Susan approached the doorway as if the men didn't exist. The man on the left took a step forward to block the doorway and held up his right hand. "Susan Turner?"

J. ALLEN WOLFRUM

"That's me." She casually pointed toward her eyes with her right index finger. "Eyes up here young man." During her time in the army, she spent the majority of her days fending off unwanted advances. The loggers in Idaho were no better.

The young man's face instantly turned bright red and he stuttered, "Ma'am, General LeMae is waiting for you."

As she walked past the guards into the office, Susan noted that both men were carrying Beretta M9 service pistols inside their suit jackets. Her boss, Mr. Frederick, and General LeMae immediately stood up.

General LeMae casually leaned against the desk; with his khaki pants and blue-checkered flannel shirt, he could have been posing for an L.L.Bean photo shoot. He took the cigar out of his mouth and smiled. "Lt. Colonel Turner."

"Curtis." Susan nodded her head. "I see you're still smoking those Montecristo's. You know they're going to kill you one day."

General LeMae grinned. "They wouldn't dare."

Susan kept a straight face. "I'll bite. What's going on? The file on Mike's death has been closed for years. I'm done talking about it, on or off the record."

SELECTED

General LeMae stared at Susan while he took a puff on his cigar. He exhaled and turned toward Mr. Frederick. "Would you mind lending us your office for a few minutes?"

"Of course, sir," replied Mr. Frederick as he stumbled out the doorway past the security guards. He gave a nervous glance back at Susan as he walked out of the room.

The security guards closed and locked the door, leaving Susan and General LeMae alone. General LeMae walked over to the couch, sat down, and took another long drag from his Montecristo. Susan sat down in the chair across the room and stared into General LeMae's eyes. "Okay, Curtis, enough with the charade. What do you want? This clearly isn't a social call."

General LeMae tapped his cigar and looked out the window. "Susan, I have good news. You've been selected as the next President of the United States."

Susan stared for a moment at General LeMae with cold eyes. She broke the silence. "You know I don't want the job."

General LeMae stood up, walked to the window, and paced back to the door. He turned back toward Susan. "We thought you might have this reaction and that's why—"

"Excuse me? Who is 'we'?"

J. ALLEN WOLFRUM

"The Joint Chiefs of Staff."

Susan snapped back, "Last time I checked the newspaper, you were a former member of the Joint Chiefs of Staff."

General LeMae raised his eyebrows. "True . . . but I don't have to remind you that after the Dove Revolution, the President, the Senate and Congress are selected at random every two years—"

"So you're here to threaten me? Nice, Curtis." Susan straightened her back in defiance.

General LeMae raised his hand in defense. "All right, slow down, no need to get aggressive with me. I was in the room when the random selections to public office were generated and I knew you'd decline. I'm here as a friend."

Susan watched General LeMae pace back and forth across the room puffing on his cigar. Her heart raced. She took a sharp, deep breath and exhaled to regain focus before speaking. "My answer is still no."

General LeMae nodded. "I know you don't need a reminder, but your official decision can't be recorded until September fifteenth, seven days from now. Take some time to think about it. As a friendly warning, this year's selection names are being announced to the public this evening at six p.m." General LeMae thumped the ashes of his cigar onto Mr. Frederick's desk.

"That still doesn't answer the question of why you're here," said Susan.

General LeMae briefly looked down at the floor. He picked his head up and looked Susan in the eye. "I'll be frank. Our relationship with the Soviet Union is headed in a dangerous direction. It's been over a generation since two nuclear powers have threatened each other in such a serious manner. The country needs a real leader. You're the right person for the job and you know it. Don't put that burden on someone who can't handle it." General LeMae paused. He could see the frustration and shock in Susan's face. "When you get your thoughts together, give me a call." He handed Susan a scrap of paper. General LeMae stared out at the airstrip for a brief moment while taking a puff off his Montecristo. He sharply turned and walked out the door and down the hall, followed by his security guards.

Susan sank into the chair and sat alone in the office.

3

On her way to pick up Greg and Tommy from soccer practice, Susan's cell phone vibrated itself from the passenger seat to the floorboard of her truck and settled under an empty McDonald's bag. She wasn't proud of it, but every once in a while she succumbed to a McGriddles sandwich and hash brown for breakfast. Susan turned up the radio to drown out the buzzing and post-McDonald's guilt in her head. Tom Petty blared on the radio.

Susan walked through the doors of the indoor soccer field just in time to see the end of practice. Greg and Tommy were all smiles. Susan wished she could freeze the moment in time. Seeing the joy on their faces made all the hardships worth it. After practice, Susan locked eyes with Greg and Tommy as they walked into the lobby and they came running toward her.

"Mom, you're going to be the president!" shouted Tommy as he reached up to give her a high five.

SELECTED

Greg jumped in. "Do I get my own bodyguard? Do you think they'll let me use those cool earpieces they wear? It's going to be awesome! Are they going to come to school with me? Do you think they'll teach me their cool jiu-jitsu moves?" Greg finally paused to take a short breath.

"Okay, okay. I get it—you're excited. I don't know what any of it means right now."

Without hesitation, Greg started again with rapid-fire questions. "Andrew's Dad said we would have to move to Washington, DC Mom, are we moving? Are Grandma and Grandpa coming with us?"

Tommy chimed in, "I don't want to leave Grandma and Grandpa."

Susan recovered from the initial barrage of questions and regained her command presence. "Boys, that's enough. Grab your bags, we're late for dinner. Grandma made fried chicken, mashed potatoes, and green beans."

"With bacon?" asked Tommy.

"I'm sure Grandma made the green beans with bacon. Grab your bags. Let's go home." Susan could feel the eyes of every person in the arena staring at her as she followed Greg and Tommy out the door.

Susan pulled in the driveway and Greg and Tommy ran screaming across the yard into the house. She walked in the door and was greeted by her mother with a beaming smile.

"Sooo . . . do you have some news you'd like to share?" Rose said.

"Seems like you've already heard the news."

"So when do you start? Did President Wilkes call you yet? I just love watching his speeches. Such an eloquent speaker. And he dresses so nicely. Reminds me of Clark Gable." Rose put her hand over her heart and fluttered her eyes.

Susan interrupted at the first sign of a pause. "Mother. Stop it. You're worse than Greg and Tommy."

"Your father and I are just so proud—"

"Thanks, Mom. But can we eat dinner first? All I had to eat today was a granola bar." Susan stopped her mother before it went any further.

Rose announced to the house that dinner was ready. "Greg, Tommy, Grandpa. It's time for dinner."

Immediately after grace, the conversation turned to Susan's

presidential selection. More rapid-fire questions from Greg and Tommy, followed by well-timed jabs from her mother. After forty years, her mother had not lost the ability to push Susan's emotional buttons in just the right spot.

Susan and her father remained silent throughout the barrage of questions. Greg, Tommy, and her mother seemed perfectly content asking and answering their own questions. Intermixed with the questions was dramatized speculation about how glorious it would be to live in the White House in Washington, DC.

The conversation finally paused. Susan's father, Earl, looked up from his plate, wiped his mouth, and took a sip of water. "So, I take it you're going to decline the selection."

"Earl, how could you say that? Of course she isn't going to decline the selection," said Rose.

Susan spoke up. "You're right. I'm going to decline the selection."

"Moooommmmm!" Greg and Tommy shouted in unison.

"Stop. Everyone calm down. We're just now getting to a good place as a family and we all know that it wasn't easy to get here. I'm not going to ruin it. We're staying right here in Idaho.

In a week, this whole thing will be over." Susan paused and looked around the table. She looked across the table at the boys and continued, "Greg. Tommy. Wipe those frowns off your faces and pay attention."

Greg and Tommy looked at Susan.

"At school there are going to be a lot of questions. Your friends are going to be jealous and they're going to tease you. Remember our talk about how you handle those situations?"

Without hesitation, the boys responded in unison, "Acknowledge, de-escalate, and deflect."

"Perfect. I do not want to hear about you causing trouble at school over this."

"But Mom, are we really not going to Washington, DC?" asked Greg.

"No. We are not. I know both of you have homework to finish. So go make it happen. No stories from Grandpa until your homework is done."

For Susan, Greg and Tommy were a daily reminder of her husband. Greg had his smile, his brains and his short temper. Tommy inherited his dad's tall muscular frame, athleticism, and his golden blond hair. It was impossible for Susan to look at the boys and not see the qualities she loved so dearly about Mike in both of them. Preparing Greg and Tommy for the world and giving them a chance for success was her only remaining goal in life.

Later that evening, after taking a shower, Susan walked over to the shadow box with her husband's army medals and the flag she was given at his funeral. She opened the lid and ran her fingers over each medal in the case. She read Mike's Medal of Honor citation and couldn't stop the tears from streaming down her face. It was the first time she'd had the courage to read it since the funeral.

At a private estate outside of Ouray, Colorado, the group known among their members as the Board gathered for their quarterly meeting. The senior members argued over the results of the random selection for the next President of the United States. The newly appointed chief operations officer, Mr. Anderson, startled the room by taking command of the decision.

His deep bass voice boomed over the group. "I don't know what we're arguing about. Susan Turner is likely to turn down the selection. The Dove Revolution is still on the forefront of the American psyche. If the American public senses any foul play in the presidential selection process, the strikes and riots will start again. And I don't think anyone wants more economic disruption."

A voice from the crowd interrupted, "And if she accepts?"

Mr. Anderson stood up and casually put his hands in his pockets. "She'll play right into our hands without even knowing it." Mr. Anderson responded to several disgruntled murmurs from the crowd. "I can assure you, Susan Turner will not delay our mission. Unfortunately, she will be collateral damage incurred on our path to Unified Peace."

4

On her way to work the next morning, Susan stopped at Calypso's for coffee. She impatiently scanned the room while standing in line. She grabbed for her phone and opened the news app. The screen filled with headlines about her.

10 THINGS YOU DON'T KNOW ABOUT SUSAN TURNER

I MADE MY MOM EXPLAIN WHY SHE THINKS SUSAN TURNER WILL BE A GREAT PRESIDENT

Susan closed her eyes and put the phone back in her pocket. Her attention turned to the man at the register talking to the barista, Claire. The man finally gave up on his awkward attempt at flirting with Claire and Susan stepped up to the register.

"Mrs. Turner? I didn't expect to see you here today."

"Yeah well . . . I still need to show up at work," replied Susan.

"I guess that's true. You know, I just . . . I don't really know how to say it . . . but we're all really glad to have you as our president."

"Thank you, Claire." Susan grabbed her coffee and turned toward the door. She didn't have the heart to tell Claire about her decision to decline the selection.

As Susan walked toward the front door, she noticed two men sitting near the piano in the front lounge area. They looked out of place. The men were in their early thirties with two-day-stubble beards, fresh haircuts, and the build of a Men's Health cover model. They were dressed in what appeared to be standard work clothes for a job site: tan, steel-toed boots, jeans, and flannel shirts. Their boots weren't dirty and no logger wore clean jeans to work. The contrast between their dress and appearance triggered a warning for Susan.

Susan drove away from the coffee shop. In her rearview mirror, she spotted a new white Ford pickup truck pull into the road as she turned the corner. Susan knew she was being followed. She went into survival mode.

Susan drove toward work and took a quick detour for gas.

SELECTED

She looked up from the pump and saw the white Ford pickup pass through the intersection. Her concern shifted to the safety of Greg and Tommy. She dialed her father.

"This is Earl."

"Dad, this is Susan."

"I know who it is. Who else calls me Dad?"

"Dad, this is serious. Did the kids make it to school today?"

"Of course. Why?" asked Earl.

"Do you know for sure? Did you see them go into the school?"

Susan looked up and saw the pickup pass the intersection one block north. They were working a parallel grid pattern. A good technique in a crowded city, but in a small town like Coeur d'Alene it was much easier to detect.

"They were late this morning and missed the bus so I dropped them off myself," replied Earl.

"I need a favor. Do not tell Mom. I need you to go check on Tommy and Greg at school. Make up an excuse. Get eyes on them and stay alert for anything that feels out of place. I think I'm being followed."

"Roger. I'm on it," Earl said as he hung up the phone.

Susan leaned on the truck as she heard the click of the gas nozzle shutting off. She raced through possible scenarios.

Back at the house, Earl walked into the kitchen. Rose stood at the counter emptying the dishwasher. She turned her head toward Earl. "Who were you talking to on the phone, honey?"

"It was the school. Tommy forgot his backpack in the car today. The teacher's assistant called to ask if I would run back to school and drop it off," replied Earl.

"I can do it once I get done with the dishes."

"No, don't worry about it, honey. I need to stop by the hardware store this morning anyway."

Earl walked into the bedroom to get the car keys and his jacket. He opened his top dresser drawer and pulled out an old cigar box. Inside the cigar box was his snub-nosed .38 revolver. He opened the cylinder, checked to make sure it was loaded, and tucked it into his waistband.

Susan pulled out of the gas station and headed back toward downtown. She parked on Fourth street and walked across the street to the Breakfast Nook, a new diner in town. No sign of the white Ford. She walked through the front doors and saw a young woman with a microphone at the counter talking to the owner. Before Susan could turn around, the reporter recognized her.

"Good morning president Select Turner, do you have time to answer some questions? You haven't made a public statement yet. Have you seen the headlines?"

Susan ignored her question. "Have we met?"

"No, I don't believe we have, my name is Brittney Johnston." She shook hands with Susan.

"Nice to meet you, Brittney. Yes, I have seen the headlines. I'd love to talk to you but I left my purse in the car. Let me go grab it, freshen up for the camera, then I'll give you a statement. How does that sound?"

"Of course, I'll get the crew ready." Brittney Johnston was at the Breakfast Nook doing a piece for the morning news about the first restaurant in Coeur d'Alene to offer cronuts on their menu. An interview with the new president Select was a career-changing moment.

Susan walked toward the restrooms and slipped out the delivery door into the alley. She quickly walked for three blocks being careful to not be seen from the street. She came around the corner and took a peek down Fourth street. She saw the white Ford pickup parked next to the curb; it stuck out like a sore thumb. The passenger had his head stuck out of the window and was straining to see the entrance of the Breakfast Nook.

Susan was two blocks behind the white Ford pickup. She quickly moved closer and positioned herself to be hidden from the pickup as she approached. Their reaction under stress would tell her all she needed to know. She walked up to the open passenger window from behind the truck and loudly announced, "Hey there! You look new in town . . . need directions?"

The man in the passenger seat turned around with a startled look on his face. Before he could reply, Susan jumped up on the side step of the truck and leaned her head into the window. "If you're looking for a place to eat, the Breakfast Nook has the best ham and cheese omelet in town and I heard they've got cronuts now."

The driver quickly shot back, "Thank you, ma'am, we'll give it a try."

Susan leaned back and looked the passenger in the eye. "Why are you following me?"

Both men looked at each other but no words came out. Susan saw a Beretta M9 pistol and a radio lying on the console. It was the same type of pistol General LeMae's men were carrying.

"Are you working for General LeMae?" Susan said.

The driver and passenger both looked as if they were being scolded by a piano teacher. Both nodded their heads and replied in unison, "Yes, ma'am." The driver immediately followed up their admission of guilt: "Ma'am, this is our first security detail with the general. I really don't want to go back behind a desk. Have some mercy. Please don't tell the general."

"Aww, aren't you cute? I bet you still wait for Mommy to tuck you in at night." Susan raised her eyebrows right before jumping down from the side step of the pickup. She gave the hood of the truck a quick slap. "Be good boys and don't let me catch you following me again." She shook her head in disbelief as she walked away from the white Ford pickup toward the Breakfast Nook.

Susan felt her phone vibrate. It was a text from Earl. "Boys are fine. All clear." Susan walked into the Breakfast Nook and locked eyes with the reporter. "This is going to be quick. I need to get to work. Are you ready?"

The reporter eagerly nodded her head as the camera and sound men got into position. "Mrs. Turner, how does it feel to be the next President of the United States?"

Susan looked directly into the camera. "Thank you for asking, Ms. Johnston. Although it is a great honor, I will be declining the selection. I have faith that the alternate will carry on the great traditions of the United States of America and lead the nation to a prosperous and peaceful future." Before the reporter could get out another question, Susan turned around and walked out the door. She dug in her purse for the scrap of paper General LeMae had given her and dialed the number.

"This is General LeMae," said the voice on the phone. Susan heard the whistling wind in the background.

"Tell your men to stop following me. I don't appreciate it.

I can take care of myself."

"What are you talking about? My men aren't—"

"Spare me the lies, Curtis. Enjoy your fishing trip and leave me alone." Susan hung up the phone, got in her car and continued her drive to work.

General LeMae turned to his security guard. "Find out who's following Susan Turner. And why."

5

Susan's statement to the local news caused an uproar in the media. Susan and her boss Mr. Frederick agreed it was best for her to take a vacation until the selection process was over. The thought of relaxing at home for the next week was a welcome break from the chaos of the last two days.

The evening after her press announcement, Susan sat down at the dinner table with her family.

"Mrs. Kline said that 200,000 people marched in Washington, DC, to celebrate your selection. Why did you have to tell that reporter you were declining? Why can't you just say yes? Everyone wants you to be the president," Tommy said.

Susan let the silence linger in the air for a moment. "Do you remember last year when you changed positions from striker to midfielder?"

SELECTED

"Yes."

"Why did you switch positions?"

"Because Chris was a better scorer. I was a better passer and defender," replied Tommy.

"Right . . . and?" prompted Susan.

"And it was better for the team," admitted Tommy.

"That's why I'm declining the selection. There is someone else out there better suited to lead. I've done my duty for the country," said Susan.

Rose broke the tension. "Boys, I made peach cobbler for dessert. Help me clean up the plates and you can have some ice cream on top."

Before Rose brought out dessert, the doorbell rang. Tommy sprinted from the kitchen to answer the door. Susan overheard their conversation from the dinner table.

"You look an awful lot like your dad. Are you Tommy or Greg?" the stranger said with a smile.

"My name is Tommy Turner, nice to meet you." Tommy extended his hand.

General LeMae chuckled and shook Tommy's hand. "Nice to meet you, Tommy Turner. My name is Curtis LeMae. Can I speak to your mother?"

"Mom! Mr. LeMae is here to see you," shouted Tommy.

She stiffened in her chair. "Come on in and make yourself at home, Curtis. I'll be right there."

The sight of General LeMae talking with Tommy in the foyer sent Susan's heart racing. Susan hid her panic. General LeMae was a good friend but he also brought with him heavy emotional baggage that she hoped would remain in the past where it belonged.

She walked into the foyer and gave General LeMae a hug.

"Good to see you again, Curtis. What brings you to town? Doing some fly-fishing up at the cabin?"

General LeMae smiled. "You know me too well. I can't resist the challenge of battling those cutthroats on the North Fork."

"Where are my manners? Come on in, Curtis. You're just in time for dessert." They walked into the kitchen and Susan introduced General LeMae to her family. Rose made another plate of peach cobbler with ice cream for General LeMae.

SELECTED

Earl broke the awkward silence after the introductions. "Curtis, you mentioned you've been doing some fishing. Any luck?"

"It's been pretty good. But nothing close to the twenty-five-inch cuts that the locals at the fly shop brag about. You do any fishing, Earl?"

"I did in my younger days. I spent a good many years chasing brown trout. I used to take Susan with me," said Earl.

"Mom, can we be excused?" Greg and Tommy had already finished their dessert and fidgeted at the table.

"Yes, you may. No video games or TV until your homework is done," replied Susan.

The boys jumped up from the table and chased each other upstairs. Earl wiped his mouth and pushed his chair away from the table. "You'll have to excuse me. I'm late for Antiques Road Show. Very nice to meet you, Curtis. It'd be a shame if I don't find out whether poor old Alice's rocking chair is worth ten thousand dollars." Earl grinned and walked into the living room.

"I need to walk off this cobbler. Curtis, would you like to join me?" asked Susan.

"Sure, I could use some exercise. Thank you, Rose. The cobbler was fantastic. I hope my unannounced visit didn't cause you any unnecessary trouble."

"No trouble at all. Any friend of Susan's is welcome here," replied Rose.

Susan and General LeMae walked down the driveway to the sidewalk in silence. Susan turned toward General LeMae. "You better have a damn good reason for coming here. If you wanted to talk to me, you could have called."

"You're right I could have called. But I needed to talk to you in private."

"What's so important? I already told you I'm declining the selection. And I told the world yesterday morning."

"You and your family are in danger. You hung up on me yesterday before I could explain. If you're being followed, it's not by me. I have my men looking into who's following you and why. But they haven't reported back. How did you decide you're being followed?"

Susan's posture and tone moved from agitated to concerned. "Two men in their mid-thirties at Calypso's coffee shop. Looked like former Special Forces Operators. Another team of two in a new white Ford pickup. Following me from a distance using a parallel grid pattern."

"Did you get a license plate?"

"No. But I talked to them. That's why I assumed they were your men."

"You talked to them? What exactly did they say?"

"I caught them by surprise and accused them of being your men because I saw a Beretta M9 on the console in the truck. The same as your security guards were carrying. They're standard military issue but no professional would carry one."

General LeMae interjected, "Pretty weak association. Anything else?"

"Yeah, when I approached their truck, I came up from behind and surprised them. First I asked if they needed directions and I followed up by accusing them of being your men."

"And?" prompted General LeMae.

"They both looked down like they'd been caught by the principal in a high school prank. And immediately begged me not to tell you."

General LeMae frowned and muttered, "Professionals."

Susan nodded. "No kidding. Where do you learn that kind of reaction response and bearing? I surprised them from behind the truck—no way could they have seen me coming. And they both rolled with it."

"Yeah, not good at all. This is a problem. We need to be careful until we figure out who they are and who they work for."

Susan picked up the pace of the walk. She wanted to get back to the house. A feeling of general unease settled into her psyche. "Before I start losing sleep over the men following me, you said there was something else?"

"Susan, you've already given more to this country than the world will ever know. And no person in their right mind would blame you for declining the selection. But you can't. The country won't survive the next year if a truck driver named Andrew Trumble from Woodlawn, Arkansas, is leading our response to the Soviet Union. Can you imagine what would happen if we ended up in a war against the Soviets? The whole world would get dragged into it. Millions would die for no reason. The world would never recover."

Susan slowed the pace of her walk as she talked. "Not

every president has been a great leader. That's why the Joint Chiefs are appointed to span multiple presidencies. There are plenty of bureaucrats in DC who've been there for decades; everyone knows they really run the government. The president is just a figurehead."

"True . . . in the past, that's essentially how it worked." General LeMae stopped at the end of the driveway, turned to Susan, and looked her in the eye. "Over the last decade, Boris Rosinski has been carefully maneuvering to increase the Soviet Union's influence over other countries. The bureaucrats have been lulled into thinking this is business as usual. They don't understand the risk of playing political games with another nuclear power. If things go bad with the Soviet Union, the course of human history could be altered in less than ten minutes."

Susan looked down at the ground before responding. She put her hands in her pockets and kicked at the dirt. "Do you have any proof of Rosinski's plans?"

"What I have is on a flash drive. I can't give it to you. I shouldn't even be telling you about it. It's too dangerous. The drive has documents proving collusion between a large international corporation and several foreign governments. I have copies that will be distributed if anything happens to me.

If the wrong people find out what's on that drive, they'll kill anyone associated. They won't take any risk of the information getting to the public."

Susan nodded her head, beginning to process the gravity of the situation.

"Like I said, think about it. The country needs you." General LeMae's security detail pulled up to the driveway in a black Suburban. General LeMae jumped in the backseat and they pulled away.

6

On September 14, one day before she needed to reach her official decision, Susan folded clothes in the laundry room. Her mother yelled from the kitchen, "Susan, if you get a chance today, can you run to the store?"

"Sure, Mom. I'll go after I finish folding the laundry."

On her way upstairs, Susan set the laundry basket down on the couch next to her father. Earl set up the television in the living room to be a split screen. The conservative station was on the left side of the screen and the liberal station on the right. Both stations showed a picture of Andrew Trumble, the alternate selection for president. Susan's curiosity got the best of her; she had to watch.

The conservative news correspondent interviewed one of Andrew's former army buddies. They'd been deployed to Iraq together. The screen rotated through pictures of Andrew in the army. In every picture, he was either driving a truck or riding in the cargo bay of an airplane—nothing to indicate he'd been involved in any combat operations or held any leadership position. The highest rank that Susan could make out from the pictures was specialist, a junior enlisted rank.

Out of the corner of her eye Susan saw Earl staring at the old family photo with a nostalgic look on his face. "What are you thinking about, Dad?"

Earl smiled. "I was just thinking about when you and your brother were kids. And the summers we spent up at the cabin in Sand Point."

Susan chuckled. "Uggh, the snakes."

"Yup, the snakes. Your brother would torment you with those things. Then you'd come running back to the cabin screaming bloody murder. Scared the hell out of your mother."

Susan shrugged her shoulders. "Hey give me a break, Brad shoved a gardener snake down my shirt. What was I supposed to do?"

"Fair enough." Earl smiled. "Brad has always been a prankster. He sure knew how to push your buttons. Do you remember those games of Risk we played at the cabin?"

Susan gave her father an annoyed look. "How could I

forget? Brad and his freakin' alliances. Right before I had an army strong enough to take him on, he'd form an alliance to stop me. God I hate that game."

Earl laughed. "Yup. Brad knew how to use your stubbornness against you. We had some good times up at the cabin with you kids."

Susan noticed that Earl's emotion quickly turned somber and he stared blankly out the window. Susan left him alone with his thoughts. After a brief moment, he turned his attention toward the television and commented to Susan with a healthy dose of sarcasm, "This guy has everything under control. He's going to put the Soviet Union in their place and make everyone at home rich. We can all rest easy."

Susan felt her father's judgment about her decision to decline the selection to the presidency. "Sure seems like it," she said. She picked up the basket of clothes and walked upstairs to her bedroom. Folding the laundry could wait. She opened her laptop and typed "Andrew Trumble" into Google. The first result was his Facebook page. Susan clicked on the link.

Susan scrolled through his Facebook timeline. Andrew Trumble enjoyed posting ridiculous conservative memes with pictures of Chuck Norris, Clint Eastwood, and Ronald Reagan.

Andrew Trumble's posts didn't show any indication that he was married or had children. Susan discovered Andrew's army job was 88H—Cargo Specialist. She continued looking through his photos. Andrew's post-military life revolved around four wheeling, fishing, and water skiing. He still lived in his hometown of Woodlawn, Arkansas, about forty minutes east of Little Rock.

Susan went back to her Google search. A message board link came up as the next result. Andrew Trumble's screen name was oathkeeper71. He was an active commenter, or depending on your point of view, an internet troll. Based on his comments, Andrew frequently participated in a thread titled "Preppers Unite." The thread focused on theories describing how the next apocalypse would happen and techniques for surviving the impending collapse of the United States.

Her mother shouted, "Susan! Are you still here?"

Susan ended her online stalking and met her mother in the kitchen. "Mom, what do you need from the store?"

"Nothing urgent. But we need more milk, bread, and turkey for sandwiches," said Rose.

"Okay, I got it. Practice ends at four thirty, right?" asked Susan.

SELECTED

"You got it. Dinner will be ready when you get home."

As Susan walked by, Rose gently grabbed her shoulder and gave her a hug. "Honey, I don't care if you decline the selection, I just want you to be happy."

Susan rested her head on Rose's shoulder. "Thanks Mom. You know I wouldn't have made it this far without you and Dad. I just want to do what's right for Tommy and Greg."

A tear welled up in the corner of Rose's eye. "We will always love you and the boys."

"Mom . . . I've already given so much. And we've worked so hard to get back to a stable place. I just can't throw it all away, not again." Susan tightened her grip around Rose.

Rose kissed Susan on the cheek. "I know, honey. I know."

Later that afternoon, Susan walked through the entrance of Pilgrim's Market. She put in an order for a pound of sliced turkey at the deli counter. "I'll take the same," said a voice behind Susan. She turned her head to put a face with the voice.

Standing behind her were the two men from the white

Ford pickup. Susan's heart raced. She felt her face turn red. Susan quickly closed her eyes, took a deep breath, and turned to face the men. "Gentlemen, you don't look like you're from around here. On vacation? Or here for work?"

"Vacation, ma'am," replied the man on the left with a smile.

Susan interrupted before they could elaborate. "Let me guess. Fly-fishing."

The man on the right replied with a sinister smile. "I guess we're not the first out-of-town fly fishermen to visit Coeur d'Alene. We must stick out like a sore thumb."

Susan turned back toward the deli counter and the clerk handed her the sliced turkey. Susan walked away and went down the aisle toward the exit. Her heart felt like it was about to explode; she couldn't catch her breath. Midway down the aisle, she stopped to gather her thoughts. Over the last few days, she'd forgotten about the men following her in the white Ford pickup. The last thing she expected was for them to approach her in a public place. Susan looked down the aisle and saw the men approaching.

The man on the left grinned. "It's a shame about Ms. Kline. I hope she feels better."

SELECTED

Susan's panic turned to anger. "What are you talking about?"

"You know Ms. Kline, right? Tommy and Greg's English teacher. She's out sick today. She'll be fine in a few days, it's probably just the flu. A friend of ours is substitute teaching for her. He's a really nice guy and great with kids." Both men abruptly walked past Susan toward the exit.

For a brief moment, Susan stood frozen in shock. Then she reached in her coat pocket for her cell phone. It wasn't there; she'd left it in the car. Susan dropped her basket in the aisle and rushed out to her car.

General LeMae leaned on the hood of Susan's car in the parking lot. He saw the panic on Susan's face as she briskly walked toward the car. "What's wrong?"

"The men from Calypso's coffee shop — the men in the white Ford pickup who followed me — they're here and they have Greg and Tommy."

"No they don't."

Susan opened the door of her car. "They just told me someone from their team was substitute teaching for Greg and Tommy's teacher. We need to get to the school immediately."

General LeMae gently put his hand on the door. "They lied to you. Agent Edwards is at the school. Ms. Kline is teaching English class today. There is no substitute teacher. Our last check-in was five minutes ago, Greg and Tommy are sitting in English class with Ms. Kline. Agent Edwards has eyes on them right now. They're safe."

Susan shook her head. "Why are you following me? Are you sure Agent Edwards is okay?"

"Yes, I'm certain. I found out more information on the men following you. You were right, they're former Special Forces Operators, but they aren't dangerous. They're hired thugs."

Susan interrupted, "Hired by who?"

"Are you familiar with Pacific International?" replied General LeMae.

"No. Should I be?"

"Most people don't know the name Pacific International, but you'll know the names of the companies they own: Chase Bank, Boeing, Lockheed Martin, General Electric, Exxon Oil, AIG Insurance, and American Aluminum, just to name a few."

Susan furrowed her brow. "I don't get it. Those are the

biggest companies in the world. They're all owned by a single company? What does that have to do with me?"

"It's complicated, but yes. The consolidation happened a few years ago. There was no media attention; the structure of the deal allowed all the subsidiary companies of Pacific International to keep their status on the stock exchanges. In the eyes of the public, nothing changed and there was no need for media coverage."

"Okay, I get it, big companies. Get to the point. What do they want with me?"

"Although you may have put the selection out of your mind, the world hasn't. You're still the primary selection to be President of the United States. And whether you like it or not, the person sitting behind the desk in the Oval Office is the most powerful person in the world. I have a feeling they don't want you in that chair."

"What does me being the president have to do with Pacific International? I'm not putting the pieces together," said Susan.

"You haven't been watching the news."

Susan shook her head. "No, I've been intentionally avoiding it."

"Andrew Trumble is getting a large volume of positive press from conservatives and liberals. The media might love him but he's no match for Boris Rosinski and the Soviet Union. Boris Rosinski is going to manipulate Andrew Trumble into making some horrible mistakes, and once public opinion gets behind the war machine, it's impossible to stop."

Susan fidgeted with the car keys in her right hand. "But what about the Joint Chiefs and the other advisors?"

"The Joint Chiefs and most of the other permanent advisors are former or current military generals. When difficult decisions need to be made, men fall back to what they know. If you ask a military man to solve a political problem, he will choose a military solution ten out of ten times. When all you have is a hammer, everything is a nail," said General LeMae.

Susan crossed her arms. "Wait a minute. You think Pacific International wants Andrew Trumble as president because he can be manipulated by Boris Rosinski? And somehow that's a positive for the company?"

"I know it sounds far-fetched."

Susan rolled her eyes. "Sure does." She opened the car door and got inside. "I'd love to stand here and talk geopolitics with you all afternoon, but I'm going to check on my boys."

SELECTED

Susan quickly closed the car door and drove away to check on Tommy and Greg.

7

Susan woke up to the buzzing of her alarm at 6:30 a.m. on September 15, the day of her official decision. She went through her morning routine and mentally linked together her schedule for the day. Take the boys to school, go to City Hall, get next week's work schedule from Mr. Frederick, pick up dry cleaning, and return a dress at Kohl's for Rose. If everything worked out, she would have enough time to get it all done and still make it home in time for a game of checkers with Earl before dinner.

Susan walked downstairs into the kitchen. The rest of the family was almost finished with breakfast. Before she sat down at the table, Rose snapped at Susan.

"Susan . . . Elizabeth . . . Turner. You cannot wear jeans and a flannel shirt to the presidential selection ceremony. Do you want the entire world to think you were raised without any manners?"

SELECTED

Susan snapped back at her, "Mom, this isn't going to be a news event. The press won't even be there. They're all focused on Andrew Trumble."

"I don't care. The President of the United States of America is a position that deserves respect," said Rose.

Susan knew her mother was correct. She didn't put much thought into what was going to happen at City Hall in a few hours because she'd already made her decision. It didn't matter; there wasn't time do her makeup and put on a suit. She was already going to be late dropping the boys off at school. Susan deflected her mother's concern. "You're right, Mom. I'll figure something out. Greg, Tommy, finish up your breakfast. We're going to be late for school."

The boys both nodded as they drank the last bit of milk from cereal bowls. Susan checked the clock in the car as they pulled out of the driveway: 7:15 a.m., just enough time make it to school before the late bell. Before they pulled into the school parking lot, Tommy asked, "Mom. What was Dad like?"

Susan paused before answering. "You haven't asked about your dad in a long time. What made you think about him?"

Tommy replied, "I was sitting on the couch with Grandpa yesterday watching the news and they were showing pictures of you and Dad in your army uniforms. I don't really remember him. I've seen pictures of him holding me and Greg but I don't remember much else. Just him pushing me on a swing."

Susan fought to hold back tears. "Well . . . your father would be very proud of you boys." She pulled into the school parking lot and the boys jumped out of the backseat. Susan rolled down the window and shouted, "Greg . . . Tommy!" Greg and Tommy turned around. "I love you." The boys replied in unison, "Love you, too, Mom," and ran toward the school doors.

Susan pulled out of the school parking lot and headed toward City Hall. A sign for Memorial Gardens on the opposite side of the road grabbed her attention. Her hands began to shake and she stopped breathing. Susan pulled into the next neighborhood side street and stopped the car. She closed her eyes and took three deep breaths. She regained control of her breathing, opened her eyes, and drove back to the cemetery.

Two large brick stanchions and an iron gate marked the entrance to Memorial Gardens Cemetery. Beyond the entrance there were five large sections separated by tall pine trees. In the middle of the cemetery grounds stood a United States flag surrounded by flags representing each branch of the military. At the far end of the cemetery, memorial walls stood as tributes

SELECTED

to the lives lost in military conflicts.

Susan parked next to the memorials at the far end of the cemetery and walked toward the Global War on Terror memorial. She found the section of the wall titled Operation Iraqi Freedom - OIF. The names engraved on the wall were listed in alphabetical order. Susan found her husband's name, Lt. Colonel Mike Turner, United States Army, Combat Aviation Brigade, 1st Cavalry Division. Her eyes welled up with tears. She pressed her lips to the cool marble and kissed her husband.

Susan regained her composure to find two more names on the wall, Captain Joshua Tilmore and Captain William Henson. The world closed in around her as the memories came back. After leading her squadron through the toughest and deadliest fighting since the Vietnam War, Susan left the combat zone to train new helicopter pilots.

Two weeks after returning stateside, two of her best friends, Captain Tilmore and Captain Henson, were killed flying a solo support mission for an infantry raid. Official protocol stated that only one helicopter was required to support an infantry raid. As squadron commander, Susan never allowed her pilots to fly solo missions. Far too many times she'd seen the enemy try to lure helicopters into dangerous situations. Susan knew the only way to safely operate was in teams. She never forgave herself for leaving her squadron during combat operations. She lived with the memories of their funerals every day. The memories of what could have been, distraught widows, and fatherless children. Not a day went by without thinking of them. The regret hung around her neck like a noose.

Susan stumbled as she stepped back from the wall. She steadied herself and continued reading each name on the memorial. The thumping sound of the flags waving in the wind brought Susan back to the present. She took a long deep breath, turned to look at the memorial wall one more time, and walked back to the car.

As Susan pulled out of the cemetery, she looked down at the clock on her dashboard: twenty-six minutes before the recording of her official decision at City Hall. Not enough time to change clothes. The world would have to see her in jeans, a flannel shirt, and a ponytail.

Susan walked through the front doors of City Hall with a sense of purpose. Reporters swarmed around her shouting questions. A man in a black robe introduced himself as the official selection judge. "Hello, Mrs. Turner, we've been waiting for you. Follow me." Susan followed the man past the media circus into a room with a large oak desk, four leather chairs, and a couch.

"I apologize for being brief out there. I'm not much of a media person and we don't have much time. My name is Judge Mickels."

Susan shook hands with Judge Mickels. "Susan Turner, nice to meet you."

"Are you familiar with the selection process?"

"I am not. What do I need to know?"

Judge Mickels explained, "Well, actually not much, it's a brief process. We will both walk out together to the podium in the foyer. I'll read from the official selection document. The last paragraph will be a question for you: Susan Turner, do you accept or decline the selection to the office of President of the United States of America? There are two options for your response. You can say, 'I accept' or 'I decline the selection.' "

"That's it?" asked Susan.

"Yup, that's it. After your verbal decision, we will both sign the formal documentation on camera. I have 8:26 a.m. on my watch so we should get going. Are you ready, Mrs. Turner?"

"I think so. Let's make it happen." Susan smiled and followed Judge Mickels out of the office back into the media frenzy. Susan and Judge Mickels stepped up to the podium in the foyer of City Hall. On queue, at exactly 8:30 a.m., Judge Mickels read from the presidential selection document. Susan strained to keep her focus. Finally he said her line. Judge Mickels boomed, "Susan Turner, do you accept or decline the selection to the office of President of the United States of America?"

Susan locked eyes with Judge Mickels and replied, "I, Susan Turner, accept the selection to the office of President of the United States."

Inside the Pacific International headquarters, the CEO, Mr. Anderson, leaned back in his chair and smiled. It was all coming together as planned. Mr. Anderson had commissioned a group of psychologists to analyze Susan's medical and military history. He knew Susan Turner better than she knew herself. Her personality and background were the perfect fit to assist in implementing the Board's strategic goal of Unified Peace.

8

Susan walked down from the podium and the crowd quickly overwhelmed her with congratulations. Her heart raced; she felt boxed in and the fear showed on her face. She didn't know how to process the barrage of questions. She repeated the phrase, "Thank you, I'm honored," in response to every question. Judge Mickels quickly rescued Susan from the crowd and escorted her back to the office where they met before the ceremony.

Judge Mickels chuckled. "That wasn't what I expected."

Susan shrugged her shoulders. "Me, either. Thanks for getting me out of there. I didn't know what to do besides smile and say thank you."

"Yeah, I could see the panic in your eyes. Reminded me of witnesses on the stand for the first time."

Susan sighed. "Well . . . it's been a long day."

Judge Mickels laughed. "President Turner, it's not even 9:00 a.m. The day just started."

Hearing the phrase "President Turner" for the first time shocked Susan. Judge Mickels gently put his hand on her left shoulder. "Why don't you take some time to collect your thoughts. I'll get the bailiff; he'll escort you past the crowd to your car. I'll be right back."

The bailiff escorted Susan down the hallway, past the crowd, and out to her car. Susan drove out of the parking lot past a crowd of reporters flowing out of City Hall. Susan wondered if her parents and the boys heard the news. She needed to get home.

Rose greeted Susan at the front door with a hug. "I'm so proud of you, honey. But I really wish you had worn a suit," Rose said with a smile.

Susan smiled back at her. "Thanks, Mom. Is Dad home?"

"He's out in the garage. I'm sure he's expecting you."

Susan opened the door to the garage. The radio blared Shania Twain singing "Any Man of Mine." Earl was measuring a piece of oak for his latest cabinet project. He saw Susan from the corner of his eye. Earl pulled the pencil from behind his ear and marked the piece of wood and yelled over the music, "If I knew the leader of the free world was stopping by, I would have cleaned up a little. Come on in, Madam President." Earl smiled and turned down the radio.

Susan walked over to the workbench, wrapped her arms around her father's shoulders, and gave him a hug. A tear ran down Earl's cheek. He squeezed Susan tighter and gave her a gentle pat on the back with his right hand.

"Dad . . . I just couldn't . . . I couldn't live with myself if I turned it down."

"I know, sweetie. You did the right thing."

Rose walked into the garage holding the house phone. She looked as giddy as a teenager talking to her first high school crush. "Susan, President Wilkes is on the phone for you."

Earl grinned. "And it begins."

Susan took the phone from her mother. "This is Susan Turner."

The voice on the phone boomed, "This is President Wilkes, congratulations."

"President Wilkes, I'm honored. I didn't expect to hear

from you so soon."

"I have to say — I'm as shocked as the rest of the country. I'm glad you took the job."

"Thank you, Mr. President."

"The White House will be sending a team of six staff members to Coeur d'Alene to help you with the transition. I know it's a lot to take in, but don't worry, the team will take care of everything."

"Thank you, Mr. President, I can use all the help I can get."

"Before I let you get back to the celebration — my staff alerted me this afternoon that several members of the press have copies of your medical records. I don't know how long it will be before the news goes public," said President Wilkes.

Susan took a deep breath and straightened her back. "Good to know. I appreciate the warning."

"It's the least I could do. I'm looking forward to meeting you in person. Take care Susan, and again, congratulations."

Susan heard a click as President Wilkes hung up the phone. Susan needed time to come up with a strategy. Defending her reputation in front of the world wasn't a part of her plan when she left the house this morning.

"Words of encouragement from the president?" asked Earl.

Susan sighed. "Yeah, and some insider information. I knew this would happen eventually. But the press got a hold of my medical records."

Earl looked Susan in the eye. "Hmpph. Well . . . you know what you have to do."

Susan nodded her head in agreement. The last thing Susan wanted to do was talk about her past in front of the world. She lived with the emotional scars every moment of every day. Talking about it made the pain more difficult to deal with.

The doorbell rang. Rose answered the door. It was a county sheriff, Jim Simpson. Rose looked past Sheriff Simpson and noted the growing number of news vans and reporters on the street.

"Good afternoon, Sheriff. What can we do for you?" said Rose.

"Ma'am. is Susan home? I'd like to talk to her about the press outside on the street. The situation is starting to get out of control."

Susan heard the conversation from the garage and walked to the front door to introduced herself, "Hi, Sheriff, Susan Turner. What can I do to help?"

"Ma'am, the reporters out there are awfully anxious to talk with you. I'm concerned they're going to start knocking on doors in the neighborhood. The last thing we need is some little old lady waving around a shotgun and yelling at the reporters on her lawn," said the sheriff.

"Understood. Do you happen to know if there are any reporters from the local news station?" asked Susan.

"I believe I saw Brittney Johnston from KXLY and her crew out there," said the sheriff.

"Great. Will you do me a favor and walk with me out to the street and help me find her?"

"No problem," replied the sheriff.

Susan followed Sheriff Simpson down the driveway and out to the street. The closer they got to the street the more distinct the shouts became.

"President Select Turner, what are your goals for your first one hundred days in office?"

SELECTED

"Have you spoken with Andrew Trumble?"

"What made you change your mind?"

Sheriff Simpson put the bullhorn up to his mouth. "President Select Turner has a statement she would like to make. Is Brittney Johnston from KXLY here?" The crowd quieted to whispers. "Brittney Johnston KXLY, right here, Sheriff," shouted a voice as Brittney emerged from the crowd.

Susan spoke over the crowd. "I know everyone has questions for me. I'm going to answer them all together this afternoon. Ms. Johnston, can you set up a space for a Q&A session at the station?"

"I'm sure we can figure it out."

"Thank you. I'll see you all at the KXLY station in two hours," said Susan.

The crowd of reporters erupted in questions. Susan walked back up the driveway to the house.

9

The staff working at KXLY rushed to modify their local morning news set into a town-hall-style news conference. The desk normally used by the morning news anchors was replaced with a podium. Chairs and microphones for the reporters were placed in front of the set. While the reporters waited for Susan's arrival, they scrambled for background information on Susan and speculated about her past.

Susan walked through the front doors of the KXLY station headquarters five minutes early. An exciting news day in Coeur d'Alene was a new restaurant opening or the high school football playoffs. An exclusive press conference with the president select was the most high-profile event they'd ever hosted. The station manager greeted Susan with a warm smile and quickly escorted her to the green room.

Susan sat alone with her thoughts in the green room. She

paced the room nervously with hopes of putting together a coherent story in her mind. Susan struggled with how much information she should give to the press. The last thing she wanted was to bring up painful memories for Greg and Tommy. Susan fought back from a dark place in her life to provide stability for the boys. She feared her past would follow Greg and Tommy for the rest of their lives.

Brittney Johnston opened the door and interrupted her manic pacing in the green room. She quickly sensed the intensity in the room and nervously announced her presence: "Madam President?"

Susan quickly turned toward the door. She recognized Brittney and relaxed her posture. "Hi, Brittney, is it time?"

Brittney explained the situation to Susan. "It's up to you, but the equipment is ready. We're using the morning news set—you have a podium in the center of the stage. The press have chairs and microphones set up in front of the podium."

"Do you know how many press members are out there?" asked Susan.

"I'd say about fifty total people including camera and sound crew. Most of the major media outlets focused their attention on Andrew Trumble in Arkansas."

J. ALLEN WOLFRUM

Susan couldn't stand to be alone with her thoughts any longer. "No time like the present. Let's head out there."

Brittney led Susan out of the green room, down the hallway, and onto the local morning news set. Susan walked to the podium. The room went silent and the reporters focused their cameras on her approaching the podium. Susan stepped up to the podium and briefly paused to scan the crowd. She took a deep breath and then surprised the audience by grabbing the microphone out of the stand and walking in front of the podium to address the reporters.

"Today I made history. I was the first woman ever . . . to accept the presidential selection in jeans and a flannel shirt." The entire room including Susan burst into laughter. "If any of you were wondering . . . Yes, my mother absolutely did yell at me when I got home." Susan and the crowd laughed again. She paused to let the laughter die down. "On a more serious note, I want to address some of the questions you have for me. My decision this morning was a surprise to many people. I'll save everyone at home the effort of Googling my name." Susan paused to catch her breath. "I'll keep it brief; I have a hard time talking about myself. As I assume you already know, I was born and raised here in Coeur d'Alene. My dad is an army veteran and a retired electrician. My mother is a retired second-grade teacher. I graduated from Coeur d'Alene high school, then went on to college at West Point where I met my husband. After West Point, I spent twelve years in the army as an Apache helicopter pilot. I have two children, Greg and Tommy, both at Coeur d'Alene middle school. Since I left the army, I've been working as a helicopter pilot for a logging company." Susan paused. The reporters listened silently.

"Just in case you got the wrong idea . . . I'm not perfect. In the third grade, on the playground at Skyline Elementary, I pulled Jill England's hair and got suspended for two days. If you're watching, sorry about that Jill." Susan and the crowd chuckled. Susan smiled and squeezed the microphone for safety. "Well, that's the end of my prepared material. Who has questions?"

The reporters in the crowd all shouted questions at once. Susan responded to the first question she could identify: "When did you decide to accept the nomination?"

"Great question." Susan looked down at her watch. "About four hours ago." The reporters chuckled. Fear of a tougher question to come prompted Susan to expand her answer. "When I found out about the selection, my immediate reaction was to decline. We've all seen what the stress did to past presidents. And I have two boys who need the full attention of their mother. This morning I was forced to face the reality of avoiding my duty. I couldn't tell Greg and Tommy that I declined to serve my country. Declining the presidency and putting that burden on another person's shoulders would have haunted me for the rest of my life."

The crowd erupted with questions again. Susan responded to the question, "How does it feel to be a single mother and president?"

"Well, I haven't been sworn in as the president yet. Check back with me after the first six months in office. In response to the single mom part of the question: without my parents to help, I doubt I would have made it this far, and I'm sure I'll be leaning on them for the next two years as well."

The next question from the crowd was, "How do you think your mental condition will impact the decisions you make as president?"

Susan knew the question was coming, but it still caused her to freeze on stage. While Susan paused, the room filled with a moment of silence, then a hushed whisper of questions. Susan's suit felt as if it was being compressed around her body like a straightjacket. She cleared her throat and removed the heavy silence from the room.

SELECTED

"The short answer is — it won't." Susan paused and looked out into the audience. "I see a lot of confused looks in the crowd. Clearly that question didn't come out of the blue. For those of you who haven't yet received a copy of my medical records, let me get you up to speed. Six years ago I was admitted as an inpatient to the psychiatric ward in a VA hospital."

"Oh, my gosh," a reporter in the front row gasped.

Susan responded, " 'Oh my gosh' is right. I would use more colorful language to describe that period of my life . . . but that's about how I feel when I look back on it now. Toward the end of my career in the army, I was diagnosed with post-traumatic stress disorder and clinical depression. In retrospect, I should have sought treatment long before that point, but I was too proud to ask for help. The stress of being involved in consistent combat operations, being away from my children, and then my husband's death pushed me to a very dark place. I lost faith in myself to climb out of the darkness." Susan paused to let her words sink in.

Susan's words weighted the air with a somber fog. A follow-up question from the crowd broke the silence. In a humble tone, almost a whisper, a reporter asked, "Are you cured?"

"Am I cured?" Susan repeated. She paused to contemplate the answer. "For me, I don't think a cure is the right way to think about it. I firmly believe I can mitigate the impact on my life but the memories never go away. Alongside many others, every day I struggle, every day our past tries to knock us down, and every day we fight back. Some days we win, some days we get knocked down. On the days we get knocked down, we get right back up and continue fighting. Back to your question: Am I cured? No . . . but I will always have the willpower to press on. I will always get back up."

Susan's response shocked the reporters into whispers among themselves. There were no more immediate follow-up questions. Susan took the opportunity to gracefully end the press conference by thanking the station employees and reporters in attendance. She walked off the stage wondering if she had done irreversible damage to her family, herself, and her country.

10

After the press conference, Susan picked up Tommy and Greg from school. She saw the excitement in their faces as they ran toward the car. The boys jumped into the backseat and immediately began to pepper Susan with questions.

"What happened, Mom?"

"Yeah, Mom, I thought you were declining the selection."

"When are we moving to Washington, DC?"

The questions came at Susan without a pause for her to respond. The boys wouldn't have listened to her responses anyway. They were caught up in the excitement of being the center of attention at school. Susan continued to quietly listen to questions from Tommy and Greg in the backseat.

"Are we really moving to Washington?"

"I heard the teachers talking at lunch, they said you're crazy. Mom, are you crazy?"

Susan pulled into the driveway. "Enough." Her tone immediately stopped the stream of questions from Greg and Tommy. "Yes. I am going to be president. No. I don't know if we're all moving to Washington, DC." The boys were more relentless than the press. It felt like having two caged lions in the backseat jumping around.

Greg and Tommy asked legitimate questions. Susan's presidential inauguration was one month away and logistics were the furthest thing from her mind. But she knew one thing: she wasn't going anywhere without her boys. Susan's body froze and she stopped breathing as her mind looped through all the horrible scenarios that might happen to her boys if she left them behind. She inhaled sharply and it broke her out of the negative thought pattern. She reminded herself, "one day at a time." Her hands turned white from clenching the steering wheel with all her strength.

Susan walked inside and found Earl and Rose in the living room. Earl sat in the recliner with his feet up and his face buried in a Louis L'Amour cowboy novel. Rose sat on the couch knitting an afghan blanket. Susan sat down on the couch next to her mother; neither Earl nor Rose seemed to notice her arrival. Susan announced, "I'm going to take Greg and Tommy with me to Washington, DC."

SELECTED

Earl lowered his glasses and peered at Susan over his book. "Why?"

"Because I'm their mother and I'm not leaving them."

Earl pushed back, "Seems like something you should have thought about before you took the job. Did you ask Greg and Tommy what they thought?"

Susan's frustration quickly came to the front of her emotions. "No . . . I didn't . . . they're eleven years old. They don't have a say in the decision."

Earl remained calm. "I think it's a mistake. The boys just started the school year. All their friends are here. That much change is going to be traumatic for them."

Susan paused to interpret the frown on her father's face. "Are you pushing back because you think it would be bad for Greg and Tommy? Or because you don't want to go?"

Rose tried to calm the building tension between Susan and Earl. "Your father and I discussed it earlier today. The boys have a nice stable environment here in Coeur D'Alene and they can focus on being children. We don't want them to be burdened by a new environment. Changing friends at their age can be traumatic. We just want what's best for the boys."

Susan looked toward her father. "Dad, I assume you feel the same?"

Earl sighed and set his book in his lap. "Honey, we love you and the boys. You know that'll never change. We want what's best for the boys. And right now, things are as good as they can be. We think it's too risky to take them out of an environment where they're comfortable and happy."

Susan nodded her head in agreement. "I understand."

Susan got up from the couch and slowly walked into the kitchen. She opened the freezer, hoping to find a pint of Ben and Jerry's Red Velvet Cake ice cream. No luck. She settled for some frozen Tag Along Girl Scout Cookies. Susan sat down at the table to contemplate the situation over milk and cookies. She split the Tag Along's into two bites, letting the peanut butter and chocolate melt in her mouth, with a gulp of milk to wash them down. Susan rocked the glass of milk around on the table as she thought about the situation. She wasn't leaving Greg and Tommy behind. After two cookies, Susan walked back into the living room with a handful of Tag Alongs in her left hand and a half glass of milk in her right hand.

Susan stood in the living room looking at Earl. She had a mouthful of cookie when he moved his gaze to meet hers.

SELECTED

They locked eyes and Susan took a gulp of milk. Susan looked Earl in the eye and shouted, "Greg. Tommy. Come down here, we need to talk."

Susan watched Earl squint his eyes in what appeared to be a mixture of annoyance and frustration. She heard two bedroom doors slam shut and the pounding of feet on stairs echoing through the living room. Greg and Tommy bounded into the living room.

"What's going on, Mom?" asked Greg.

Susan focused her attention to Greg and Tommy. "I want to talk to you about my presidency. After the inauguration, I'll have to move to Washington, DC. I can't stay here. What do you think about moving with me?"

Greg and Tommy immediately gave each other a high five and yelled, "Awesome!"

Susan looked at Earl and smiled.

The boys went right back to their rapid-fire questions about DC and the White House. Susan had to cut them off. "I get it. I get it. You're excited. We're not leaving for another month. There's plenty of time to figure it all out."

After Susan's interruption, the boys focused their fire hose of questions on their grandpa.

"Grandpa, remember the show we watched about elephants? We can go see the elephants at the Natural History Museum," said Tommy.

"And then we can go to the spy museum," said Greg.

Tommy followed, "It's going to be awesome. At the Air and Space Museum we can fly in a rocket ship."

Greg and Tommy moved closer to Earl and their questions kept coming.

Earl finally relented and replied with a sigh, "Okay, okay . . . boys, that's enough, we can do all those things when we get there." Earl's answer diverted Tommy and Greg's attention. They chased each other upstairs to continue researching Washington, DC.

Susan took another bite of her Tag Along, washed it down with a gulp of milk, and walked back into the kitchen.

Earl sighed and returned to his cowboy book, but he couldn't hide a small smile. Rose smiled and went back to knitting her afghan.

11

President Wilkes walked off the stage to standing ovation after his keynote speech at the UNICEF fundraiser. He resembled a Hollywood leading man more than a former high school teacher. During his term as president, his looks combined with the stage presence he acquired as a high school teacher made him a great asset to fundraising campaigns.

As a high school teacher he was self-conscious about the image he presented to his students. He maintained a strict diet, rigorous workout regimen, and fashionable wardrobe. During his first few years of teaching, he took motivational speaking courses in the summers to learn how to present his course material in a way that was interesting and compelling for his students.

As president, his policy decisions were not always well received by the public, but he was the most likable president in recent memory. In the media, he was consistently compared to president John F. Kennedy.

After dinner at the UNICEF fundraiser, President Wilkes walked toward the cocktail bar in search of a glass of water. A man dressed in a well-tailored dark blue suit, white shirt, and red tie followed him to the bar.

The man in the dark blue suit caught President Wilkes's attention at the bar. "President Wilkes, that was an inspirational speech."

Before turning to look at the man President Wilkes replied, "Well, thank you." He then turned and extended his hand to the man in the dark blue suit. "Nice to meet you."

"Nice to meet you as well. My name is Mr. Jones, I work for your friend Mr. Anderson. He asked me to send his regards."

President Wilkes instantly stiffened his easygoing demeanor but stopped himself before alerting the Secret Service agents watching him. He smiled and patted Mr. Jones on the shoulder as if they had known each other for years. "Ohh really, I haven't had a chance to talk with Mr. Anderson in a while. How's he doing?"

"He's doing pretty good. His kids are both out of school

now and he's been enjoying the freedom, spending more time at the ranch with his horses."

"Sounds like he's living the good life, if only we all were so lucky." President Wilkes chuckled. "Any friend of Mr. Anderson's is a friend of mine. Come with me, let me introduce you to some of the event organizers." President Wilkes patted Mr. Jones on the shoulder again and walked toward his Secret Service detail who watched closely for any suspicious activity at the event.

President Wilkes made eye contact with the Secret Service agent in charge and gave him an inconspicuous friendly half wave, as if he was greeting a friend across the room. This was a signal President Wilkes worked out with his security details early on in his presidency. The signal indicated that he needed a moment alone with whoever was accompanying him at the time.

President Wilkes navigated through the crowd toward the restroom with Mr. Jones following behind him. Down the hallway toward the restrooms, President Wilkes slipped into a door with the nameplate Astoria Conference Room. Mr. Jones followed. He closed the door and sharply turned toward Mr. Jones.

President Wilkes put his finger in Mr. Jones's chest. "What the hell are you doing here? I've done everything you people asked of me. I made it clear you were never to contact me again."

Mr. Jones put both hands up in the air. "Whoa there, stud . . . calm down, this is a friendly visit. There's no reason to get upset."

"You call threatening me at a charity event a friendly visit?"

"Who's threatening you? Certainly not me. Do I look like an enforcer? I'm just a messenger."

"Okay messenger, what's your message? I don't have all day, the Secret Service is going to be suspicious if I'm gone for too long."

"Watch your tone." Mr. Jones paused and stared down at President Wilkes. "I assume you've seen the news? The new president, Susan Turner. We need you to keep tabs on her."

"You mean kill her?"

Mr. Jones shook his head in dismissive confusion, then laughed. "What? Who do you think you are? James Bond? No . . . I want you to do exactly what I said. Keep tabs on the president: I want to know who she meets with, and I want to know what she's planning behind closed doors. That's it . . . for now."

President Wilkes took a step back from Mr. Jones and shook his head. "You have to be kidding me. I'm not going to be your personal spy in the White House. Not after what I already did for you. My debt is paid."

Mr. Jones took a quick look toward the entrance to make sure they were still alone and moved two steps closer. President Wilkes bumped against a stanchion while backing away. "I'm trying to be polite, but I don't think you understand. That wasn't a request, it was an order . . . Mr. President."

President Wilkes tried to hide his fear with aggression. "You can't threaten me like that. I'm not going to be a part of this." He turned away and took a step toward the door. Mr. Jones shrugged his shoulders in frustration, then violently grabbed President Wilkes by the shoulder and shoved him against the wall.

Mr. Jones felt the fear quivering through President Wilkes's shoulder as he spoke. "I think you lost your mind. Let me help you find it. You're going to gain the confidence of Susan Turner and you're going to keep a detailed log of her activities. And you're going to do it without her finding out.

Understood?"

President Wilkes reached down and found a sliver of backbone. "I already told you, I'm done with you people. Tell Mr. Anderson to find another lackey to carry out his orders."

Mr. Jones nodded his head and sighed. "You must enjoy torturing yourself. I'll be even more direct Mr. President. You remember the videos we have? You know, the ones with you and your students?" Mr. Jones paused as he watched President Wilkes's face turn gray. "Ohh fantastic . . . you do remember. What do you think they do to people like you in jail, Mr. President? That's if you make it that far." Mr. Jones paused again.

President Wilkes slouched against the wall. "Fine, I'll do it."

Mr. Jones smiled. "Good. I'll consider your apprehension a failure to communicate on my part. Thanks for the constructive feedback. We're going to make a great team. For now, all you need to do is keep a log on Susan Turner. We'll arrange a weekly drop. Do you think you can handle that?"

President Wilkes sighed. "Yeah, I can do that."

Mr. Jones slapped President Wilkes on the shoulder and

SELECTED

smiled. "Cheer up, mate. You'd better get back to the fundraiser. I'll be in touch." Mr. Jones left the room and walked out the back entrance of the building.

President Wilkes straightened his tie, wiped the sweat from his forehead, and walked back out to the fundraiser crowd with a smile.

After Mr. Jones exited the building, he pulled out his phone. After two rings he heard the voice on the other end of the line.

Mr. Anderson answered, "Hello."

"This is Jones."

"Was the message delivered?" replied Mr. Anderson.

"It was. It took some convincing to get him to see things our way. But I think it'll work out."

Mr. Anderson replied, "Good, keep eyes on him. Continue the surveillance and check-in protocols until otherwise notified."

J. ALLEN WOLFRUM

"Roger that." Mr. Jones calmly walked back to his car and continued planning his strategy for surveillance on President Wilkes.

12

In the days after Susan accepted the selection, the briefings preparing her for the transition to the Oval Office were overwhelming. She spent most of her time with the transition team from the White House. They set up a temporary office in the Coeur d'Alene City Hall.

The thought of President Wilkes staying in her administration as the vice president eased many of Susan's concerns. The presidential selection came with a four-year term: two years as the president and the following two years as the vice president. The selected representatives in the Senate and Congress got off easy, only serving two years.

Three days before Susan and her family were scheduled to leave for Washington, DC, she finally caved into the media pressure and agreed to be on a fifteen-minute segment for CNN news. The segment would be hosted by two news anchors from CNN, Megan Richards and John Fritz. The panel consisted of Susan, whom the media labeled a conservative, and the Idaho senator select, Ethan Reynolds, who was labeled a progressive liberal by the media. Senator Ethan Reynolds was also from northern Idaho; the local Coeur d'Alene news station hosted the taping.

Susan arrived at the station and was greeted by two men from the CNN news team. They escorted her into a green room by herself and told her to expect the live segment to start in about five minutes.

Left alone in the green room, Susan ran through a series of terrifying questions she might be asked. She wondered why they didn't put her and Ethan Reynolds in the same room. After less than five minutes of waiting, a CNN crew member opened the door to the green room and escorted Susan out to the set. She saw Ethan Reynolds for the first time as they walked out to the stage. Susan noted his dark brown hair and sharp blue eyes. He dressed much better than any man she had ever met from Idaho. Susan self-consciously smoothed her blouse and straightened her posture.

Ethan extended his hand with a warm smile. "Ethan Reynolds. Nice to meet you, Madam President."

Susan smiled and shook Ethan's hand. "Susan Turner, nice

to meet you. I'm still not used to being called Madam President."

"I'm a little nervous. How do you think this will go?" asked Ethan.

"I have no idea. I assume they'll talk over us, try to get us to say mean things to each other, then talk about it for another week straight. Shouldn't be anything to worry about."

Ethan put his right hand on his abdomen. "Tell that to the butterflies fluttering around in my stomach."

The television crew's countdown interrupted their conversation. The light on top of the camera went red, indicating they were live.

Susan tried to appear relaxed while Megan Richards led the segment with an introduction. "President Select Turner, Senator Select Reynolds, thank you for taking the time to be on the show this evening. John and I are honored to speak with you."

"Thank you, it's an honor to be on the show," said Susan.

Ethan followed. "Thank you, glad to be here."

"We don't have much time, let's dig right into the issues.

President Select Turner, we haven't heard much from you. How is the transition process going?" asked Megan Richards.

"Thanks for asking. Things have been hectic, which is why you haven't heard much from me lately. The transition process has been overwhelming, I couldn't do it without President Wilkes and the White House staff."

John Fritz chimed in with the next question. "President Wilkes started his presidency with a very high approval rating, but recently it has been abysmal. Many Americans are very disappointed in this administration's recent hawkish stance on military aggression. Ethan, you're seen as a devout liberal. How do you feel?"

"Well, John, thanks for asking my opinion. I think President Wilkes is trying to do the right things. I'll save my opinion until I get my feet firmly planted on Capitol Hill."

Megan Richards turned the question toward Susan. "President Select Turner, how do you feel about a strong military stance against the Soviets?"

"As president, I'll do everything in my power to protect the United States and our allies. I'm in full support of the policies and tactics President Wilkes and his team have put in place."

SELECTED

"President Select Turner, wasn't your husband killed during combat operations in Iraq? And it has been rumored that Soviet Special Forces were responsible for his death. Don't you think we need a strong military response?" asked Megan Richards.

Susan searched for a response, but her mind went blank. The information about Mike's death and their mission was classified. She could feel her heart beating. She grabbed the chair for security; but couldn't force words out of her mouth. After the awkward pause, Susan regained her composure enough to stammer, "I'll evaluate all possibilities once I have all the information."

Megan Richards followed up with another question before Susan could regain her composure. "President Select Turner, can the American people really expect you to make decisions impacting national security while you're suffering from post-traumatic stress disorder and depression?"

Susan froze again. She couldn't get her thoughts untangled. Her instinct was to go on the offensive and she went with it. "My medical history has no place in this discussion."

Susan saw the smirk on Megan's face and feared the worst. She knew her aggressive response would be turned against her by the veteran news anchor.

Just as Megan Richards was about to pounce on Susan, Ethan immediately spoke up to rescue her. "That's a great point, Megan. Soviet involvement has been escalating and we need to take appropriate measures to respond. I've spent some time in the Soviet Union. I'm sure you know, my family owns Reynolds & Mitchell, a global shipping company. Growing up around the family business, I've heard many discussions about the current hot spot of Ukraine."

John Fritz jumped in to take over the conversation. "Ethan, what is your role in the family company? Seems like a conflict of interest to be an owner of a global shipping company and a senator responsible for foreign policy."

"I'm glad you asked, John. I currently have no role in Reynolds & Mitchell. I worked there after I got my bachelor's degree for about a year. Umm . . . let's just say it wasn't the right fit for me." Ethan smiled.

The rest of the conversation was focused on Ethan Reynolds and his family. Ethan's family was well known by the general public; there were several extremely successful people in his immediate family who were at one time in the media's

SELECTED

focus. The shipping company Reynolds & Mitchell was accused of smuggling illegal oil and natural gas out of war-torn countries. Ethan's uncle operated a hedge fund that was accused of manipulating currencies within the European Union. His family history provided no shortage of targets for the news anchors, and Ethan intentionally led them down every rabbit hole to kill time. Finally, the red light on the camera turned off. Susan stared blankly at the camera in shock of what just happened.

Ethan Reynolds broke Susan out of her own thoughts. "I'm sorry about dominating the interview. But I couldn't let them attack you like that. Once they started in on my family . . . well, you know, there's lots to criticize."

Susan quickly shook her head. "Thank you, Ethan. I wasn't prepared to talk about myself. I figured they would try to put us against each other about policy questions. I didn't think they'd go straight into attacking me."

"At least it's over. We survived to fight another day."

"Seems like it."

Ethan shot Susan a flirtatious smile. "I have to get going,

but you owe me."

"Owe you?"

"Yeah, you owe me dinner. I'll even let you pick, French or Italian."

Susan rolled her eyes and laughed. "All right, Senator Reynolds . . . I'll see you in Washington."

13

The morning before the inauguration ceremony in Washington, DC, a Secret Service motorcade escorted Susan and her family to Spokane International Airport. The entire forty-five-minute ride to Spokane, Greg and Tommy peppered the two Secret Service agents with questions. The agents responded kindly to the nonstop questions, but it was obvious they were not prepared for the intensity of two eleven-year-old boys.

The motorcade rolled onto the tarmac at Spokane International Airport. The boys' attention diverted to Air Force One and the accompanying F-16s flying security overhead.

Greg pointed toward the sky. "Mom, are the jets flying with us the whole way to Washington?"

"They sure are."

Tommy tugged Susan's shirtsleeve. "Mom, did you fly one of those planes in the army?"

Susan kept her gaze into the sky as the F-16s faded into the distance. "No, but I would talk to them on the radio during our missions."

Greg asked, "Mom, did you have a call sign?"

Tommy echoed the question. "Yeah, Mom, what was your call sign?"

Susan chuckled and hesitated before answering, "I did. My call sign was Razor."

"That's the coolest call sign ever, can we call you Razor?" asked Greg.

Susan laughed, "No you absolutely cannot call me Razor. Go ahead and get on the plane."

The boys ran off toward the boarding ramp. Susan shook her head and could not help laughing to herself. The boys would not have been as impressed if she told them the story of how she got the call sign Razor. Susan's leg-shaving routine tended to be less frequent than socially acceptable and the guys in the squadron definitely noticed.

SELECTED

After boarding Air Force One, Susan took Greg and Tommy up to the cockpit. The pilots gave them a tour of all the gauges, radar, and radio equipment. The boys had a blast asking questions and watching the pilots show off the gadgets in the cockpit. The pilots even let the boys listen in on the radio chatter.

While walking back to their seats in the main cabin, Susan pulled Earl aside. "Dad, do you mind keeping the boys occupied on the flight?"

Earl chuckled. "Sure . . . but they seem to be doing a good job of making those Secret Service agents think long and hard about whether they want to have kids."

Susan smirked. "Yeah, I got that impression, too. There will be plenty of time for the boys to ask them questions. I don't want to wear out our welcome on the first day."

Earl laughed again. "No problem . . . I'll see what I can do."

Susan used the six-hour flight to work on her inauguration speech. She'd failed to prepare for her last two public appearances; her inauguration speech might fall flat but it wouldn't be due to a lack of preparation. She had no doubt about her ability as a leader, but public speaking was a beast she had yet to tame.

They made it to the White House too late in the evening for the full tour. Mason Adams, Susan's chief of staff, met them in the White House foyer and promised to introduce her to the rest of the staff after the inauguration. Susan and the family were more than happy to skip the official tour and get some sleep. After a quick security brief, the Secret Service agents escorted them to their bedrooms. Susan settled into the president's bedroom, Earl and Rose in the Lincoln Bedroom, and the boys occupied the West and East Bedrooms across the hall from Susan.

Susan's alarm woke her up at 6:30 a.m. She took a shower, got dressed, and went downstairs for breakfast. Susan walked into the dining room and saw a breakfast table filled with smiles and laughter. Rose exchanged recipes with the kitchen staff, Earl had his morning newspaper, and the boys were practically jumping out of their chairs when they discovered the White House had a swimming pool, movie theater, and bowling alley.

Susan interrupted the chaotic chatter at the breakfast table. "I'm glad you're all excited about the White House. But we need to talk about my speech today and the logistics afterward."

"Am I going to be on TV?" asked Greg.

"Great question. Yes, we'll all be on TV. You don't have to do anything special, just stand up straight and pay attention while I talk. Grandma and Grandpa will be right there with you." Greg and Tommy nodded.

Susan explained the logistics for the day. "After my speech, we'll watch the parade together, then you'll come back here with Grandma and Grandpa. I'll have to go to work afterward."

Tommy asked, "After the parade, can we go bowling?"

"Sounds good to me. Grandma and Grandpa will be here—make sure you let them know where you are at all times, just like back at home, understood?" The boys nodded.

Susan stood up from the table. "I need to work on my speech. I'll see you at the ceremony. Greg, Tommy, don't pester the Secret Service agents, we don't want them to quit on the first day." Susan smiled at the boys and raised her eyebrows toward the agents in the room.

The boys replied together, "Okay, Mom."

Later that day at the inauguration ceremony, Susan Turner stepped up to the podium and recited the oath of office.

"I, Susan Turner, do solemnly swear that I will faithfully execute the office of President of the United States, and will to the best of my ability, preserve, protect, and defend the Constitution of the United States."

Immediately following the ceremony, Susan addressed the world for the first time as President of the United States of America.

"Fellow citizens of the world, I am humbled by the importance of the tasks we will accomplish together. Allow me to quote from former president John F. Kennedy's inaugural speech in 1961. His words ring as true today as they did in

SELECTED

1961.

" 'Let every nation know, whether it wishes us well or ill, that we shall pay any price, bear any burden, meet any hardship, support any friend, oppose any foe, in order to assure the survival and the success of liberty.'

" 'This much we pledge—and more.'

" 'To those peoples in the huts and villages across the globe struggling to break the bonds of mass misery, we pledge our best efforts to help them help themselves, for whatever period is required—not because the Communists may be doing it, not because we seek their votes, but because it is right. If a free society cannot help the many who are poor, it cannot save the few who are rich.'

" 'To that world assembly of sovereign states, the United Nations, our last best hope in an age where the instruments of war have far outpaced the instruments of peace, we renew our pledge of support—to prevent it from becoming merely a forum for invective—to strengthen its shield of the new and the weak—and to enlarge the area in which its writ may run.'

" 'Finally, to those nations who would make themselves our adversary, we offer not a pledge but a request: that both sides begin anew the quest for peace, before the dark powers of destruction unleashed by science engulf all humanity in planned or accidental self-destruction.' "

The crowd responded with patriotic applause. Susan continued her speech by praising the previous administration and their accomplishments. The crowd and the world cheered as Susan turned and walked away from the podium. Walking through the crowd backstage, Susan heard the roar of applause from the crowd. The feeling of pride in herself and in her country rushed over her like a waterfall.

SELECTED

14

Following the inauguration ceremony and parade, Secret Service agents escorted Susan to her first presidential daily briefing. The presidential daily briefing is a mandatory daily meeting prepared by the CIA specifically for the president. The president, directors of the CIA, NSA, and FBI, and the Joint Chiefs of Staff are present for the meeting. In accordance with the presidential transition protocol, Vice President Wilkes accompanied Susan to her first presidential daily briefing.

Susan walked into the John F. Kennedy Conference Room, known publicly as the Situation Room. The chairman of the Joint Chiefs of Staff shouted, "Attention on deck," and everyone in the room snapped to their feet with their hands at their sides in the position of attention.

Susan responded out of instinct, "At ease." She felt right at home. This was just another military officer's meeting. She'd led these types of meetings hundreds of times as a squadron commander; this one would be no different.

Susan looked around the room and recognized Arianna Redmond, the first female director of the FBI. Director Redmond became a public figure during the presidential scandal that began the Dove Revolution. She led an investigation that found the President of the United States guilty of colluding with government officials from North Korea and China for personal gain. She became a figurehead for the Dove Revolution and earned the admiration of the world for her integrity and ethical standards. On the surface, Director Redmond looked like a kind and gentle grandmother, but she did not suffer fools kindly. During the height of her celebrity, several television news anchors made the mistake of underestimating her intellect and found themselves on the receiving end of her sharp wit.

After Susan and the other members of the Joint Chiefs of Staff took their seats, the chairman, General Gillingham, began the meeting. "Thank you, Madam President, we're all honored to serve in your administration."

Susan responded, "And I'm humbled to have all of you in my administration. Vice President Wilkes did an amazing job during his tenure as president. I can only hope to bring as much honor to the office of the president as he did." Susan paused and nodded toward Vice President Wilkes. "Let's get to work—I don't want to waste your time."

General Gillingham continued the meeting. "Madam President, there are several news items on the agenda today and one action item. Would you prefer the action item or the news items first?"

"Let's start with the news."

"There is only one news update on the agenda for today. The CIA confirmed reports that Soviet Union soldiers are posing as Ukrainian soldiers in the Ukrainian civil war."

Susan nodded and asked a follow-up question. "Are there any other indications of Soviet involvement in the Ukrainian civil war?"

"Yes, Madam President. We believe the Soviets are supplying arms to the Ukrainian separatist movement and they're also using cyber warfare tactics to sway public opinion in favor of the separatist movement. The details are in the folder behind the agenda. Would you like me to walk through them?"

"No, that won't be necessary. I don't want to hold up the

meeting. Let's move on to the action item."

"In August of this year, President Wilkes authorized the use of a Special Forces reconnaissance team at the Ukrainian border with the Soviet Union. The team was tasked with reconnaissance on the border crossing. Yesterday the team reported a large movement of Soviet tanks and artillery across the border, disguised with Ukrainian markings. The Soviet soldiers are also using Ukrainian uniforms and equipment." General Gillingham paused to look down at his notes. "The team on the ground is requesting authorization for a covert air strike targeting the Soviet tank and artillery units. Two weeks ago, we presented this potential scenario to President Wilkes and he preauthorized an air strike in response. Madam President, do you we have your approval to move forward with the air strike?"

Susan looked toward Vice President Wilkes and then General Gillingham. "In the past, have we conducted air strikes directly on Soviet troops?"

General Gillingham didn't let the silence linger. "No, we have not. This would be our first overt response to Soviet aggression. The air strikes will not be traceable to the United States. The equipment and soldiers are disguised as Ukrainian; it would appear that the air strike is a part of the Ukrainian civil war. The team on the ground would be responsible only for target identification. They would not be directly involved."

Susan turned again toward Vice President Wilkes. "And you previously authorized an air strike in this scenario?"

Vice President Wilkes cleared this throat. "I did. This is our best option; we can't sit back and let the Soviets invade NATO-protected countries." Vice President Wilkes paused to gauge Susan's reaction. He saw a glimmer of confusion in her expression. He continued his explanation to drive home the point. "The Soviets want to control the natural resources in the Ukraine. Crimea is a peninsula in the southern Ukraine, there are natural gas and oil reserves off the coast of Crimea in the Black Sea and the Sea of Azov. If the Soviets gain control of Crimea and the Ukraine, they'll own the existing natural gas and oil pipelines that lead to Eastern Europe. In short, the Soviets would own the entire fossil fuel supply chain for Eastern and Central Europe. And we believe this will lead to a forceful expansion of Soviet control in Eastern Europe."

Susan nodded and paused to contemplate the scenario. "How much time do we have before the tanks and artillery move out of range?"

General Gillingham replied, "Based on our latest

intelligence, we have a forty-five-minute window for the decision to be made."

Susan settled into the rhythm of the meeting. She folded her hands on the table, leaned slightly forward, and calmly looked around the room.

Susan directed her question toward General Gillingham. "What is the expected enemy casualty count?"

General Gillingham replied without hesitation and without looking at his notes. "Seventy-five. Along with human casualties we expect to destroy two Giatsint-B 152 mm howitzer artillery pieces, one T-90 tank, and three BTR-80 armoured personnel carriers."

Susan quickly responded with a follow-up question. "What is the risk of detection for the troops on the ground?"

"Our team is in a concealed location. The risk of detection is close to nonexistent."

Susan looked around the table. "Is there anyone here who opposes the decision to move forward with the air strike?"

Around the table, everyone replied without hesitation, "No, Madam President."

SELECTED

Susan looked directly at General Gillingham and gave the order. "General Gillingham, you have my authority to initiate the air strike."

General Gillingham picked up the receiver to the secure telephone line on the conference table and dialed the Joint Special Operations Command post to authorize the mission. He hung up the line and informed the room, "The drone will be on station in less than two minutes. The video will be on the monitors any second."

Every eyeball in the room fixated on the monitors showing a live feed of the drone's targeting system. The screens showed a grainy black-and-white aerial video of what looked like farmland mixed with trees and gently rolling hills. At the center of the screen were white crosshairs moving toward a section of wooded valley. Susan could make out the shapes of artillery pieces, vehicles, and troops moving around on the ground.

Susan sat silently in her chair, fixated on the monitor. Suddenly the screen flashed white from the impact of the first missile from the drone, followed quickly by several more flashes. The screen came back into focus, the artillery pieces, tanks, and personnel carriers replaced by black splotches and gray smoke. Next to the personnel carriers, the dead bodies looked like dark sticks spread on the ground.

General Gillingham nodded his head while listening to the after-action report on the secure phone line. He hung up the phone, sat up straight, and turned toward Susan.

"Madam President, the mission was a success. All rounds landed on target."

The room erupted in applause. Susan calmed down the rowdy cheers and ended the meeting. Before leaving the Situation Room, every general and director shook Susan's hand and expressed their gratitude for her leadership.

Susan and Vice President Wilkes walked down the hallway of the White House after the meeting. When they were alone, Vice President Wilkes commented, "You're really making me look bad—I was a wreck in my first daily briefing. I thought they were going to fire me."

Susan shrugged her shoulders. "I spent my army career in those kind of meetings. Feels like home."

15

The next morning, Susan's chief of staff, Mason Adams, waited in his office for her to arrive. Mason tapped his pen on the desk and watched the clock. At 8:10 a.m., his patience ran out. He left his office and went looking for Susan. He found her in the White House lobby chatting with General LeMae.

President Turner and General LeMae both looked at Mason as he approached. Mason quickly addressed General LeMae with a nod of his head. "Good morning, sir." Mason quickly moved his attention toward Susan. "Madam President, I believe you're late for a meeting. Please come with me."

Susan exchanged a glance with General LeMae and rolled her eyes. "My presence has been requested. I'll see you around."

Susan turned and caught up with Mason in a few steps. "Mason, I'm sorry about being late. General LeMae and I are old friends. We needed to catch up."

Mason didn't acknowledge her explanation for being late. "Today you've got a full schedule. Did you get my email with the itinerary for the week?"

"I think so."

Mason continued, "Have you prepared for the secretary of state briefing?"

Susan hesitated. "Umm, I think I saw the meeting on the agenda email you sent—"

Mason cut her off. "In my itinerary summary emails, the meetings with read-ahead materials are highlighted in red. Links to the read-ahead files are listed as bullet points under the meeting time and location. In the meeting description, you'll find the agenda and meeting administrator. Any questions or concerns about the agenda are to be sent to the meeting administrator directly."

Susan raised her eyebrows. "Okay, good to know. I'll look at it in more detail when I get to the Oval Office."

Mason continued his lecture as they walked. "The itinerary for the next day arrives on your cell phone at 4:00 p.m. each day. The daily schedule includes forty-five minutes for lunch and two fifteen-minute breaks throughout the day."

"All right, umm . . . what's on the schedule this morning?"

"This morning, you're late for your 8:00 a.m. tour of the White House and protocol review. " Mason continued to walk quickly down the hallway. "You need to meet Kate Swenen."

Susan gave him a confused look. "Who?"

Mason turned right down the hallway and knocked on the first door. "Your stylist."

Before Susan could react, the door opened and a short, dark-haired woman appeared in the doorway. She immediately gave Mason a hug. "Mason! How have you been? Come on in."

Susan stood behind Mason. She felt like the third wheel on a date.

Kate moved back from Mason and recognized Susan. She stepped forward toward Susan. "I'm Kate, such a pleasure to work with you, Madam President." Kate leaned closer and gave Susan a hug.

Susan hugged her back and tried to hide her anxiety.

Kate motioned for them to come into the room. "Follow me. President Turner, it's such a privilege to work with you. It's going to be amazing. Take a seat."

Susan followed her order and sat down in a salon chair. Kate stood behind her and examined her hair for a moment. "I would absolutely die for your hair color. I wish I could get that color of brown." She paused to examine the length of Susan's hair. "I've got it. I know what we're going to do. Your hair is the perfect length for what I like to call a tuck-up. Just put a few pins here in the back." Kate reached to the counter, quickly grabbed four bobby pins, and put them in Susan's hair. "Just like that. You've got a whole new look. Amazing. What do you think?"

Susan blushed and shyly responded, "It looks great."

Kate asked, "Did you like the dress I picked out for your inauguration?"

So much happened that day, Susan had no idea what she wore, but she didn't want to be rude. "It was a fantastic choice, thank you picking it out."

Kate bubbled with excitement. "Great, I've got some other ideas I'd like to try out with you. When do you want to do a fitting? I have a pair of—"

"Kate, can we pick this up another time? I'm sure

SELECTED

President Turner wants to hear all about the designs you've picked out for her but we're running late this morning."

Kate responded, "Ohh, absolutely. Please don't let me make you late. I'm so glad you stopped by." Kate took the bobby pins out of Susan's hair and put it back in place. "President Turner, it is such an honor to meet you. I'll coordinate with Mason to find a time in your schedule for us to do a formal dress fitting."

Susan stood up and awkwardly hugged Kate. "Thank you so much. I can't wait." She had no doubts about picking up the rhythm of work in the White House but being fashion conscious wasn't going to come as easy.

Susan followed Mason out of the room and he kept talking about the remaining items on her agenda as they walked down the hallway toward the Oval Office. Susan tuned out the words that came out of his mouth. Every time she checked into a new unit in the army there was an overly excited administrative clerk who made the job sound impossible. Mason was no different. Susan continued to follow Mason around the White House as he explained the different meeting rooms and security protocols.

Susan felt a sense of relief when her tour ended in the Oval

Office. Susan sat down on the couch and looked at her watch: 8:50 a.m., ten minutes before her next meeting. Mason handed Susan a government-issued cell phone.

"There's nothing special about the phone except the itinerary app. It has all of your meeting details and contact info." Mason gave Susan a stern look. "And it also has an itinerary reminder function. Just a friendly reminder to help you stay on schedule."

Susan looked up from the phone. "Anything else I need to know?"

"Vice President Wilkes is your next meeting, right here in the Oval Office." Mason paused. "No chance of you being late."

Susan watched Mason close the door to the Oval Office and slumped in her chair. She opened the itinerary app on her phone and clicked on the meeting titled "Vice President Wilkes—Welcome Aboard." She clicked a small pencil icon in the upper-right-hand corner of the meeting title. She added to the title of the meeting, "Mother would swoon—I wish he was a little younger :)" Susan chuckled to herself.

SELECTED

Susan stood up when Vice President Wilkes walked through the doors of the Oval Office. Susan noted that he was exceptionally well dressed. Vice President Wilkes wore a tailored dark gray suit, white shirt, blue tie, and matching pocket square. His hair was perfectly combed and Susan could smell a hint of cologne when she shook his hand.

Vice President Wilkes smiled. "President Turner. It has a nice ring to it. Sounds right."

Susan blushed. "Thank you. It's an honor. I've got some big shoes to fill."

Susan's phone vibrated on the coffee table. The speaker was on full volume as her itinerary app announced the meeting, "Your meeting . . . Vice President Wilkes . . . Welcome Aboard . . . Mother would swoon . . . I wish he was a little younger . . . smiley face emoticon . . . begins in one minute at 9:00 a.m. Eastern." Susan dove for the phone and silenced the speaker.

Vice President Wilkes burst into laughter. "You'll have to introduce me to your mother."

Susan's face felt like it was on fire. "I'm so sorry. I was just playing around with the itinerary app. I had no idea—"

Vice President Wilkes put up his hand to stop Susan. "It's

okay, it's okay, no worries. Mason's gadgets threw me for a loop, too." Vice President Wilkes rolled his eyes. "He sure is a stickler for the rules. Speaking of which, I brought you a present." He handed Susan an engraved wooden box with a Montblanc pen inside.

Susan was still short of breath from embarrassment. "Thank you. I don't even know what to say. I feel like I should have gotten you something."

"Ohh no, it's quite alright. During my presidency, I found myself spending most of my time behind that desk and I could never find a pen when I needed one. After about two months, I finally caved in and put one of these on my desk. Well, anyway . . . I thought you might find it useful."

"Thank you." Susan struggled to find the appropriate response. She put the pen and case on her desk. "I have no doubt it'll get some use."

"So . . . how are you feeling? Has it settled in? Or are you still in shock about being the president?"

Susan shrugged her shoulders. "Honestly, I'm really not that worried about it. This all feels the same as being in the army. It's a routine. Once you settle into the routine, it all works itself out."

SELECTED

Vice President Wilkes nodded his head. "Yeah, I agree. Once I got the lay of the land, it went pretty smooth. But it was a rough road for me. You're already doing better than I ever did. I'm a high school teacher — being around all these military people is intimidating. I got bullied a lot in the beginning of my presidency. Can I give you some advice?"

Susan eagerly nodded. "Absolutely."

"Well . . . as you've seen, there's a lot to get used to. Most of it comes pretty easy. But there are two big challenges I faced." Vice President Wilkes smiled. "The first was figuring out how to deal with Mason. As you saw this morning, he's a bit . . . umm . . . particular about some things. In the classroom, I'm used to being in charge of the curriculum and schedule. It wasn't easy for me to give that up. He's a good guy and he'll do right by you. But you have to find a way to work with him."

Susan smiled. "Noted. That's number one on my to-do list. I was late this morning. We got off to a bit of a rough start."

Vice President Wilkes chuckled. "Well . . . like I said, he's a good guy. I'm sure you'll figure it out. And once you do, your life is going to get much, much better." Vice President Wilkes paused and leaned forward. "This is between you and me. Understood?"

Susan sat up straight. "Of course."

"Every day you're going to be swamped with decisions. And some of those decisions are ugly. It's just the nature of the job. You're going to make decisions that you regret. No matter what happens, don't let anyone push you into decisions that compromise your integrity. It's a slippery slope and once you start down that path, it's impossible to turn around."

Susan looked down to the ground and solemnly nodded her head. "Understood. It's good to hear the warning from someone who's been in these shoes."

Vice President Wilkes quietly clapped his hands together. "I'm sorry, I didn't mean to turn this into a depressing meeting. Sooo . . . it seems like your mom is a fan of mine. What can I do for her?"

Susan laughed. "Oh, I think just telling her that I met you is enough."

"What's her name?"

Susan's face turned pink with embarrassment. "Rose."

"What a beautiful name." Vice President Wilkes picked up a pen on the coffee table and scribbled a quick personal note: "Dearest Rose—Best Wishes—President Wilkes." He reached into his left breast pocket and wrapped the note with his pocket square. "For your mother."

Susan smiled. "Oh my gosh, you didn't have to. But she'll love it."

Susan listened eagerly as Vice President Wilkes continued to flatter her with compliments and stories from his own tenure in the White House until Mason Adams opened the door. "Madam President, I'm sorry to interrupt but it's time to get ready for your next meeting."

Vice President Wilkes stood up from the couch and shook Susan's hand. "Until next time, Madam President."

16

Vice President Wilkes met Mr. Jones at the Gelman Library in Washington, DC. He meandered around the library before finding Mr. Jones in the classic literature section reading a copy of Julius Caesar. Mr. Jones closed the book. "Always good to catch up on the classics." He gave Vice President Wilkes a sinister smile. "Et tu, Brute?"

Vice President Wilkes glared back without responding.

Mr. Jones carefully put the book back on the shelf. "Do you have something for me?"

Vice President Wilkes handed Mr. Jones a small flash drive.

"What's on it?"

Vice President Wilkes smirked. "You wanted to know what's happening in the Oval Office. Now you have a front row seat for the show."

"What?"

SELECTED

Vice President Wilkes responded, "I planted a listening device in the Oval Office."

Mr. Jones furrowed his brow. "Tell me more about this listening device." He poked his index finger into Vice President Wilkes's chest. "You're not as clever as you think. That office gets swept for electronics twice a day. If they find—"

Vice President Wilkes cut him off. "They aren't finding anything. This is state of the art; the surveillance sweeps won't pick it up. And there's no chance of it leaving the Oval Office. The device is hidden inside a Montblanc pen case I gave to President Turner as a welcome gift. She didn't really want it, but now she feels guilty. Zero chance of her taking it off the Oval Office desk."

Mr. Jones snarled. "Fair enough. If it becomes a risk, we'll take the device out of play." Mr. Jones looked around to make sure they were alone. "We're switching our meet locations every week. Next week, Georgetown Neighborhood Library, got it?"

"Why do we have to meet in person? Why can't I just drop off the disk on a park bench somewhere?"

Mr. Jones smiled. "Because I don't trust people like you." He leaned closer and whispered into Vice President Wilkes's ear, "Remember . . . I'm always watching." Mr. Jones grabbed Vice President Wilkes by the suit jacket lapels and pretended to straighten his jacket. He leaned back and patted Vice President Wilkes firmly on the shoulder. "Good talk old friend. See ya next week." Without waiting for a response, Mr. Jones stepped past Vice President Wilkes and disappeared.

After leaving the library, Mr. Jones quickly walked west for a block and doubled back to a concealed location with a view of the library entrance. He spotted Vice President Wilkes walking down the front steps of the library. His head was on a swivel; he was clearly looking for someone. Vice President Wilkes's gaze focused on a newspaper stand across the street. Mr. Jones watched while Vice President Wilkes quickly walked across the street and had an animated conversation with a serious-looking man in a dark gray jacket and jeans. The man remained deathly still while Vice President Wilkes gestured wildly with his hands. The conversation ended as abruptly as it started.

Mr. Jones carefully followed the man in the dark gray jacket and jeans. He kept up for four blocks, then the man in

SELECTED

the dark gray jacket ducked into the Metro station and effortlessly slipped away. Mr. Jones had been right not to trust Vice President Wilkes.

Later that evening, Mr. Anderson pulled a cell phone from his desk drawer and dialed a number from memory.

"Good evening, Mr. Jones, do you have an update?"

Mr. Jones replied, "Yes. I received the first drop from Vice President Wilkes. He planted an audio device in the Oval Office. I'll have my contacts in security get the electronic sweep protocols and logs. I'll make sure it isn't detected."

"Good. I want a copy of the audio files. What else?"

"It seems that Vice President Wilkes has hired his own private surveillance. I spotted them outside the drop—"

Mr. Anderson interrupted, "Did you ID them?"

"No. It was just one man. I followed him for four blocks but he lost me on the Metro. I'll take care of the situation."

"I don't need to remind you of what happens if he is able to provide evidence of your relationship."

"No, sir. I'll take care of the problem."

"Updates on your secondary mission?" asked Mr. Anderson.

"Yes. I was able to get eyes on. But there are too many Secret Service agents around for me to be there every day. There isn't enough foot traffic around the school to stay hidden. If I'm in the area more than once a week, it will arouse suspicion."

Mr. Anderson tapped his fingers on his desk before responding. "I was hoping for less of a Secret Service presence." He paused before continuing. "I need you to come up with a plan to take the children without using force. You'll need to be at least an hour away before the Secret Service is alerted of their disappearance."

Mr. Jones paused before responding, "I'll have to give it some thought. I may have to get others involved."

"Come up with the plan first. Then we'll discuss. That will be all." Mr. Anderson ended the call.

Mr. Anderson twisted the West Point class ring on his right hand. He disliked the thought of using Susan's family as leverage. If she reacted according to plan, he wouldn't have to get her children involved. But if he needed to use this ugly option, it would happen in a rush and the plan would already have to be in place. Mr. Anderson stared out the window and mentally prepared himself for what he might need to do. He took off his West Point ring, placed it neatly in the desk drawer, and continued his work.

17

During her time as a Black Hawk pilot in the army, Susan gained the respect of her fellow soldiers with her willingness to take calculated risks on the battlefield. As a squadron commander, she led from the front and gained a cult-like devotion among the soldiers in her squadron. She wasn't the person you wanted on a conference call, but in a firefight, you wanted her on your side. She earned the reputation of being a soldier's soldier.

After breakfast, Susan walked upstairs to grab her daily itinerary folder. Walking down the hallway, she focused on the open East Bedroom door. She walked closer and stopped in the hallway outside the door. Bedsheets were on the floor, dirty clothes were on top of the dresser, and Legos were scattered across the floor.

Susan yelled downstairs, "Greg! Get up here right now!"

SELECTED

She heard a loud sigh from Greg downstairs. "What?"

"Don't make me say it again!"

Greg stomped his feet as hard as possible on every step of the stairs toward his bedroom. Susan paced the hallway with her hands on her hips. She caught herself before the anger made it to the surface. She stopped moving, closed her eyes, and took two deep breaths to regain control.

"What?" said Greg with as much attitude as he thought he could get away with.

Susan briefly closed her eyes to gain her composure and simply described the situation to Greg. "Your room isn't clean."

"I know."

Susa calmly nodded her head. "Good . . . so we're starting on the same page. One of our rules is to clean your room before you go to school every day. Why isn't your room clean today?"

"Because I don't have to clean my room, Norma cleans my room."

Susan nodded her head again, walked into Greg's room,

and sat down on the bed. "Greg, come in here and sit down. We need to talk."

Greg gave her a confused look. "Okay, Mom."

"Listen Greg, Norma isn't going to clean your room anymore. You are going to be responsible for cleaning your own room, just like at home."

Greg looked at her with questioning eyes. "Why?"

"Because there won't always be someone as nice as Norma here to help you. Norma isn't going to clean Tommy's room anymore either. Every morning I'm going to come up here and check your rooms before school. Understood?"

Greg nodded in agreement. "Yes, Mom."

"Good. You'd better get back downstairs before you miss your ride to school."

Susan leaned back on the bed and listened to Greg running down the stairs. She closed her eyes and wondered how she let life get to the point where her kids relied on the maid to clean their bedrooms. It wasn't their fault; they were only eleven years old.

Susan looked at her vibrating cell phone and picked it up.

SELECTED

She remained lying on her back with the cell phone over her head as she read a message requesting a meeting in the Situation Room. Susan put the phone down and stayed on the bed for another thirty seconds. The meeting wasn't for another hour and she needed time to clear her mind.

Susan met her chief of staff, Mason Adams, in the hallway en route to the Situation Room. On the walk to the Situation Room, Mason was unusually quiet. The silence started Susan's mind racing through worst-case scenarios. After a few seconds, her thoughts spiraled out of control, and she quickly shook her head and cleared her mind before opening the door to the Situation Room.

Susan walked into an unusually empty Situation Room— only the joint chiefs of staff and directors were in attendance. Before today, for every meeting in the Situation Room, the Joint Chiefs of Staff brought intelligence, military, and foreign relations experts to answer any specific questions regarding the situation at hand. Susan paused before taking her seat at the head of the conference room table. She sensed a mood of anger and contempt from the men in the room. Susan locked eyes with Arianna Redmond, director of the FBI, hoping for a clue about what was happening. Her eyes revealed an intense anger—Susan took note of the beads of sweat on her forehead.

General Gillingham nodded solemnly and began. "Ninety minutes ago, two U.S. Air Force pilots were shot down by a surface-to-air missile near the Yeline region of the Ukraine. We believe they safely ejected from their aircraft on Ukrainian soil. We have not had radio communication with them since their ejection." He paused to let the message resonate and continued. "We were able to get the speed, altitude, and location of the aircraft prior to impact. The F/A-18 was flying far above the range of any shoulder-fired surface-to-air missile. The missile fired must have been ground based, with a sophisticated radar system. The missile fired was likely from an S-400 class surface-to-air missile system."

Susan filled the silence. "My anti-aircraft weapon knowledge is a bit out of date. But from what I remember, the only surface-to-air missile systems capable of reliably shooting down a fixed wing aircraft were owned by the Soviet Union. And even when those weapon systems ended up in the hands of foreign governments, they were very difficult to train personnel to use them properly. Is that still the case?"

General Estes, the air force commanding general, replied, "Yes it is. The S-400 surface-to-air missile systems are complicated to operate, but in the hands of a trained crew they are very effective. The Soviet military trains their operators for six months exclusively on the S-400 and it takes an entire trained team of four to operate the system. This is the first fixed wing aircraft we have lost to a surface-to-air missile since the Vietnam War."

Susan followed up again. "Do we know with certainty who fired the missile? Or where the missile system was located?"

General Estes responded with confidence, "The missiles were fired from either the Soviet Union or just across the border into the Ukraine. Our current intelligence found no evidence of the Ukrainian military or the Ukrainian rebels possessing an S-400 surface-to-air missile system. We believe the missile was fired by the Soviet Union with the explicit intention of destroying a United States aircraft."

Before Susan could reply, General Gillingham interjected, "Madam President, we have put the air force's Eighty-Sixth Fighter Group out of Ramstein Air Base in Germany on full alert—"

Susan interrupted, "I appreciate the initiative. But I want to make sure I understand the situation. . . . What I believe I heard was that we have circumstantial evidence that leads us to believe the Soviets were responsible for the missile? Is that correct?"

J. ALLEN WOLFRUM

Susan listened while all four Joint Chiefs of Staff started talking at the same time, defending their response plan.

In recent months, the Joint Chiefs of Staff witnessed the Soviet military continually press closer to the borders of Eastern Europe. The recent movement of Soviet troops near Latvia and Belarus could only be interpreted as a precursor to a Soviet invasion. Arianna Redmond remained silent. Her crossed arms and stern facial expression made it clear that she did not approve of the military action agreed upon before President Turner walked into the Situation Room.

From the perspective of the Joint Chiefs of Staff, this incident provided an opportunity to push back on the Soviet military. The response plan created by the Joint Chiefs of Staff included military strikes against Soviet troops on Soviet soil near the borders of Ukraine, Belarus, and Latvia.

General Gillingham's voice silenced the room. "Yes, the evidence we have at this time is circumstantial, but the situation should be interpreted within the context of recent Soviet troop movements, the mobilization of Soviet troop reserves, and the Soviet intervention in the Ukrainian civil war. If the Soviets don't believe we will react with force to military aggression, they will continue to escalate the situation."

Susan looked around the room, studying each face at the table. "I can see you all have made a decision on our response before this meeting. What's your plan?"

General Gillingham spoke for the group. "We are prepared to conduct air strikes against Soviet troops and air defense systems near the borders of Ukraine, Latvia, and Belarus. And we will immediately launch a search-and-rescue mission near the crash site."

Susan took a long drink of water before responding; it was the only way to stop herself from screaming. She responded in a rushed voice, "What I think I just heard was that we should start a war with another nuclear power. Please tell me I'm wrong?"

General Estes continued to defend the plan. "We are absolutely not suggesting we start a war with the Soviets. What we are suggesting is an appropriate response to Soviet aggression, a defensive measure."

"Attacking Soviet air defenses is a defensive measure? That is insane. What do you expect the Soviets to do when we begin air strikes? Back down? Do you think they aren't going to defend themselves? We're going to end up in an all-out air war within minutes. . . . What don't you understand? If we escalate, the Soviets will escalate. What then?" Susan paused. There was no immediate response.

Susan answered her own question. "I'll tell you what will happen: within five minutes of launching your plan, Rick, the very nice Secret Service agent standing outside the door holding a suitcase handcuffed to his wrist is going to walk in this room. And I'm going to have to decide whether or not to respond to a nuclear attack from the Soviet Union."

Susan paused again to catch her breath. Susan's forearms trembled from her grip on the table.

General Gillingham's face turned bright red with anger. "Madam President, allowing the Soviets to shoot down a United States aircraft without an equal military response is a sign of weakness. The Soviets have been probing us for years, waiting for this type of weakness. Make no mistake, they will exploit your weakness."

Susan looked General Gillingham in the eye and responded, "I appreciate your warnings but we are not responding with air strikes. Call General Kenney at Ramstein Air Base and have him stand down the Eighty-Sixth Fighter

Group."

General Gillingham's eyes went cold with hatred. He made no move toward the secure line on the desk. Susan locked eyes with General Gillingham and they stared at each other; neither moved a muscle. Susan swiftly got up from her chair, grabbed General Gillingham's briefing folder, and quickly found General Kenney's phone number. She picked up the secure line and dialed the number. She stared at General Gillingham as the line rang. General Kenney picked up the line in Germany. Susan continued staring at General Gillingham as she spoke to General Kenney.

"This is General Kenney."

"This is President Turner. Be advised that the Eighty-Sixth Fighter Group is to stand down; you are no longer on full alert. Return to normal operations. Do you understand?"

"Yes, Madam President."

"Thank you, General."

Susan hung up the secure line and stared at General Gillingham before walking back to her chair at the head of the conference room table. The room was silent. Susan took her time to scan the room. She intentionally looked at each person and studied their expressions.

"Gentlemen, we have work to do. We need to find those pilots. General Estes, I want a full update on the situation tomorrow morning. In the meantime, if anything significant happens, alert me immediately." Susan stood up and left the room.

Everyone in the Situation Room stood as Susan left the room except General Gillingham.

Arianna Redmond looked down at him from across the conference room table and scowled.

General Gillingham stayed silent and stared daggers back at her. He remained seated as the others left the room. When the room cleared he opened a new page in his notebook and wrote, "The two most powerful warriors are patience and time." The quote from Tolstoy served as a helpful reminder throughout his military career. He witnessed the downfall of many great military men because of their short tempers. Obtaining the rank of general is technically a military decision, but at that level, the promotion criteria is weighted heavily toward political savvy. Military leadership skills are much less important.

SELECTED

General Gillingham began making a list of White House staff members and the political leverage he held over them. One way or another, President Turner would regret embarrassing him in front of the entire Situation Room.

18

President Rosinski heard the sharp beeps on the electric collar switch from five second intervals to a steady quarter-second interval. Instinct and adrenaline took control. He sprinted forward ten steps, hurdled over a downed tree trunk, and pushed through a small thicket to get in position. His pace slowed to a creep and he focused on a small clump of brushes to his right. The bushes came alive with a sharp rustling sound, followed by a booming thunder. In one smooth motion, he snapped the shotgun into the crook of his shoulder, flipped the safety forward, put the small gold bead at the end of the barrel just ahead of the partridge, and squeezed the trigger. The adrenaline masked the kick of the shotgun in his shoulder. His German Shorthaired Pointer, Jake, watched the partridge fall out of the sky and leaped forward to find the downed bird. In less than thirty seconds, Jake retrieved the bird and dropped it back at President Rosinski's feet.

President Rosinski stuffed the dead bird into the pouch on

the back of his hunting vest and patted his dog on the shoulder. "Good boy, Jake." Jake took off to find more birds and President Rosinski yelled toward the rustling he heard in the bushes twenty yards to his left. "Nikolai, is that you over there?"

Nikolai Tremonov, director of the Soviet KGB, replied, "Yeah, it's me."

President Rosinski shouted over the wind and rustling leaves, "Let's walk the edge of this swamp for another hundred yards, then head back up to the ridgeline. What do you think?"

KGB Director Tremonov ducked under a tree branch and shouted back, "Sounds good. It's about time to quit for the day."

Back at the cabin, President Rosinski sat on the porch with his dog Jake between his legs. Jake rolled over on his belly and President Rosinski carefully cut the burrs out of the hair on his legs and underbelly. He checked Jake one last time and patted him on the shoulder to let him know the job was done. "Good boy . . . let's get you some dinner."

After President Rosinski fed Jake he grabbed the birds from the back of the truck and laid them out on the table to be cleaned. He also set out on the table: a pair of kitchen scissors, a clean bucket of water, and his Karatel knife. KGB Director Tremonov walked over to help clean the birds and picked up the kitchen scissors. The men settled into the process of cleaning the birds.

President Rosinski kept his focus on the birds and asked, "What do we know about the American pilots?"

KGB Director Tremonov grunted, "They're being held by Chechens. Our men have them under twenty-four-hour surveillance."

President Rosinski nodded and paused before responding, "We need to let the pilots go. I don't want the Americans focusing any attention on the Ukraine or Eastern Europe. They need to stay in the dark about our Eastern European plans as long as possible."

KGB Director Tremonov set his knife on the table and turned toward President Rosinski. "That's going to be a problem."

President Rosinski washed the blood and feathers off his hands and turned toward Tremonov. "Explain."

"What's to explain? They're Chechens. The perimeter of the building is booby-trapped and every security guard is wearing a suicide vest rigged with explosives. All they have to do is stand next to the American pilots and push the button."

President Rosinski crossed his arms and exhaled deeply. "Eventually the Americans will know our plans to take control of the Ukraine, Belarus, and Latvia. But I want to keep our efforts a secret until it's too late for them to respond. Any attention from the Americans on the Ukraine is bound to cause problems for us."

KGB Director Tremonov looked down at the ground and jabbed the toe of his boot into the ground. "Understood. The Chechen group's leader, Alexander Umirov—he has a family. I'll find out how much he loves them."

President Rosinski uncrossed his arms. "Do what is necessary."

Later that evening, inside his hunting cabin in a remote region of the Caucasus Mountains, President Rosinski sat alone at his desk. He kept a dossier on every foreign leader. He'd brought one dossier with him to study during the hunting trip.

He pulled out the folder titled SUSAN TURNER — PRESIDENT OF THE UNITED STATES and opened the cover. Rosinski carefully reviewed the notes he'd previously made in the margins of each page. He took a break, looked up from the documents, and focused on the picture of his first wife Anna, who died during the famine four decades ago. Forty years later, Boris still carried the burden of her death with him every day. He kept her picture on his desk to remind him of his duty to the Soviet people.

As a young metal worker, Boris witnessed the life improvements brought forth by providing productive work for a community. His small town moved from a starving agricultural community to a community able to consistently feed itself and support the Soviet people with the excess wealth. The economic prosperity of the Soviet people was the fuel for his drive to become president. He believed the key to long-term prosperity for the Soviet people was economic freedom—no matter the short-term costs.

His plan for producing economic prosperity for the Soviet people involved gaining control of the oil and gas natural resources in the Ukraine. With a virtually unlimited supply of natural resources, he planned to build a pipeline through the Ukraine, Belarus and Latvia for distribution. Pipeline construction would bring immediate jobs and maintenance of the pipeline would provide employment for generations. He began moving ground troops toward the Soviet borders with those countries in anticipation of violence. He believed an overpowering swift show of force would quickly stop the local uprisings and result in a lower probability of retaliation from the Americans and their allies. President Rosinski accepted the risks involved with the strategy. The Soviet economy was on the brink of collapse, this was the best option. He couldn't bear the thought of being responsible for fellow Soviets meeting the same fate as his dear wife Anna.

19

A white van turned left into the parking lot of Lincoln Elementary at ten Wednesday morning and came to a stop at the Secret Service checkpoint. The driver rolled down his window. "Mornin' gentlemen. I've got a work order for a heating vent repair." Mr. Jones reached into the passenger seat, grabbed a clipboard, and handed it to the agent. The agent took a brief look at the work order repair and replied, "I'll need to see your driver's license."

Mr. Jones reached into his wallet and handed over a fake Virginia State driver's license along with the clipboard and work order. The agent took the documents and walked back to a black Chevrolet Suburban parked fifteen feet away. Mr. Jones knew exactly what would happen next. They would run the plates on his vehicle, do a background check with the fake driver's license, and make sure the company listed on the work order was legitimate. Mr. Jones couldn't focus on anything except the urge to itch the fake beard he wore to match the picture on the driver's license. A wig of long blond hair pulled back into a ponytail and a Washington Nationals baseball cap made up the rest of his disguise.

The agent swiftly walked back to the van with the clipboard in his left hand and driver's license in his right. He handed Mr. Jones the driver's license and clipboard. "You're all set, Mr. Dickinson. Check out with us before you leave."

Mr. Jones took the clipboard and driver's license. "No problem, shouldn't take me more than an hour. Have a blessed afternoon." Mr. Jones parked the van at the back of the school near the maintenance entrance, out of the Secret Service agent's view.

He methodically pushed his tool cart down each hall of Lincoln Elementary, verifying that each hallway and exit in real life was identical to the architectural drawings. It was overkill but being lazy is how men in his line of business died at an early age. Before every mission, Mr. Jones reminded himself of the stories he heard about great contractors, legends in the business, getting killed because they failed to do the basics.

Mr. Jones walked into the school nurse's office and introduced himself. "Hi, Ben Dickinson, Renaissance Heating and Cooling. I have a work order for a faulty temperature controller."

The school nurse looked up. "Thank goodness, I've been freezing in here all morning. The temperature control is over on the back wall."

Mr. Jones smiled and nodded. "Thank you, ma'am, I'll take a look." He pushed his tool cart into the corner of the room and set his tool belt down on the floor next to a row of chairs. He grabbed a screwdriver and walked toward the temperature control unit in the back of the room.

The school nurse caught his attention. "Excuse me, sir. I need to use the restroom, I'll be right back. I'm going to leave the door unlocked. If any children come in while I'm gone, don't let them open any of the drawers."

Mr. Jones nodded. "No problem." He went back to work taking apart the temperature controller and looked down at his watch. It read 10:14 a.m.

Mr. Jones heard a knock on the door, a pause of silence, and then the door slowly crept open. A voice came from the other side of the door. "Nurse Freemont?"

Mr. Jones replied, "She'll be right back. Come on in."

Greg Turner's shaggy brown hair and blue eyes poked

around the corner of the door. Mr. Jones smiled. Greg was right on time. "It's all right, come on in and have a seat. The nurse will be right back."

Greg cautiously sat down in a chair against the wall and remained quiet. The repairman made him uncomfortable.

Mr. Jones walked toward Greg, leaned down, grabbed the electrical volt tester from his tool belt, and showed it to Greg. "Do you know what this is?"

Greg nodded his head. "Yeah."

His response surprised Mr. Jones. "Really? What is it?"

Greg confidently replied, "It's a volt tester, you use it to test electrical current. My grandpa showed me how."

Mr. Jones raised his eyebrows and smiled. "Sounds like your Grandpa has got you on the right track."

Nurse Freemont interrupted their conversation. She rushed through the door and looked at Greg. "I'm so sorry I'm late. Give me a minute to get your allergy shot prepared."

She turned and looked at Mr. Jones. "And thank you for keeping him occupied."

Mr. Jones smiled. "Not a problem, give me about five

more minutes and I'll have your heat back on."

Later that afternoon, Mr. Anderson called Mr. Jones for an after-action report.

Mr. Jones began to describe the events at the school. "Overall, it was a success. Other than the Secret Service agents outside, security is nonexist—"

"Sounds like some good reconnaissance work. Can you do it again?"

"Yes, but I need twenty-four hours' notice and obviously only on a school day. Greg Turner gets an allergy shot every day at 10:15 a.m. That's our best chance to get him alone without drawing attention."

Mr. Anderson asked, "What about the other boy, Tommy?"

Mr. Jones shook his head. "I couldn't find a way to get him alone without raising suspicion. If snatch and grab is acceptable, I can easily lure him out of a classroom. But within

SELECTED

minutes someone would notice he's gone."

Mr. Anderson took a deep breath. "Don't worry about the other boy. Having one of her boys is good enough. You'll need some time to get away from the school and I don't want your identity compromised. Any issues with the escape route?"

"None. I have a tool locker on wheels for the kid. He'll be unconscious, so he won't be making any noise. And Secret Service doesn't do vehicle checks. Shouldn't be a problem at all."

"How long do we have until someone notices he's gone?"

Mr. Jones tapped his finger on the desk. "Right after his allergy shot is recess. Nobody will notice he's gone until after recess. Maybe longer, just depends. But we definitely have forty-five minutes."

Mr. Anderson sensed apprehension in Mr. Jones's voice. "Listen . . . I know this isn't easy. I don't like the idea of involving children either. But if this is what needs to be done to accomplish the mission . . . then we have no choice."

Mr. Jones took a deep breath. "Don't worry about me, I've got it under control."

Mr. Anderson replied, "I'm not worried about you. I know

you're dedicated to the cause. I just want you to know where I stand. This phase of violence is an ugly necessity in order to accomplish the goal. Your contributions will not go unnoticed. When we unify the world under our control and restore peace, you'll be a part of the global leadership. You've earned it."

Mr. Jones replied, "Understood. Thanks, boss."

"Keep your head up, it won't be much longer. I'll be in touch with the next steps." Mr. Anderson hung up the phone.

Mr. Anderson's executive assistant walked into the office. "Sir, General Gillingham is waiting in the second-floor conference room for you. He's here to discuss the expansion of our military logistical contract."

Mr. Anderson stood up and straightened his jacket. "Thank you. I'll be right down."

He walked into the conference room and shook hands with General Gillingham.

General Gillingham looked around at the expensive artwork and raised his eyebrows. "Jack, you ever regret getting out the army?"

SELECTED

Mr. Anderson shrugged his shoulders. "I miss the people. The bureaucracy . . . not so much." He smiled and patted General Gillingham on the shoulder. "You know, when you finally retire, I've got an office for you right next to mine. Just like old times."

"Might be sooner than you think. Freakin' President Turner. She doesn't have a clue on how to deal with the Soviets. Those bastards are going to eat us for breakfast." He continued on a tirade about Susan's stubbornness and her shortsighted views on the Soviets.

Mr. Anderson patiently listened and finally interrupted his rant. "Okay, okay. I get it—you don't like her. You think she's weak. You've gotta relax. And it sounds like she needs to be taken down a few notches."

General Gillingham's face still showed his anger. "Damn right she does."

Mr. Anderson crossed his arms and slightly spread his feet. "Tom, we've been friends for a long time, right?"

General Gillingham took a couple deep breaths and began to calm down. "Yeah, of course. What are you trying to get at?"

Mr. Anderson paused to look down at the ground then

back up at General Gillingham. "So, I know you're already plotting some kind of revenge against her." General Gillingham started to defend himself and Mr. Anderson put up a hand to stop him from talking. "So I take that as a yes." He paused before continuing. "I don't want to see you do something you'll regret. Let me deal with President Turner. It's a situation that's better handled by someone outside the government. You have too many restraints and the blowback, if you get caught, is too risky."

General Gillingham took a deep breath and sighed before responding. "What do you have in mind?"

Mr. Anderson shook his head. "It's better if you don't know. But I promise, I'll deal with her. She needs to learn how dangerous hubris can be."

General Gillingham relaxed his posture. "You know what . . . you're right. I need to let it go. But I'm not backing down on my opinions about military strategy."

"And you shouldn't. Just try to be respectful about it, that's all I'm saying."

General Gillingham nodded.

Mr. Anderson smiled and changed the direction of the

SELECTED

conversation. "Good. Let's talk through these contract details."
Mr. Anderson took a seat at the conference table and General
Gillingham followed.

20

Susan stood in front of the mirror in the women's bathroom outside the Oval Office, wishing she hadn't had the ice cream sandwich and red wine for dessert. Arianna Redmond walked into the bathroom and stood at the sink next to Susan. Susan glanced over and locked eyes with Arianna in the mirror. Arianna Redmond initiated the conversation. "Arianna Redmond, nice to meet you." She touched up her lipstick.

Susan stuttered, "It's an honor."

Without missing a beat, still applying her lipstick, Arianna responded, "Gillingham's a coward. Good on you for standing up to him. You know . . . they call me all kinds of nasty names behind my back . . . I don't give a damn. I just keep on doing the right thing. They're nothing but a bunch of sixty-five-year-old men who still act like high school kids. Don't let it bother you." Without waiting for a response, she walked out of the bathroom. Susan stood at the sink in shock from Arianna's blunt perspective.

Susan greeted Ambassador Dashkov in the Oval Office. She noted his casual dress, a light blue suit, white collared shirt, no tie, and brown shoes with no socks. This was Susan's first meeting with the Soviet ambassador, and his pleasant and casual demeanor was not what she expected.

Susan gave Ambassador Dashkov a warm smile and shook his hand. "I'm sorry for cutting your vacation short, thank you for taking the time to meet with me."

"You're welcome, Madam President, always happy to be at your service. What can I do for you?"

"Please have a seat. I'd like to talk to you about the American pilots."

Dashkov sat down on the couch and comfortably leaned back as if he were at home. "Yes, I saw the report on the news."

"Have you talked with President Rosinski about the situation?"

Dashkov leaned forward. "I'm sorry, Madam President, I have not yet spoken with the Kremlin about the situation."

Susan nodded. "Can you give a message to President Rosinski for me?"

Ambassador Dashkov narrowed his eyes. "Sure. What is the message?"

Susan folded her hands. "Please tell President Rosinski that I am requesting temporary access to Soviet air space to launch a rescue mission when we find the location of the pilots."

Dashkov's face hardened and he straightened in his chair. "Madam President, you're asking us to allow you a free path to kill Soviet people on Soviet soil. In all my years in politics, I have never been so deeply offended. Do you have such little respect for the Soviet Union that you think you can simply give us orders? This is not how diplomacy works."

Ambassador Dashkov abruptly stood up and straightened his jacket. "Madam President, I have another meeting to attend. If you wish to discuss diplomacy, please alert my staff." Before Susan could respond, Ambassador Dashkov turned and walked out of the Oval Office.

Still sitting down, Susan scrambled to make sense of what

just happened. Was Ambassador Dashkov really offended? Or was it just a political game of intimidation? Mason Adams interrupted her moment of despair. The pale look of disappointment on his face was more than Susan wanted to deal with at the moment. If curling up in a blanket and hiding under her desk had been an option, she would have taken it.

"Are you all right?" asked Mason.

Susan noticed the dark circles under Mason's eyes. "I was about to ask you the same thing."

"The press will not let go of the story about the captured pilots. They want to know what we're doing to get them back. And when. They're relentless."

"I know Mason, I know. I'll prepare a statement for this afternoon. I'll make the presentation to the press—you look like you need a break. Take the rest of the day off, go home and relax. I'll be fine."

Mason looked down. "Are you sure?"

"Yes . . . I promise, I'll stay on schedule. Before you leave, can you have Senator Reynolds come to my office as soon as he's free?"

Mason smiled. "Absolutely."

Susan tried to wrap her mind around the meeting with Ambassador Dashkov. How was she supposed to approach the situation? The rescue team was going to need a clear air space to rescue the pilots. The only way to get a clear air space was to ask for it.

Susan needed to get away from her own thoughts. She wandered out of the Oval Office and down the hallway. She spotted her father in the West Wing lobby, sitting in a chair with his feet up on the ottoman reading a Louis L'Amour cowboy novel. Susan startled Earl by putting her hand on his shoulder.

"Hi, Dad. I'm glad you're making yourself at home. No checkers this morning?"

"Nope, not yet. The mornings are always slow. These stiffs don't want to be late to their first meeting. I catch some interesting characters in the middle of the day. Your friend Curtis stopped by the other day."

"Oh yeah? How's General LeMae doing?"

"He's five dollars richer after beating me. He should be ashamed of himself for taking money from an old man."

Susan rolled her eyes and laughed. "Yeah, he's something.

SELECTED

Do me a favor, take it easy on the gambling. I really don't want to explain why my dad is running a gambling ring out of the West Wing lobby."

Earl chuckled and went back his Louis L'Amour novel.

Susan walked a lap around the West Wing, then wandered outside for a few minutes of fresh air before returning to the Oval Office. Senator Reynolds sat up on the couch when Susan walked into the room; he'd dozed off while waiting for her.

Susan walked into the Oval Office. "Make yourself right at home, Senator. Can I get you a pillow and a blanket? Maybe some cookies?"

Senator Reynolds sighed. "Sorry, it's been a long morning. Well, actually it's been a long couple of months."

"Yeah, I'm beginning to feel the same way. I met with Ambassador Dashkov this morning . . . it did not go well."

Senator Reynolds sat up. "What happened? I met him briefly a few weeks ago. He seemed like a nice guy, invited me to play squash with him but I haven't been able to make it happen yet."

Susan waved her hand. "It's not really worth getting into the details. He'll eventually have to see things my way—he just needs to feel some pain first. Which is exactly why I asked you to look into the options for using sanctions against the Soviet Union. Did you have a chance to look into it?"

Senator Reynolds opened the folder on the coffee table. "I did, and I found out the president has more authority to implement sanctions than I believed."

Susan raised her eyebrows. "Really? Best news I've heard in a while."

Senator Reynolds looked up from the documents. "In layman's terms, you can make a broad statement to identify people who are involved with the situation in the Ukraine. And once you identify those people, you can seize all money in their bank accounts, real estate holdings, and businesses assets, and have them deported from the United States."

Susan put her hands on her hips. "You're kidding? With an executive order, I don't need Congress or the Senate?"

Senator Reynolds shook his head. "Nope. Just you. This is how sanctions are typically executed."

Susan shook her head in disbelief. "And that's legal?"

"Yeah, this is how things are done in Washington. Most foreign businessmen are cautious enough not to have substantial holdings in the United States. The Soviets have been getting bolder over the last few years and several prominent officials in the Kremlin have substantial holdings in the United States that could be seized. You could put some serious pressure on the Kremlin."

"Okay, I'll have my legal staff draw up the executive order. I need the Soviets to know we're serious about getting our pilots back. I'm not taking no for an answer. Dashkov is going to have to start seeing things my way. If he doesn't want to do it willingly, then I'll put as much pressure as necessary on him until he breaks."

Senator Reynolds stood up. "I'll have my team work out the details from a foreign relations perspective. And I'll get a list of names for the first round of sanction violators."

Susan shook his hand. "Sounds good to me. If the Soviets don't want to cooperate and help us get the pilots back, I'll make it as painful as possible."

Senator Reynolds raised his eyebrows. "No problem. Remind me to stay on your good side. Until our next date, Madam President." He turned and left the room, looking back with a smile as he walked out the door. Susan was too tired to play high school games. It could wait for another time.

Ambassador Dashkov called President Rosinski to debrief him on the meeting with Susan. He tersely described their interaction. "She walks around the White House barking orders like an army drill sergeant. I will not allow her to treat me like that. If she thinks she can shout orders at me—"

"Enough complaining, get to the point. What did she want?"

Ambassador Dashkov caught his breath. "She wants a secure air space on the Ukrainian border to launch a rescue mission for the pilots. I told her that under no circumstances would we allow the United States military free passage to kill Soviets within our borders."

President Rosinski's face hardened. "I understand your agitation. This is most certainly not how diplomacy is conducted. We do not simply take orders from the United States. The American needs to be taught a lesson."

Ambassador Dashkov responded, "Thank you for understanding my frustration."

President Rosinski leaned back in his chair. "I need you to keep a relationship with the American government. In a few days, President Turner will reach out to you and apologize. Put your pride aside, and accept her apology. No matter how inappropriate her requests, take them in stride. She needs to feel comfortable around you. I don't want you banned from the White House. The intelligence you gather in Washington is too important."

Ambassador Dashkov nodded in agreement. "Understood. Thank you, Mr. President."

21

Jack Anderson opened his eyes to rays of sunshine penetrating the blinds. He sat up straight in the bed and quickly scanned the room. For a moment, he felt lost. He recognized the end table and lamp on the opposite side of the bed and relaxed. He sighed, ran his hands through his hair, and cursed himself. Jack Anderson represented many things to many people, but beneath it all, he was still a man.

Jack heard noises from two people downstairs. One person walked around the kitchen, opened the fridge, and put a frying pan on the stove. The other turned off the shower and paced around the bathroom.

The open closet door caught his eye. His shirt, suit jacket, and pants hung on the doorknob. Directly below, on the floor, his socks, underwear, and white T-shirt were placed on top of his shoes. Jack got out of bed, quickly jumped in the shower, got dressed, and walked downstairs.

SELECTED

Before Jack made it down the stairs, Zoe greeted him with a sarcastic shout from the kitchen, "Uncle Jack, how do you like your eggs?" She then immediately turned to her mother. "Do I really still have to call him Uncle Jack? Aren't I old enough to stop pretending?"

Emily did a poor job of hiding her frustration and snapped back, "Watch your tone. Mr. Anderson is a guest in our house."

"Not my guest," snapped Zoe.

Jack walked into the kitchen and attempted to diffuse the tension. "Zoe, you can absolutely call me Jack. How old are you now? Fourteen?"

"I'll be fifteen in two months."

Jack smiled. "Of course, how could I forget."

Zoe grabbed her backpack from the back of the chair and looked at Jack. "It was good to see you again . . . Jack." She announced, "I'm late for the bus," and walked out of the kitchen. She turned around before opening the front door. "Jack, did you get the backstage passes for the Taylor Swift concert next week?"

Jack replied, "I did and I'll leave them with your mother."

"Thanks Jack." Zoe ran out the door.

Emily looked at Jack with a raised eyebrow. "She's sure got your attitude. I know it's just a phase but she's more than I can handle right now."

Jack smiled. "She'll get through it. I don't imagine you were an angel at that age, either."

Emily rolled her eyes. "No, I certainly was not."

Jack poured two cups of coffee. He added half a spoonful of sugar and a few drops of milk to Emily's coffee. Emily scooped out a pile of scrambled eggs and hash browns onto their plates. Jack opened up the Wall Street Journal and handed Emily the front page while he read the markets section.

Jack could feel Emily's eyes staring at him through the paper. He did his best to ignore it and kept his head buried in the paper. Jack couldn't hold out any longer, he felt Emily's eyes burning an actual hole through the paper. He put down the paper and asked, "Is there something you want to talk about?"

Emily pursed her lips. "Zoe is starting to get in trouble at school. I think it's because she's bored. I want to send Zoe to private school next year. I need your help."

SELECTED

Jack nodded. "Okay . . . what school? I might know someone on the admissions board."

"Trinity . . . it's a good school and it's not far away. She needs more of a challenge."

Jack nodded. "I'll see what I can do."

"Thank you." Emily quickly looked down at her plate, then looked into Jack's eyes. "Things haven't been going great at the paper. I've only got two stories published in the last four months. I'm behind on the rent, things are tight."

Jack scowled. "I provide more than enough for you and Zoe to live comfortably. We've had this conversation before. The money is to be used for living expenses and the excess is to be spent on Zoe. It is not for you to—"

Emily cut him off. "I don't need a lecture from you about money. I think you forget that the only reason Cheryl hasn't divorced you is because I've stayed quiet. Not to mention what your friends would think if I—"

Jack put down his fork and snapped. "Stop. That's enough. I think you forgot who I am . . . take a second to think about it." Jack paused, exhaled deeply, and briefly closed his eyes. "I'll increase your monthly draw from the trust."

Emily nodded. "Thank you."

Jack tapped his finger on the table. "Are you interested in getting back into covering the White House?"

Emily rolled her eyes. "I don't have the drive. That beat is tough. There's a hundred reporters stabbing each other in the back for the same story."

Jack nodded. "Yeah, I know, it's a tough gig. What if I gave you an exclusive story? You wouldn't have to fight for it. You'd just have to write it."

Emily couldn't hide her skepticism. "I'm not going to do anything illegal for you."

Jack raised his hands in defense. "I promise, it's nothing illegal."

Emily shook her head. "Jack, I don't know."

Jack replied, "You won't have to deal with me at all. I'll have someone else send you the information. You decide what you want to do with it. If you think it's too dangerous, don't print it. No harm done."

Emily asked, "What's the story?"

"It's about President Turner. You'll figure it out after you listen to the audio."

Emily exhaled. "Okay, I'll listen to it . . . but no promises."

They continued eating in silence. Emily swallowed a mouthful of scrambled eggs and washed it down with a sip of coffee. She looked across the table at Jack. "Do you think Zoe knows?"

Jack stared at her in silence.

Emily continued, "You always said we would tell her when she gets old enough to understand."

Jack inhaled and exhaled sharply. "I'd say she probably has a suspicion but I don't think she's ready to hear the truth."

Emily pursed her lips and nodded. "You're probably right."

That evening, Emily walked up the driveway and saw a plain white envelope sitting on the doormat. She picked up the envelope and took out a black flash drive. She turned toward the street and scanned for anything suspicious. She saw nothing out of the ordinary and calmly slid the flash drive into the front pocket of her jeans before walking inside the house.

Emily glanced at the clock in the kitchen; she had another twenty minutes until she had to pick up Zoe from soccer practice. She opened her laptop and slid the flash drive into the USB port. There were at least twenty files on the drive, and each appeared to be labeled as a date. She opened a file titled 01052028_OvalOffice.mp4. Emily listened to the recording for ten minutes. She identified the voices of President Turner, Mason Adams, General LeMae, and Vice President Wilkes, along with several other world leaders. The file was heavily edited and contained snippets from multiple conversations that appeared to be held within the Oval Office. There were also several segments of the audio where President Turner appeared to be talking to herself, alone in the Oval Office.

Emily closed her laptop, walked out to the front porch, and scanned the street again. She left the front door open behind her. She knew Jack had someone watching her and wanted to let them know she was aware of their presence. She stood on the porch and contemplated her next move. The audio files from the Oval Office had the potential to revive her career or get her killed. Maybe both.

22

Senator Reynolds stared blankly at the wall and focused on taking slow continuous breaths. He reminded himself that his mother's words came from a place of concern. At least he wanted to believe they did.

"Ethan, you really should have talked to your father about the Senate Foreign Relations Committee. Your father negotiates with government officials on behalf of the business all the time. You really should talk to him."

Senator Reynolds remained neutral. "Well, what I'm doing is a little different, we're . . ." He caught himself midsentence. An explanation wasn't going to help. "You're right, Mom, I should. I'll give him a call—"

Before he could continue, his mother interrupted. "I don't know what's going on with those pilots. The newspapers are right, we need to go get them. If the Soviets don't want to turn them over to us, they need to be taught a lesson."

Senator Reynolds cut in before her rant got out of control. "Mom, I don't think it works like that. I have no doubt we're doing everything we can to get them back."

She backed down. "Well . . . all I'm saying is that those Soviets can't just take our pilots hostage. We need to do something." She paused before changing subjects. "You know, being the chair of the Senate Foreign Relations Committee is an honor. I really hope you're wearing a jacket and tie to work every day. You've never liked getting dressed up but it's important."

Senator Reynolds closed his eyes and took a breath before responding. "Yes, Mom, I'm wearing a suit and tie right now. And I shave every day. Don't worry. Listen, I have to get going. I just wanted to check in with you."

"Okay, I love you, honey. Call your father."

"I love you, too. I'll call Dad." Senator Reynolds hung up the phone and put his hands over his face to recover.

The Chechen rebels posted a video of Lt. Colonel Rodriguez and Lt. Colonel Harris on a Soviet social media website. On the video, both pilots had hollow eyes with dark gray circles under their eyelids. Their faces were intentionally spared from open wounds that would reveal the torture they'd endured at the hands of the Chechen rebels.

The video of the captured pilots was exactly one minute and thirty seconds in length. The pilots took turns reading a scripted message from the Chechen rebels. The video ended with the rebels demanding that the United States withdraw all military troops from foreign countries within ninety days or they would execute the pilots.

The Chechen rebels were well aware that the United States manned nearly eight hundred military bases in seventy countries across the globe. A complete withdrawal of troops was impossible. They were using the American pilots as a marketing tool for their cause. Capturing and killing two American pilots was better than winning the lottery for a terrorist group looking for new recruits.

Susan watched the video several times with the NSA analysts as they explained to her the most probable courses of action the Chechen rebels may take. The NSA analysts were convinced that the pilots would be killed prior to the ninety-day troop withdrawal demand. The NSA analyst pointed out that as Lt. Colonel Harris read from the teleprompter, Lt. Colonel Rodriguez blinked in Morse code the word t-o-r-t-u-r-e.

Susan mentally prepared herself to take any measure necessary to bring the pilot's home safe. At the end of the NSA's briefing, there was no actionable intelligence. The highest probability of a breakthrough was from the NSA's cyber warfare division. Susan endured a thirty-minute briefing to learn that their attempt to hack into the servers hosting the video was stopped by an encrypted SSL firewall. She lost her temper at the lack of progress and stormed out of the Situation Room.

Susan's face and demeanor showed the cumulative stress of the decisions she made over the last few months as president. Dark gray circles formed under her eyes and her hands constantly twitched. She could barely hold a cup of coffee still for long enough to take a sip. She wasn't able to hide from the press, the American people, or her most ferocious critic, herself.

During her last combat deployment to Iraq, Susan served as the squadron commander responsible for eight Black Hawk helicopter crews. Two of her best friends were killed when their helicopter was shot down over Mosul. The local insurgent group recovered their bodies before the Quick Reaction Force team made it to the crash site.

The bodies of her two best friends were tied to the back of a pickup truck and dragged through the streets of Mosul. In the city square, their bodies were put on display for the town, then mutilated and burned. Videos of the atrocity were posted on the internet for the world to see. The memories haunted her every night and during the days she caught herself blankly staring at nothing, thinking of their children, wives, parents, and what could have been. Those men were her responsibility and she didn't bring them home. Part of her didn't come home either.

After storming out of the NSA briefing, Susan retreated back to the Oval Office for lunch. She made a habit of eating lunch in the Oval Office; every time she walked down the hallway of the West Wing she was accosted with more questions and decisions. Closing the door of the Oval Office gave her a place where she could relax and think.

Mason Adams walked in the room. Susan looked up from

her lunch, a chef's salad with chicken. She desperately wanted a slice of pizza, but the paralyzing fear of having to buy a new pair of pants forced the salad.

Mason pointed toward Susan's desk. "What is that hideous thing in the corner?"

Susan smiled. "It's for you." Mason shot her a questioning look. "You know . . . you're always pestering me about schedules, timelines, meetings." Susan mocked Mason's voice and his body language. "Madam President, you're late . . . Madam President, why didn't you read the briefing documents? Soo . . . I made myself a to-do list on a whiteboard."

Mason kept a cold serious look and responded, "Good . . . I'm glad to see you're taking some initiative."

Mason promptly continued with his original message to Susan. "I have good news. The NSA has a location on the source of the video. They want to meet back in the Situation Room in fifteen minutes; the Joint Chiefs and FBI director will be there as well."

Susan caught a glimpse of a smile from Mason before he turned and walked toward the Oval Office door.

SELECTED

Susan walked into the Situation Room, and felt the mood was much lighter than earlier in the day.

"General Gillingham, can you bring everyone up to speed?"

"With assistance from the Israeli Mossad, we were able to get an IP address from the user who uploaded the video. The video was uploaded from an internet cafe in the Soviet Union. We gained access to the computer used to upload the file, and found the original video file which contained the geotags. The coordinates from the geotags on the video led us to the location you see on the monitors."

General Gillingham pointed toward the monitors, which showed a series of satellite images of a fortified compound on the outskirts of Churovichi, a small agricultural community twenty-five kilometers across the Ukrainian border in the Soviet Union.

"Our satellite surveillance has shown no movement at the compound except for the guards posted outside. We believe that Lt. Colonel Harris and Lt. Colonel Rodriguez are being held inside the building. We have a reconnaissance drone on the way."

Susan kept her eyes glued to the surveillance monitors. "Is

a rescue mission possible?"

"Yes. I have General Keene from JSOC standing by on the phone. General Keene, can you brief President Turner on the options?"

"This is General Keene. Madam President, we have a Special Forces team that can be ready within the hour. We can launch the mission under cover of darkness with two helicopters below Soviet radar. The team will recover the two pilots and gather any intelligence possible while inside the building. We estimate the total mission will take less than twenty-five minutes."

Susan asked, "What are the risks from your perspective?"

"Madam President, detection by Soviet radar or air defense systems will be our most significant risk but it is minimal. Just in case we run into a problem, we have spoken with our counterparts in the Ukrainian military. They're willing to create a diversion to even further minimize that risk. An alternative plan would be for the team to drive civilian vehicles across the border. I don't like that plan because of the increased time exposure on Soviet soil, but it's an option. My recommendation is to launch the mission via helicopter and request air space clearance from the Soviet Union."

SELECTED

Susan agreed with the risk assessment. "General Keene, let's move forward with the helicopter recovery plan. Asking the Soviet Union for air space clearance is not a diplomatic option and the risk is minimal. How long until your team is ready?"

"Understood. Madam President, the team needs about thirty minutes before they're prepared to launch. The rescue team will be wired up so you can follow the mission in real time from the White House."

Susan nodded. "Thank you, General. We'll talk to you in thirty minutes."

The Situation Room hummed with excitement. Susan spoke above the chatter. "Good work, everyone. Let's take a quick break. Meet back here in fifteen minutes."

23

The Special Forces rescue team wore helmet cameras equipped with night vision. The Situation Room was patched into the live audio and video feeds. On the wall of the Situation Room, each monitor was dedicated to an individual Special Forces team member. The top of each monitor displayed the camera number and the team member's last name. Every person in the Situation Room leaned forward in their chair with their eyes glued to the monitors.

During the flight to the target, the video feed was mundane and difficult to follow. There were seven team members all wearing helmet cams. The different angles and perspectives made it difficult to follow the mission unless the viewer focused on one specific monitor.

Susan locked into the video feed titled, CAM 1 — McGEE. Sergeant First Class McGee was the team lead for the mission. Susan paid close attention to the audio as all necessary team communication and checks occurred. There was a natural lull in the audio communication, which was quickly filled with jokes from the team about the constant hydraulic fluid leaks on the helicopter. The jokes reminded Susan these were just kids. Before age twenty-five, they'd seen more than a normal person does in a lifetime, but they were still kids.

The helicopter hovered over the landing zone and the gunner's mate shouted distance to the ground. "Ninety-five feet . . . eighty feet . . . sixty feet . . . five, five five!" The helicopter landed hard, throwing the team out of their seats and onto the deck of the helicopter. The team quickly regained their bearing and exited the helicopter. Less than twenty steps from the helicopter and before they could huddle as a team, a burst of AK-47 fire crackled over their heads. Several people in the Situation Room jumped back in their chairs at the sight of the tracer rounds on the monitors.

Camera five went black. They could hear, "I'm hit . . . I'm hit," followed by a pause in the audio. "It's not bad . . . glanced off my gear, I can keep going." Camera five came back into focus as Sergeant Krugman quickly recovered.

The team returned fire and moved out of the kill zone. They were engaged with two guards on the outside of the building and another team of two firing at them from an upstairs window of the house. The team bounded swiftly toward their planned entry point of the building, one team member providing covering fire while another moved. They reached the double French doors on the east side of the building, set an explosive charge, and prepared for entry. The blast blew down the French doors and the team entered the first floor of the house.

Through his earpiece, Sergeant First Class McGee received directions via satellite communications with the forward operating base. "On the thermals we see four bodies gathered on the first floor on the northwest side of the building. Two are moving and two are still. There is another hostile on the second floor moving toward you."

Sergeant McGee used hand signals to relay the information to his team and start them moving toward the objective. Sergeant McGee took the lead down the long hallway toward the pilots and their guards, two other team members stacking single file behind him. Sergeant McGee stopped briefly before the right turn in the hallway. In the Situation Room, only the sounds of breathing and footsteps came through the audio feed. There was no discussion or movement in the Situation Room. Susan's vision narrowed as she focused on the video from Sergeant McGee's video feed.

The pilots were held two rooms down the hallway to Sergeant McGee's right. He made a quick move into the hallway. The distinct click of an AK-47 safety froze him in mid-step. He focused on the black shape of a rifle barrel moving in his direction as the guard stepped into the hallway. Sergeant McGee and his teammate both fired at the guard, hitting their target. Another guard blindly sprayed the hallway with AK-47 fire. The poorly aimed rounds landed on the wall two feet above the team. Sergeant McGee returned fire as the guard stepped into the hallway. Both guards were down.

Gasps from the staff broke the silence in the Situation Room, most of whom had never witnessed the brutality and anxiety of a close-quarters firefight. The team moved quickly down the hall toward the wounded guards; both were still alive but badly wounded. A child's cry grabbed Sergeant McGee's attention. He moved toward the sound alone while the team searched and zip tied the wounded guards. Sergeant McGee entered the room where the pilots were being held. On the ground was a teenaged boy, short black hair, the right leg of his pajamas soaked in blood. His sister sat on the bed screaming, with her hands covering her eyes.

Sergeant McGee called for the team medic. Sergeant McGee quickly discovered the source of the bleeding: a gunshot wound had grazed the boy's right thigh. Sergeant McGee's hands began to shake. The team medic tapped him on the back and took over the triage.

Sergeant McGee stood up and left the room to regain his composure and check on the team. The team finished clearing the rest of the first floor and quickly moved up to the second floor. The entire building was secure and clear—no sign of the pilots.

Sergeant McGee picked up the satellite handset to talk with the JSOC command post.

"Raptor this is Wookie."

"This is Raptor. Give us a situation report."

"The pilots are not in the building. I repeat, the pilots are not in the building. We encountered six armed hostiles. And two civilians . . . both children. I have one team member walking wounded, three hostiles seriously wounded, and a wounded civilian that requires medical attention. The wounded civilian is a child."

SELECTED

"Roger that," replied the JSOC command post.

Sergeant McGee pressed for guidance. "Do we have the authority to take the civilian back with us for medical treatment? We have two minutes and thirty seconds until we need to be out of the building for extract."

Susan heard the request to help the wounded child in the Situation Room. She jumped out of her chair toward the handsets in front of General Gillingham's chair. "Which one of these talks to the team?"

General Gillingham handed Susan a blue handset marked Sat Comm.

"Sergeant McGee, this is President Turner."

"Yes, Madam President."

"How serious is the child's injury? Can we stabilize him?"

"He's lost a lot of blood. He's probably got an hour, maybe two at the most, to get to a hospital."

Susan stared at the mahogany tabletop and closed her eyes.

Sergeant McGee waited for a response. "Madam President?"

Susan responded, "Sergeant McGee, stabilize the civilian the best you can and leave him for the Soviet emergency response team."

"Roger that, Madam President . . . Wookie out."

Sergeant McGee relayed the information to the team. The medic was able to stop the bleeding and stabilize the boy's wound. The team gathered near their exit point of the building to prepare for extraction. The two Black Hawks stayed spinning on the ground inside the compound. The team planned to leave with the two pilots; even without the pilots they stuck with their plan and split into separate helicopters for the extract. The team medic worked on Sergeant Krugman's flesh wound on the ride back.

In the Situation Room, Susan's shortness of breath caused her heart to race. The room broke into sidebar discussions about why they were misled about the location of the pilots. The monitors continued to display a video feed of the helicopter ride back to the JSOC base.

Susan ignored the side conversations in the room and focused on the monitors that were still showing the team's helmet cams. Two minutes into the flight back to base, the video on three of the screens simultaneously shook wildly and went dark. The remaining helmet cams moved quickly from side to side as the Special Forces Operators wearing them watched surface-to-air missiles and tracer rounds light up the sky. After thirty seconds of chaos, the sky fell back to dark.

During the team's extraction flight back across the Ukrainian border, they triggered a battery of the Soviet air defense system. Susan immediately picked up the handset for the JSOC command post. No answer. The Situation Room erupted in gasps of horror. Susan saw the JSOC command post handset light up. She grabbed the handset. "What just happened?"

"Madam President, we lost a Black Hawk helicopter in Soviet territory. Based on Sergeant McGee's initial report, there will be no survivors. The Black Hawk took a direct hit to the fuel tank from a surface-to-air missile. Including the pilot and crew, there were seven soldiers on board. I'm sorry, Madam President."

Susan hung up the handset. She stared at the conference room table before relaying the news. "One of the Black Hawks was shot down by a surface-to-air missile. It was a direct hit to the fuel tank. We lost seven soldiers." Susan paused for a breath. "General Gillingham, please bring me a full debrief of the mission and intelligence tomorrow morning. That is all."

Susan abruptly stood up and walked out of the Situation Room into the hallway. She found the first bathroom, opened the door, and threw up in the sink. Susan collapsed to the floor in the bathroom and curled against the wall.

The rest of the staff in the Situation Room remained seated in a shocked silence.

General Gillingham slammed his fist on the table. "Not asking for air space clearance was an unacceptable risk. That is a direct failure of the president."

Arianna Redmond sharply interjected, "That's bullshit and you know it! We all sat here and listened to the options before launching the mission. I didn't hear you speak up. Everyone in this room is responsible for what happened. We made the best decision possible with the information on hand." Arianna Redmond paused to catch her breath while staring at General Gillingham. "And if you can't see that . . . you're a coward and don't deserve those stars on your collar." Before General Gillingham could respond, she abruptly stood up and left the room. The traumatized staff slowly followed her lead and left the room.

24

Susan's brother, Brad, walked off the beach with his surfboard under his right arm. The water dripping from his long brown hair glistened in the warm Southern California sunshine. He strapped the board to the roof rack of his vintage VW Bug and turned on the local NPR radio station.

"The U.S. Army has confirmed that seven soldiers were killed in a training accident near the Ukraine border with the Soviet Union. The army refused to give any further details on the incident at this time."

Brad turned off the radio; he didn't need to hear any more details. He instinctively knew the captured pilots and the training accident were linked to each other. In their previous conversations, Mr. Anderson hinted at this type of scenario. There was no doubt his services would be requested soon.

J. ALLEN WOLFRUM

Susan met with General LeMae two days after the press statement about the training accident. She'd barely slept since the failed rescue mission. General LeMae walked into the Oval Office in his usual dark blue Brooks Brothers suit, white shirt, and red tie. Susan didn't get up to greet him. Her head stayed buried in intelligence briefing documents. General LeMae sat down in the chair across from Susan and waited for her to acknowledge his presence. After ten seconds, he cleared his throat announced himself. "I see you're busy but we need to talk."

Susan looked up from the intelligence documents. There was no hiding the signs of sleep deprivation—hollow eyes, a slight tremble in her hands, and a general look of irritability. General LeMae put his agenda aside. "Susan . . . are you okay?"

"Am I okay? Of course I'm okay. I told Mason I was busy and not to be interrupted. I don't have time for a lecture."

General LeMae didn't react. "I'm here to help."

Susan dropped her pen. "You're here to help? Great . . . how exactly are you going to help?"

General LeMae pursed his lips and sighed. "Susan, I know it's hard."

SELECTED

Susan cocked her head and folded her arms across her chest. "Ohhh really?"

General LeMae nodded his head. He realized there was no sense in trying to talk to Susan in this state. He stood up and walked toward the door of the Oval Office. Before he made it to the door, Susan burst into tears and began shaking.

General LeMae turned and half-jogged back toward the Oval Office desk. He grabbed Susan by the shoulders, stood her up, and gave her a hug. General LeMae held Susan in silence while she cried. There were no words to console her grief; being present was the best he could do.

Susan regained control of her breathing, took a step back from General LeMae, and wiped the tears from her eyes. "Curtis, I'm sorry. I don't know why I yelled at you."

"It's okay. I'm going to get you a cup of green tea." General LeMae handed Susan his handkerchief to wipe the remaining tears and makeup from her eyes.

General LeMae came back into the Oval Office with two cups of green tea and sat them down on the coffee table in the middle of the room. "Come over here and sit down. Get away from that desk for a minute."

Susan walked over to the couch and sat down.

General LeMae started the conversation again. "How are you doing?"

Susan took a sip of tea and held the cup in her hand. "Obviously not great. I just got seven soldiers killed on a failed rescue mission . . . and we still don't have any idea where the captured pilots are being held . . . or if they're still alive."

General LeMae leaned forward. "What I asked was, How are you doing?"

Susan slumped in her chair. "I can't even answer that question because there is no me. My entire identity and my entire life is consumed by this job."

"I've seen a couple presidents come and go. It's a tough job. I couldn't do it. But you can't keep going like this, it's going to ruin your life. And it's going to ruin your relationship with your boys."

Susan exhaled deeply. "I know but I can't just quit. For the rest of eternity, in their history books, kids will be reading about the president who couldn't hack it. Even worse, Greg and Tommy will have to live the rest of their lives answering questions about me."

SELECTED

General LeMae stopped Susan's negative spiral. "I didn't say you had to quit. But you do need to find a way to make the job sustainable. Because right now, you're not in a place where you can even make a rational decision." General LeMae paused to let his words sink in. "This isn't your first rodeo. Remember when you first took over as squadron commander in Mosul and thought you could sleep three hours a night? How long did that last?"

Susan rolled her eyes and shook her head. "I can't believe I was that stupid."

"Exactly . . . and this is no different. You can't work without sleeping for days at a time. The stakes are higher and the decisions are more difficult but this is not any different than what you've done in the past."

Susan sighed. "I know, I know. I need to get my life together."

General LeMae saw that his message had gotten through to Susan. "All right, I'm done with the pep talk. Are you up to talking about work?"

Susan perked up. "Yeah sure, what is it?"

"Our intelligence assets on the ground alerted us to the

Soviet military calling up reserve troops about a month ago. Ever since then, we have been closely monitoring their movement. It seems like a slow systematic move westward to the borders. They're preparing for something."

Susan nodded. "I think I remember something about Soviet reserve troops being activated in my daily briefings. It was just another bullet point, no other information."

"Yes, but what you haven't heard is that we've observed an oddity in the type of troops being moved toward the borders. They aren't the typical war fighting units—infantry, tanks, artillery. They're moving engineering and construction units toward the borders."

Susan furrowed her brow. "Seems like a good thing?"

"I wouldn't call it good. The Ukrainian rebels are working to get the Southern Ukraine state of Crimea legally annexed to the Soviets and the NSA believes they're close to making it happen."

Susan shot General LeMae a look of confusion. "Let me make sure I understand what you just said. The Ukrainian people are going to vote to give Crimea to the Soviets? And all the Soviets have to do is say thank you?"

SELECTED

General LeMae raised his eyebrows. "Exactly. And if history repeats itself, when the Soviets take over Crimea, they're going to kill every Ukrainian in the region who fought against the rebels."

"Oh my god."

"It's just a hunch but I think it all fits together. The Soviets get the Ukrainian people to hand over their land, and of course, that includes oil and natural gas reserves. Then the Soviets move in, construct oil and gas pipelines for exportation, and in the process eliminate anyone who gets in the way. Then reap the financial benefits for generations to come."

Susan sat up straight on the couch. "Do the Joint Chiefs of Staff know about this?"

"Yes, but they've dismissed it as unsubstantiated speculation. Which is why you haven't heard about it in your briefings."

"Hmmpph. What can we do?"

"Well, I think having a conversation with the Russian ambassador is a good place to start. I'm sure he'd also like to give you an update on their search for our pilots."

Susan nodded in agreement. "We didn't end our last

meeting on a positive note. But I still think I can get him to help us in exchange for loosening up on the sanctions. I'll have Senator Reynolds set it up." Susan stood up from the couch. "Thank you, Curtis. I'm glad you stopped by. I let myself get too wrapped up in this."

"Anytime, Susan."

Susan gave General LeMae a hug and walked with him to the door of the Oval Office. Before leaving, General LeMae turned toward Susan. "Tell Earl to hit up the bank before our next checkers game. I play for keeps. Cash only." Susan shook her head and laughed as General LeMae walked away.

25

Susan picked up her cup of coffee and glanced at the newspaper on the dining-room table. A picture of her sitting in the Oval Office on the front page grabbed her attention. The headline read PRESIDENT TURNER, A DIFFERENT PERSON BEHIND CLOSED DOORS. Susan's heart raced.

She grabbed the paper and carefully read the article. Her hand trembled. She folded the paper and laid it back on the table with the article facedown. If the article had made false claims, she could have easily brushed it off, but every piece of the article was true. She couldn't understand how that type of information made it to the press. Nothing in the article was public information; everything in the article happened behind closed doors. The article listed the source of information as an anonymous insider within the White House administration.

Susan's mind raced through the list of people that would have been present for all the events in the article. The article covered meetings with multiple people, spanning the White

House, Pentagon, and NSA headquarters. The most disturbing pieces were the accounts of Susan's activities behind closed doors in the Oval Office. Susan narrowed down her list to one person: her chief of staff, Mason Adams.

Before having breakfast, Susan walked directly to Mason's office. The door was open. Mason sat at his desk eating yogurt and reading the newspaper. Susan knocked on the opened door and stepped into his office. "Good morning, Mason. I apologize for interrupting. Could you let FBI Director Redmond know that I will be visiting her at FBI headquarters this morning. Please arrange transportation with the Secret Service."

Mason looked up at Susan and narrowed his eyes.

Before he could speak, Susan added, "I know the protocol is to secure my schedule at least one day in advance. This is important."

Mason nodded. "Okay. I'll make it happen. Do you have an agenda that I can share with Director Redmond?"

Susan shook her head. "Nope. Just tell her I need thirty minutes of her time this morning."

Mason wrote down the instructions on a legal pad of

paper. He looked up at Susan. "Who will be attending the meeting? I need to give the FBI headquarters notification of any visitors."

Susan replied, "Just me. I'll be traveling alone. I don't want to interrupt anyone else's schedule on such short notice."

Mason raised an eyebrow. "Okay. I'll, uhh . . . I'll make the arrangements. The Secret Service escort will be ready as soon as possible. Anything else I can do?"

"No, that's it. Thank you, Mason." Susan walked out of the office.

Mason looked down at the headline: PRESIDENT TURNER, A DIFFERENT PERSON BEHIND CLOSED DOORS. He rubbed his hand over his forehead and closed his eyes.

Arianna Redmond sat at her desk and watched President Turner walk down the hallway toward her office. Halfway down the hallway, President Turner stopped and quickly spoke to the Secret Service agents. President Turner continued walking; the Secret Service agents did not follow her. Arianna

Redmond furrowed her brow. She opened the door to her office and greeted President Turner before she had the chance to knock.

Arianna Redmond smiled and shook her hand. "Madam President, thank you for stopping by this morning."

President Turner nodded. "Thank you, Director Redmond."

They walked into the office. Arianna Redmond sat behind her desk and President Turner in the chair on the other side of the desk. Arianna Redmond pressed a gray button on the right side of her desk and the blinds closed.

Susan quickly filled the silence. "I assume you saw the paper this morning?"

Arianna Redmond showed no emotion and kept her eyes on Susan. "I did."

Susan folded her hands in her lap. "I need your help . . . and your discretion."

Arianna Redmond narrowed her eyes.

Susan continued, "I believe the source mentioned in the article is my chief of staff, Mason Adams."

SELECTED

Arianna Redmond remained silent and slightly nodded her head while she contemplated the situation. A politician trying to save their reputation is more dangerous than a wounded bear.

Susan realized Arianna was not yet on her side, so she relaxed her posture. "I'm not convinced he's the source. I don't want to believe that he's responsible, but he's the only person who was present for all of the events described in the article. He knows about my disagreements with General Gillingham and Ambassador Dashkov storming out of the Oval Office." Susan paused and sighed. "And he's the only person who would know that I have a bottle of whiskey in the Oval Office."

Arianna Redmond took a moment to read the situation before responding. She looked Susan in the eye. "I couldn't care less about a newspaper article that tarnishes your reputation. What I am concerned about is the possibility of national security secrets being leaked from the same source. Whoever leaked this information to the press clearly has access to other confidential information."

Susan remained calm and listened.

Arianna continued, "I want to find the source of the leak

to the press and we need to keep the investigation off the radar. I'm concerned that if the investigation happens in the open, we'll scare off the source."

Susan nodded. "I agree."

Arianna Redmond briefly looked around the room. "I have an agent I can put on the case. She will report directly to me. Give us a few weeks to work the case. In the meantime, act as normal as possible around your chief of staff. I'll be in touch when we have more information to share."

Susan exhaled and felt a weight come off her shoulders. "Thank you."

Arianna Redmond put her hands on the desk. "Madam President, anything else I can help you with today?"

Susan stood up and shook her hand. "No, Director Redmond. I'll let you get back to work." Susan turned and walked out the door.

Arianna Redmond opened the blinds and watched Susan walk down the hallway with her Secret Service detail. Arianna walked back to her desk, picked up the phone, and dialed the chief of the FBI National Security Branch, Brian Connolly.

Brian Connolly answered, "Director Redmond, this is

SELECTED

Section Chief Connolly, how can I help you?"

Arianna replied, "I've got an assignment from the White House and I need an agent for two weeks."

"Okay . . . we're short staffed, do you have someone in mind?"

"Yes, Agent Sanders. She's new, started a month ago. She's still green, shouldn't hurt you too much to lose her."

"Well, I guess if you have to take someone, it might as well be a newbie."

"Thanks Brian, I owe you one."

"More than one. I'll send her up to your office ASAP."

Brian Connolly walked out of his office into the bullpen and shouted, "Agent Sanders . . . report to Director Redmond's office immediately."

Rebecca Sanders stood up from her cubicle and responded, "Yes, sir." She stood frozen for a moment. The entire office stared at her.

Brian Connolly shouted again, "Well . . . don't just stand there. Get upstairs. And remember . . . you're representing the National Security Branch. If you embarrass me, don't bother coming back."

Agent Sanders walked up to Director Redmond's open door and knocked to gain her attention. Director Redmond looked up and Agent Sanders announced herself. "Ma'am . . . National Security Branch Chief Brian Connolly ordered me to report to your office."

Director Redmond smiled. "Come on in. And close the door."

Agent Sanders closed the door and sat down in the chair across the desk from Director Redmond.

Arianna Redmond smiled. "How's the first month been? I had lunch with your parents last weekend. They couldn't be happier. You know, getting through the academy is the easy part. Keeping your integrity on the job is the true test of a career FBI agent."

Rebecca Sanders shrugged and sighed. "I know. I've heard it from my parents a million times. 'Your career at the agency is the most important thing.' But yeah, things are good so far. I'm doing the normal new agent stuff, follow-up phone calls, taking notes and writing reports."

Arianna Redmond replied, "Sorry for the lecture. I couldn't

help myself. It's good to see you on the job. Did you see the paper today?"

"Are you talking about the article claiming President Turner is hotheaded, short-tempered, argumentative, and a booze hound?"

Arianna Redmond nodded. "I would use a more neutral tone . . . but yes, that's the article."

Rebecca Sanders shrugged her shoulders. "Yes . . . I read it. Why?"

"Because President Turner came in my office this morning and she's under the impression that her chief of staff is the source of the leak. You're going to find out if her suspicion is true."

Rebecca Sanders squirmed in her chair. "Okay . . . but I don't see why the FBI is involved."

Arianna Redmond leaned forward. "Let me be clear. I don't care about the president's reputation. But I am concerned that someone with access to classified information is willing to leak it to the press. And if they're leaking it to the press, there is a very real possibility they're also leaking classified information to foreign governments. We need to find the source of the leak."

Rebecca Sanders nodded. "Do we have any leads other than the chief of staff?"

"No. Start with the chief of staff. Focus on his activity outside the White House. I want a daily update. Any questions?"

Rebecca Sanders nodded. "Yeah, I have lots of questions."

Arianna Redmond stood up, smiled, and motioned toward the door. "Good. Get out there and find the answers."

26

Gazprom, Inc., is a public corporation responsible for all drilling, refining, storage, and exportation of oil and natural gas in the Soviet Union. The corporation is technically a publicly traded corporation on stock exchanges worldwide, but the Soviet government is still the largest shareholder and all board members are current or former high-ranking Soviet government officials.

President Rosinski attended the monthly Gazprom board of directors meeting at their Moscow headquarters, just a few blocks from the Kremlin. He took his seat at the head of the conference room table for the board of directors meeting. President Rosinski remained silent during roll call; his presence and remarks were explicitly excluded from the official records. The official Gazprom CEO, Ivan Ritkov, seated to Boris Rosinski's right, started the meeting with a company status update.

"Gentlemen, thank you for taking the time to attend our

monthly board of directors meeting. The first two issues are related to our continuing troubles in the Crimea region of the Ukraine. The civil unrest in the Ukraine has prompted the Ukrainian president to cancel all Gazprom contracts in the Ukraine. A US-based company will take over our work; we have three months to complete the transition."

President Rosinski looked around the room to judge the reaction from the board members. The room remained silent; the board members kept blank expressions on their faces as if they were at a poker table.

President Rosinski broke the silence with a question. "Mr. Ritkov, you mentioned that there were two items related to the Ukraine? What is the second?"

"Yes. I regret to inform you that five Gazprom employees were killed yesterday while working in the Chernihiv natural gas fields. They were ambushed leaving the job site."

Boris Rosinski paused before responding, "It's a tragedy anytime we lose a fellow Soviet. Please be sure to compensate their families and extend to them a job offer at Gazprom if possible." Boris Rosinski paused before moving onto the next topic.

"How long before the American company takes over?"

SELECTED

Ivan Ritkov replied, "Their work officially starts in three months. We are expected to transfer what knowledge we have to their management team prior to the transition."

The silence between questions made the men in the room fidget in their chairs. President Rosinski paused before responding, "We will not be transitioning to the Americans. Our employees will continue working in the Ukraine under our current contract structure until further notice."

Ivan Ritkov couldn't hide his surprise. "Should I inform the Ukrainian government?"

"No. Their operations won't be interrupted. By the time of the transition, the Ukrainian people will have voted to annex the Crimea region to the Soviet Union. Once we own the source of their oil and natural gas, we can negotiate favorable terms to build pipelines north toward Belarus and Latvia. From Latvia we can ship directly to Europe. This will triple our oil and natural gas sales to Europe."

"Is there planning that needs to be done prior to the annexation vote?" asked Mr. Ritkov.

"Don't do anything that can be detected by our foreign investors or the public. Assemble a small team of your best engineers and architects to work on the plans for the pipeline.

The project is to be kept off the official records. KGB Director Tremonov will be in touch with specific details."

President Rosinski scanned the room. "If there are no questions, Mr. Ritkov, please continue the meeting."

President Rosinski stood up from his chair at the head of the conference room table and walked out the door.

Later that afternoon, President Rosinski called KGB Director Tremonov into his office. He sat down in the chair across from President Rosinski's desk and opened his black notebook.

"Nikolai, what are the latest poll numbers on the Crimea annexation vote?"

"The Ukrainian people are slowly coming around. Our cyber warfare team has made a twenty-percentage-point swing in the polls." Director Tremonov flipped to the front of his notebook for the details. "The polls are predicting a no vote . . . but our cyber warfare team's model is predicting a yes vote. The cyber warfare group believes there is an underlying favor toward joining the Soviet Union that isn't reflected in the current polls."

Boris Rosinski nodded his head. "Keep me updated. What about the American pilots?"

"Our agents contacted Alexander Umirov, the leader of the Chechen rebel group holding the pilots. Our expectations were explained to him in detail. When our agents showed him pictures of his family at their homes, he understood the importance of following our instructions. We told him to stop moving the pilots, and no more videos or torture unless explicitly told to do so by our team. But he refused to release the pilots."

"Why did he not agree to release the pilots?"

"I don't know, he's a Chechen." Director Tremonov paused while President Rosinski nodded his head and looked off to the corner of the office.

Director Tremonov broke the silence. "I have an update from the cyber warfare group on the American public. The extreme anti-Soviet groups are gaining support and pushing for military intervention against us. The various factions in America pushing for military intervention are uniting under the name of the Euro-Skeptics."

President Rosinski cracked a smile. "An anti-Soviet group calling themselves Euro-Skeptics. Only in America." He paused to gain his composure. "Do we have insight into the American president's reaction?"

"Nothing outside of her psychological profile. She's weak; all she will do is make threats."

President Rosinski interrupted, "We need them to back down. We can't have the Americans launching another crazy rescue mission."

"Do we need to prepare for a retaliation from the Americans?"

President Rosinski motioned with his hand. "No. The Americans crossed our border on a secret rescue mission. They will never admit their mistake in public."

"We can always let the Chechens kill the pilots," suggested Director Tremonov.

President Rosinski looked down at the top of his desk. He needed the Americans to move their focus away from Eastern Europe. "Force Umirov to release the American pilots, I don't care how you do it. Then eliminate Umirov and his men."

Director Tremonov held back his opposition to releasing

the Americans. "The building where the American pilots are being held is heavily booby-trapped. I'm concerned that in a stressful situation Umirov might panic and kill the Americans."

"Nikolai . . . life is a risk. I trust that your team can get the American pilots out safely. Protect their lives as if they were your own."

27

Susan got up from her desk to greet Senator Reynolds and Ambassador Dashkov. Senator Reynolds wore a tight polo shirt; his broad shoulders drew Susan's attention. She felt her face blush and quickly turned her thoughts back to work.

She tried to put their previous adversarial meeting behind them by warmly inviting Ambassador Dashkov to a more relaxed location. "It looks like we've got a break from the dreary winter weather. Let's get out of this stuffy office and enjoy the sunshine while it lasts. Follow me."

Senator Reynolds and Ambassador Dashkov exchanged glances. Ambassador Dashkov shrugged his shoulders and followed Susan out of the Oval Office. Susan led the men down the White House hallway. "Ambassador Dashkov, how's your morning been so far?"

"I'm a bit worn out. Senator Reynolds is tougher on the squash court than I anticipated. I'll be sure to clear my evening social calendar before our next match."

Susan chuckled. "I'm glad to hear you two are getting along." Susan made a right down the next hallway. "Ambassador, I apologize for the harsh request I made in our last meeting. My intention was not to offend you, or the Soviet Union. I'm sure you understand that getting our pilots home safe is extremely important to the United States. I overstepped my bounds. I have no doubt that the Soviet Union is working as hard as possible to find our pilots."

Ambassador Dashkov replied, "Madam President, no apology necessary. The Soviet Union also wants your pilots returned home safely. The Chechen rebels are not friends of the Soviet Union—they are terrorists operating within our borders."

"Thank you, Ambassador, I'm glad we share the same goals." Susan opened the French doors to the White House Rose Garden. "Gentlemen, let's sit outside while we talk." Susan continued through the door and onto the cement patio. She took a deep breath of fresh air, bent down to take off her heels, and wiggled her toes in the grass. She led the men across the lawn toward the opposite end of the Rose Garden. "I love the crisp air and the feeling of grass underneath my bare feet. It reminds me of back home. Ambassador, what do you miss most about living in the Soviet Union?"

"Hmm . . . that's an interesting question." Ambassador Dashkov looked up at the blue sky for a moment before answering. "There are two things that keep me connected to home while I'm in America. A Soviet bath house just south of Logan Circle here in Washington. Seeing the familiar faces is nice, but the smells and sounds are what really bring my thoughts back home." Ambassador Dashkov paused his response to look around the Rose Garden. "And, of course, family meals on Sundays. There is nothing like family to bring you back to reality when you're thinking too highly of yourself." Ambassador Dashkov smiled.

Susan laughed. "That's for sure. Have a seat." The midcentury handcrafted Woodlawn chairs were arranged in a circle with a matching wood table in the center. "Ambassador Dashkov, you mentioned the captured pilots. Is there anything you can share about the search?"

"Unfortunately, I don't know any additional details that haven't already been communicated to the Pentagon from the KGB office in Moscow. We're still looking for the Chechen terrorist cell responsible. The KGB field officers in the area have been questioning their contacts that have ties to the Chechens."

SELECTED

"Do you think the group holding our pilots is pretending to be Chechen?" asked Susan.

Ambassador Dashkov tilted his head and raised an eyebrow while contemplating the question. "That is a good question. I'm not a military strategist, so please don't take my opinion as the truth. In the Soviet Union, we have dealt with terrorism and extremist groups for centuries. We have a widely known zero-tolerance policy. The Chechens are the only group we know of that is willing to sacrifice themselves and their family for their cause. I don't know of another group that dedicated. That's a long way of saying, no."

"This is a difficult topic for both of our countries. I appreciate your candor."

"Madam President, if you have the time, I'd like to bring up another difficult topic."

"Absolutely, go ahead."

"Senator Reynolds and I were discussing this earlier in the morning. . . . As you may have seen in the news, Soviets living in America are becoming the targets of racial slurs and vandalism. I don't think either of us wants to see this continue. Is there something we can do?"

Susan pursed her lips. "I've seen the news reports and it's terrible. I assure you the people carrying out these crimes do not represent the views of the American people. You have my word that we will prosecute the individuals responsible to the full extent of the law."

Ambassador Dashkov nodded his head. "Thank you for understanding."

"Ambassador, is there anything else you would like to discuss?"

"No, I don't want to take up any more of your precious time, Madam President. Thank you for taking the time to listen."

"I'm always available. Let me walk with you back inside the White House."

"That's not necessary, Madam President. Enjoy the beautiful sunshine. I know my way around," replied Ambassador Dashkov.

"Squash, next week, same time?" asked Senator Reynolds.

"Absolutely." Ambassador Dashkov turned and walked across the Rose Garden lawn into the White House.

SELECTED

Susan turned toward Senator Reynolds, "So, what do you think?"

"I think he's awfully quick for his age. I'm going to have trouble beating him."

Susan rolled her eyes.

"Sorry. I don't know. I think he's a politician. He isn't going to give up any information; he's going to do his best to stay neutral and be an advocate for the Soviet people. All that being said, I don't trust him."

Susan pressed, "Why?"

"I don't know, something just isn't right. I can't put my finger on it. But I don't trust him." Senator Reynolds shrugged his shoulders. "I mean he's the Soviet ambassador, is it that surprising that I don't trust him?"

"No, probably not. I get the same feeling. He's hiding something. I have a feeling the Soviets know the location of the pilots and are keeping it to themselves." Susan shook her head and paused. "Did you find any other options for sanctions? I still think we can force President Rosinski to tell us what he knows about the pilots. If we can push him hard enough with the sanctions, he won't have a choice."

J. ALLEN WOLFRUM

Senator Reynolds frowned. He'd only been the chair of the Senate Foreign Relations Committee for a few months. He was still learning the rules. "Ahhh . . . there are options but I wouldn't call them good. It looks like we've done everything we can in terms of straightforward sanctions related to the Ukraine. The next step is to target exports of the Soviet Union and target their trade partners. We can legally do that, but I can't predict all the unintended foreign relations consequences."

Susan's face hardened. "What do you mean by 'unintended consequences'? I want to put President Rosinski in a position where he's forced to cooperate with us, whether he likes it or not."

"Well, if we start putting sanctions on foreign companies and exports, we are bound to raise some eyebrows at very powerful corporations. And very powerful corporations have significant influence over governments in foreign countries. If I had to guess, you'd be getting a lot of very upset leaders of foreign countries calling you to voice their concerns. And the extreme end of that is disrupting foreign economies."

Susan sighed. "Seems like that isn't going to solve any of our other problems with the Soviet Union."

SELECTED

"What other problems are you talking about?"

"Well . . . the Soviets have activated a large number of reserve troops and seem to be moving them toward the western borders with Ukraine, Latvia, and Belarus."

Senator Reynolds leaned forward. "Do we know why?"

"No, not really. But General LeMae thinks it might have to do with the annexation of Crimea and the construction of an oil and gas pipeline."

Senator Reynolds rubbed his hand over his chin. "Makes sense to me. If they own the natural resources, they need a way to get them out to customers." Senator Reynolds looked down at the ground for a moment before continuing the conversation. "This is all starting to tie together. Have you heard of Pacific International?"

Susan furrowed her brow and shook her head. "No, doesn't ring a bell. Why?"

"When we were working through the financial details with the NSA, trying to find targets for sanctions, the company kept coming up. Pacific International was listed as the owner of a substantial number of the shell companies we were tracing. I haven't done all the homework but it seems like they're heavily invested in Eastern European manufacturing, raw material, and transportation companies."

Susan leaned back in her chair. The question reminded her of the flash drive with dangerous information about corporations colluding with the government that General LeMae warned her about back in Idaho. She brushed off the question. "Hmm . . . I can have Mason look into it."

"Susan, there's something else you should know. I really don't want to bring this up, but you know people are upset about the pilots. And it's starting to be a problem. There are some representatives that think we should be doing more to get them back. There's a lot of discontent being spread around the Senate and Congress."

"I know people are upset. We're doing everything we can." Susan saw Mason Adams walking toward them. "Here comes Mason."

Senator Reynolds glanced toward Mason as he walked toward them. "What is he wearing?"

Susan laughed. "Those are his happy colors. You need to loosen up, Mr. Lawyer. You have something against bright blue bow ties and pink socks?"

SELECTED

Susan smiled to herself on the walk back into the White House with Mason.

Later that evening, Vice President Wilkes met with his contact, Mr. Jones, who'd called the meeting at the last minute and deviated from their usual library meeting locations. They met in a dark Italian restaurant in a corner booth near the rear exit. Mr. Jones arrived twenty minutes before Vice President Wilkes to scout the location.

Vice President Wilkes sat down in the booth across from Mr. Jones and nervously scanned the room. "I've been making the drops. Why are we changing locations? If someone sees us—"

Mr. Jones interrupted. "Calm down and stop looking around the room." Mr. Jones slowly pointed his index finger to his face. "Look at me. Act normal and everything will be fine."

"What do you want?"

"The audio recordings have been very helpful. Keep the device in place—we need to know who she's meeting with and—"

"What are you doing with those recordings?"

Mr. Jones calmly raised his index finger. "I'm asking the questions. Understood?"

Vice President Wilkes pursed his lips in frustration and nodded his head.

"As I was saying, I'll keep passing you instructions when we meet, nothing changes. What I need now is for you to start the legislative paperwork for impeaching President Turner."

Vice President Wilkes cocked his head in disbelief. "For what?"

"None of your business. Tomorrow morning at ten, three lawyers will meet you in your home office. Find a reason to be there. If anyone asks, the lawyers are there to help you draft the education reform bill. The lawyers will take care of the paperwork; all you need to do is strengthen your list of President Turner's enemies. We need a majority vote in the Senate and House to impeach President Turner. Make sure we have it. Understood?"

Vice President Wilkes grimaced and stared at Mr. Jones before answering, "Yes."

"Good, I'll expect an update at our next meeting. If you're

thinking about double-crossing us . . . remember, we still have the tapes. What you did to those kids . . ." Mr. Jones paused and snarled, "The tapes go to your wife first. I want her to know what you did. You don't deserve to have anyone grieve for you." Mr. Jones slid out of the booth and walked silently out the back door of the restaurant.

Vice President Wilkes closed his eyes and fought back tears.

28

Susan made a point to be at Greg and Tommy's first indoor soccer game of the season. At halftime, she walked back to the stands with two soft pretzels, cheese dipping sauce, and one root beer. Susan handed Earl a pretzel and Rose the root beer. "Now we're even."

He squinted in confusion and grabbed the pretzel.

"Well . . . I did kind of strong-arm you two into moving with me to Washington, DC."

Rose smiled and put her arm around Earl. "I think it turned out to be the right choice."

Earl smiled and agreed. "Sometimes us old folks get stuck in our ways and we need a push to get going."

After the game, Susan, Earl, and Rose stood in the lobby waiting for Greg and Tommy. Susan and Rose discussed the logistics of dinner for the boys; they still needed to eat and get their homework done before bedtime.

Before the boys made it out to the lobby after the game, a Secret Service agent interrupted Susan's conversation with Rose. "Madam President, General Gillingham is on the phone for you. Are you available to take the call?"

Susan excused herself and took the cell phone from the agent. "This is President Turner."

"Madam President, we have an update on the pilots being held by the Chechen rebels. The situation is evolving at the moment. Our satellite surveillance picked up unusual movement at one of the possible holding locations we are monitoring. We need you in the Situation Room."

Susan nodded her head slowly. "Thank you. I'll be there." Susan ended the call and handed the phone back to the agent. She walked back toward Earl and Rose. Greg and Tommy emerged from the crowd in the lobby escorted by Secret Service Agent Young.

"Mom, did you see that pass I made to Scott for the last goal?" asked Greg.

"I sure did! Good job, honey." She grabbed Greg by the shoulder and gave him a quick hug.

"Agent Young showed me how to make a no-look pass. It was awesome, I totally fooled the defender."

Agent Young blushed and remained silent.

"Greg, Tommy. I have to head back to work. When you get back home, you can have a snack, then straight upstairs to do your homework. Got it?"

"But Mom . . . can we at least ride with you back home?"

Susan frowned. Agent Young spoke up before Susan delivered disappointing news to the boys. "You two can ride with me. I'll show you how the radios work."

"Cool, can I have my own call sign?" asked Tommy.

"Absolutely. We'll think of one on the ride back," replied Agent Young. He turned toward Susan. "Madam President, is it all right with you?"

"Yes, thank you, Agent Young."

Susan hugged each of the boys. As they walked away with Agent Young she reminded them, "Don't forget your homework."

SELECTED

In the Situation Room at the White House, the Joint Chiefs of Staff scrambled to get their intelligence images and analysis on the monitors. Susan walked into the room amid the chaos and got sucked into the tension of the scrambling staff. She interrupted the action by announcing above the noise, "What information do we know?"

The conversations among the staff died down and General Gillingham took charge. "Madam President, the situation is—"

"I don't care! Get me access to every cell tower within twenty miles." The entire room focused on an NSA analyst shouting into a cell phone. She felt the room's attention on her and looked up from her computer. "Sorry, Madam President."

General Gillingham resumed his update. "As I was saying, the situation is fluid. About an hour and a half ago we picked up five vehicles staging near one of the locations we have under satellite surveillance. The location is a warehouse near the town of Bryansk in the Soviet Union. The vehicles are unmarked Toyota Camrys, no military affiliation. Our NSA analyst kept an eye on the situation but didn't initially raise any alarms to his supervisor." General Gillingham looked at the clock. "At 6:45 p.m. Eastern time, the five vehicles drove together toward the warehouse. A total of ten men exited the vehicles and entered the warehouse. At that point, our NSA analyst raised a warning." General Gillingham paused again to read his notes.

Susan's excitement overwhelmed her and she interrupted. "What else do we know? Did the ten men leave? Did anyone else leave?"

General Gillingham looked up from his handwritten notes and continued. "Ten men from the vehicles entered the building. Eight of those ten men left the building fifteen minutes later and drove away heading eastbound. After the five vehicles left, another white Mercedes SUV left the warehouse, headed westbound."

Susan replied, "Ten men entered the building, eight left the building, so there are two men left in the building?"

"Possibly. We don't know who or how many men were in the Mercedes SUV headed westbound."

"How confident are we that this location is where the pilots are being held?" asked Susan.

"Given the information we have right now, I'm eighty percent confident our pilots are either in that warehouse right now, or were in the warehouse at some point in the last twenty-four hours."

Susan pointed toward the monitors on the wall. "Can we get a recap of the satellite images on the monitors? I want to see it with my own eyes."

The technicians scrambled to put together a time lapse of the satellite images. The NSA analyst working on the cell tower wiretap yelled, "Got it." All eyes went to her as she quickly typed on her keyboard.

"Go ahead, what do you have?" asked General Gillingham.

"We tapped into the cell towers near the warehouse. I was able to filter out all the residential chatter and I found two encrypted text messages. We broke the encryption. The first message is a single word: 'done.' The second message, sent twenty seconds later, is 'cleanup crew needed asap.' Both messages were sent after the eight men left the warehouse."

Lt. Colonel Rodriguez stomped on the gas pedal of the Mercedes SUV and looked in the rearview mirror for signs of a vehicle following them.

29

Lt. Colonel Rodriguez drove the Mercedes SUV with Lt. Colonel Harris in the passenger seat. The Soviet street signs made no sense to him. "See anything?" asked Lt. Colonel Rodriguez.

Lt. Colonel Harris spun around in his seat. "Nothing . . . no headlights."

The men sat in silence for a few minutes as they drove southwest according to the compass in the dashboard of the Mercedes. They drove down a two-lane blacktop road. Occasionally another vehicle would pass them in the opposite direction. Their anxiety grew with every mile. They had no plan.

"What do you think, Harris?"

Harris replied, "I think we need to head straight for the Ukrainian border. If we keep heading southwest, we have to hit it at some point."

Rodriguez replied, "Agreed. Heading for the border is our best chance." He paused before asking, "What do you think happened back there?"

"Which part?" asked Harris.

"All of it. Whatever happened, it didn't go according to plan. Either someone was trying to rescue us and it went bad or someone was trying to kill us and it went bad. All I know is we got lucky."

Harris shook his head. "Now we're screwed. No doubt they put the word out and are looking for us. You saw those guys who have been hanging around, right? They weren't part of the group holding us. They had to be some kind of Soviet Special Forces. If they find us, they're definitely killing us, no questions asked."

Rodriguez took his eyes off the road and looked at Harris. "Hey. Cut the shit and snap out of it. This has to work. It's not an option. We're getting out of this alive."

Harris paused to catch his breath. "You're right, man, sorry. We're going to get out of this."

Rodriguez replied, "Let's just keep going southwest toward the border. Either way we're getting the hell out of the Soviet

Union. We made it this far. It'll work out."

Harris saw red and blue lights in the mirror. He turned to get a better look. "Goddamn it, the Soviet police are behind us."

Back in Washington DC, the Situation Room buzzed with activity.

"Get it on the monitor," shouted an analyst. The screen flickered black and then showed video from a surveillance drone focused on a vehicle driving on a two-lane blacktop road. The analyst spoke up. "We found the white Mercedes SUV—it's traveling southwest toward the Ukrainian border. We have a drone with weapons onboard twenty minutes from the target. The satellite on the monitors is a five-minute delay."

Susan yelled over the chatter, "Stop." Her voice shocked the analyst, and everyone else in the room. "Everyone take a breath. We're all excited and working as fast as we can. But are not going to let that excitement dictate our decision making." Susan paused. "Everyone sit back down and let's talk through the new information." Susan gestured toward the analyst who put the satellite video on the monitor. "Tell us how you found the vehicle."

"I pieced together several different satellite feeds at the time the vehicle left the warehouse. Then I started looking for cars driving the same direction. There weren't many at this time of night. I got lucky."

"How certain are you that this is the same vehicle from the warehouse?" asked Susan.

"I'm 99.9 percent sure, Madam President."

Susan continued with more questions. "Okay. Do we know who is in the vehicle?" Susan looked around the room; no one spoke up. "Okay . . . so we don't know who's in the vehicle . . . any ideas?"

Another analyst spoke up. "It could be the two remaining men from the sedans that raided the building."

Another voice chimed in, "Or someone who was already in the building."

Susan jumped in, "Or Lt. Colonel Rodriguez and Lt. Colonel Harris." The room nodded their heads at the possibility. "General Gillingham, how long before the Special Forces team in the area can be on target?"

"Ten minutes. They have two Black Hawks with rotors spinning on the airstrip right now."

Susan stood up from her chair and put her hands on the table. "No matter who is in that vehicle, we want to talk to them. General Gillingham, get the Special Forces team on target. Have them stop the vehicle. Tell them to assume Lt. Colonel Harris and Lt. Colonel Rodriguez are in the vehicle."

In the white Mercedes SUV, Rodriguez and Harris argued over what to do about the police.

"We have to stop," said Rodriguez.

Harris shook his head. "No way."

"What are we going to do? Outrun him?"

Harris shot back, "We can't just let him arrest us."

Rodriguez slowed down the car. "Okay, so what's your plan?"

Harris froze. He didn't have a plan.

Rodriguez answered the question. "If you don't have a

plan, we're stopping. If we have to . . . we'll jump him. It's two on one, he can't take us both."

Harris nodded his head, unbuckled his seat belt, and looked for something in the car he could use as a weapon.

While Harris and Rodriguez plotted their attack plan, the Soviet police officer ran the license plate on the white Mercedes SUV. A tap on the window startled the Soviet police officer. He looked up to see a man standing outside his vehicle holding a KGB badge.

The police officer rolled down the window.

"Officer Kaminski, my name is Agent Larov, I work for the KGB counterterrorism unit. The men in that vehicle are under my protection. You will not get out of your vehicle. You will turn on the loudspeaker and calmly tell them they are free to leave. Do you understand my instructions?"

Officer Kaminski nodded his head. "Yes, sir."

"Good." Agent Larov walked back to his vehicle and waited.

Rogriguez and Harris heard through the police loudspeaker, "You are free to go" in broken English.

They exchanged glances. "Is he serious?"

The police vehicle turned off its lights and drove off in the opposite direction.

Rodriguez put the white Mercedes SUV into drive. "I guess he was serious. Maybe we stole a diplomat's car?"

Harris put his seat belt back on and put the tire iron back under the seat. "I don't know and I don't care. Let's get out of here."

Rodriguez pulled back onto the two-lane highway. Five minutes later, Harris rolled down the window and stuck his head outside. "You hear that? Slow down." Rodriguez slowed down and then stopped the vehicle in the middle of the road. He heard the noise as well. "That's a Black Hawk. And it's getting closer."

"Yup. Do they know where we are? Or that we're in here?"

The pilots froze in a moment of indecision. Harris broke the silence. "Get out now." Rodriguez gave him a confused look. "Get out of the car. Now. Put it in park and get out. They need to positively ID us."

SELECTED

The concept registered with Rodriguez: if there was a Black Hawk helicopter coming in to rescue them, the rescue team would need to positively identify everyone in the vehicle. Standing in front of the headlights in plain sight was the safest place to be when the rescue team landed. Rodriguez and Harris jumped out of the car and stood in front of the headlights with their hands in the air. A Black Hawk landed in middle of the highway thirty yards in front of them.

The Situation Room was reduced to essential personnel only. Susan did not want the Situation Room full of analysts if there was another tragic ending to the rescue mission. The helmet cameras of the Special Forces team members were put on the monitors for those remaining in the Situation Room.

During the mission brief, the team leader, Sergeant First Class Washington, pressed hard for more details on the mission. His best friend died in the previous failed rescue attempt and he wasn't letting anyone on his team die the same way. The mission details were limited: grab the occupants of a white Mercedes SUV and bring them back to base. They were told no other details about the mission. The audio feed in the

Situation Room connected as the team received their final orders before walking onto the tarmac. "And gentlemen, don't be surprised if we run into resistance on the ground. Remember the rules of engagement. If you see a weapon, don't hesitate to pull the trigger."

Susan felt a hollow pit in her stomach. She had a feeling that the pilots were in the Mercedes SUV and the thought of a friendly fire incident shook her to the core. She resisted the urge to get on the radio and correct the team. She didn't want to break their concentration or put doubt in their minds based on her hunch.

The Special Forces team split into two groups of four and rode in separate helicopters to the last known position of the Mercedes SUV. After five minutes of flying low and fast, the pilot of the lead helicopter identified the SUV and made a wide circle before landing on the highway in front of the vehicle. The second helicopter landed behind the vehicle.

Two men from each Special Forces team closed in on the vehicle while the other two provided security. Sergeant First Class Washington could only see the outlines of two men standing in front of the vehicle with their hands in the air. The thumping sound of helicopter blades overpowered all other sound. The men moved toward him. He looked to his right and

SELECTED

saw his teammate take a knee and aim his weapon at the men. The men kept moving forward and Sergeant First Class Washington recognized them as Lt. Colonel Harris and Lt. Colonel Rodriguez. He quickly looked again toward his teammate and watched his thumb flick the selector on his rifle from safe to fire. He sprinted toward his teammate and shouted in his ear, "Friendly! Friendly! Friendly!"

Sergeant First Class Washington's teammate flipped the selector back to safe and they moved together toward the pilots. The sound of whirring helicopter blades made verbal communication nearly impossible. The pilots kept their hands in the air until the rescue team lowered their weapons. The rescue team huddled around the pilots and took a quick moment to scan the area. The rescue team medic shouted a simple question into each pilot's ear, "Can you move?" Lt. Colonel Rodriguez and Lt. Colonel Harris both responded with a nod and a thumbs-up.

The rescue team was on the ground for less than one minute and the entire mission took less than fifteen minutes. In the helicopter, the whirring of the blades overpowering any attempt at conversation, Rodriguez and Harris thanked the rescue team with a smile and a thumbs-up. Besides their gaunt faces, the rescued pilots appeared to be in good health.

J. ALLEN WOLFRUM

The White House Situation Room remained dead silent throughout the mission. Memories of the last failed rescue mission lingered in the minds of everyone in the room. When the Black Hawk landed safely at the JSOC command post, the room erupted in cheers and applause.

At the JSOC command post, Lt. Colonel Rodriguez and Lt. Colonel Harris were immediately given a quick medical exam to uncover any severe injuries masked by the adrenaline. At the conclusion of the medical exams, they were brought to the JSOC base commanding officer for a formal debriefing.

Neither Rodriguez nor Harris was able to provide any immediately actionable information. Their captors kept them secluded. During the first few days of captivity, they were tortured and repeatedly moved from location to location. Neither of the men was able to recall many details from that time period. Their escape from the warehouse was equally as vague in their memory.

The Joint Chiefs of Staff left the Situation Room. Susan stayed at the conference room table by herself until midnight, drafting a speech to the American people. Before going to bed, she directed Mason Adams to set up a press briefing for ten o'clock the following morning.

30

The next morning, Susan called Vice President Wilkes's office to schedule a meeting prior to her final draft of the press briefing. Susan admired his communication style. The speeches he gave during his presidency were always clear, concise, impactful, and upbeat. Vice President Wilkes met Susan in the Cabinet Room at seven thirty. The table was already littered with coffee cups and previous drafts of the speech with handwritten notes scribbled in the margins. Susan sat at the conference room table surrounded by her staff and the speech writing team.

Mason Adams was the first to notice Vice President Wilkes's presence. "Vice President Wilkes, I'm glad you could make it on short notice. I hope we didn't interrupt your schedule for the day."

Vice President Wilkes shook Mason's hand and replied, "Things look a bit hectic. I take it you're not running this meeting."

Mason smiled, but before he could answer, Susan stood up and yelled over the noise, "Vice President Wilkes. I'm so glad you could make it." Susan walked over to greet Vice President Wilkes. "Do you mind taking a look at a draft of the press briefing?"

"I'd love to. Anything specific you want me focus on?"

"No, nothing specific but I'd really appreciate your general reaction. Take a seat anywhere, I'm almost done. Give me five minutes and I can talk. Mason, can you get him a copy of the latest draft?"

Vice President Wilkes sat down in a chair against the wall away from the swirling mass of people in the room. Mason handed him two sheets of paper marked "Draft." He read through the speech, slowly nodding his head in agreement with each section. He finished the last paragraph and Susan sat down in the chair next to him. "What do you think?"

"I think the world is going to be glad to hear that the pilots are back home safe."

Susan took a deep breath. "Hmm . . . the world. I didn't think about it that way. I try to forget that the entire world watches everything I do." Susan paused and nodded her head while staring at the floor. "What did you think of the overall message?"

"I thought it was good. The only thing that stood out to me was that you didn't address the Soviet Union's involvement in the incident. Was that on purpose?"

"To the best of my knowledge, they didn't play a part in the capture or detainment of our pilots. I didn't see a reason to address the Soviet Union specifically. I wanted to focus on the importance of patience in these situations."

"Are you planning to take questions from the press?"

"Yes, I want to be as open and honest about the situation as possible."

Vice President Wilkes nodded. "I'd do the same. I know you asked me for my opinion. I feel bad for not really giving any advice, but I think you've got it covered."

Susan smiled at Vice President Wilkes. "I'm just glad we're on the same page. I'm sure you've got a busy day, I don't want to hold you up any longer. Will you be at the briefing?"

"I'll be there. Good luck, you've got it under control." Vice President Wilkes and Susan stood up and shook hands. Vice President Wilkes left the Cabinet Room and walked back to his office. Before sitting down at his desk, he put on his jacket and told the Secret Service detail he was going back home to retrieve a folder. In the White House, even the walls have ears and he needed privacy.

Susan approved the final version of her press briefing at 9:00 a.m. She went back to the Oval Office to gather her thoughts before the 10:00 a.m. live broadcast. She couldn't get Vice President Wilkes's comment about the Soviet involvement out of her mind. She felt addressing the issue would only bring up more questions that she couldn't answer. Susan didn't know how much or how little the Soviet government knew about the pilot's capture or holding location. From her perspective, the Soviets may have been trying as hard as the United States to find the holding location, or they could have been orchestrating the entire event. It was impossible to know the truth.

Mason Adams escorted General LeMae into the Oval Office. "Madam President, General LeMae is here without an appointment. He promised to be brief."

"Thank you, Mason. General LeMae is always welcome."

Mason Adams turned and quickly left the room.

General LeMae walked toward Susan and pulled a small blue gift box out of his pocket. Susan furrowed her brow while examining the box. "Curtis, I know you're vain . . . but I'm a couple of decades too young for you."

General LeMae sighed and rolled his eyes. "Razor . . . we both know you aren't my type." General LeMae smiled and gave her a firm pat on the shoulder like a football player. "Seriously . . . I know you don't like presents, but you deserve this one. You earned it a long time ago." General LeMae handed the box to Susan. She took the cover off the box and saw a military challenge coin. The face of the coin was engraved with her squadron's insignia. Tears streamed down Susan's cheeks. She leaned forward and hugged General LeMae.

General LeMae explained, "I didn't get the chance to give one to you when you were squadron commander. I always felt bad about it. But, you know . . . the timing never seemed right to give it to you."

Susan stepped back from General LeMae and wiped the tears from her eyes.

"That's not all. Look on the back."

Susan turned the coin over. The phrase Don't let the green grass fool you was engraved on the back of the coin. Susan looked back up at General LeMae with a confused expression. She recognized the phrase from one of their running cadences in the army, but she didn't understand the significance.

"Do you remember our conversation back in Idaho? In your driveway . . . about the files?"

Susan nodded. "Of course."

"If anything happens to me, you'll find the files at my cabin. They're hidden. That phrase will lead you to them. I know it doesn't make sense now. And I hope it won't ever make sense to you." General LeMae shook Susan's hand. "I'll let you get ready for your speech. You did a good job—those pilots are alive because of you."

Susan walked to the podium in the Press Briefing Room filled with excitement and relief at exactly 10:00 a.m. She confidently walked up to the podium and let the whispers from the crowd die down before beginning. "I have great news to share. Lt. Colonel Rodriguez and Lt. Colonel Harris are free, safe, and healthy. They were rescued by a United States Army Special Forces team last night and are now resting safely inside in the Joint Special Operations Command base in Eastern Europe. They will be reuniting with their families in America as soon as we are able to get them fully debriefed."

Susan continued her speech, addressing the animosity building in America against the Soviet Union and especially against Soviet immigrants living in the United States. Susan ended the press briefing by highlighting the importance of patience and compassion in all areas of foreign relations. The press corps listened to the brief, then immediately began shouting questions at the end of Susan's briefing. Susan pointed at the first reporter she saw from the podium.

"Madam President, how were the pilots located? And why weren't they located sooner?"

"Great question, thank you for asking. I can't get into the specifics but we were alerted to abnormal activity in the area where the pilots were being held. We launched a search-and-rescue mission based on that information. I'm sorry I can't give any more details at this time. Most importantly, we were able to get Lt. Colonel Rodriguez and Lt. Colonel Harris home safe."

For the next few minutes, Susan answered more questions about circumstances of the rescue mission and the timing of the pilots' return to the United States. Her staff prepared her well for the questions asked.

Emily Bingham, a junior reporter in the press briefing,

looked down at her vibrating cell phone. The message read, "Were there any previous rescue attempts? Ask now." After two more questions, Emily was able to catch President Turner's attention.

"Madam President, were there any previous attempts to rescue the pilots?"

The room, including Susan, froze in a stunned silence. The public was told the Black Hawk crash killing seven Americans near the Ukrainian border was a training mission and there was no mention to the public about previous rescue missions. Susan looked as shocked as the rest of the press corps in the room.

"No, there were no previous rescue missions. Next question."

Susan answered questions for a few more minutes and left the press briefing on a high note. Being careful not to arouse any suspicion, Susan chatted eagerly with her staff on the way back to the Oval Office. Excitement and relief dominated the mood in the White House. Susan waited patiently until she was alone in the Oval Office before calling General LeMae.

"Did you see the press briefing?"

SELECTED

"I did, and I heard the question about a previous rescue mission. Where'd she get that question? I can guarantee it wasn't from her own brain. Somebody tipped her off."

Susan ran her hands through her hair. "I don't know who tipped her off and I don't care. Now we've got a real problem, every news agency in the world is going to be looking into it. And it won't be long until they begin focusing on the seven soldiers killed in a training accident near the Ukrainian border. The public has a short memory but it won't be long until they come around to it. Then what are we going to do?"

General LeMae attempted to ease her concern. "There's no point in worrying about hypothetical situations. If more questions are asked, we'll have plenty of time to strategize our answers. And there's no proof that those soldiers died in anything other than a training accident. Everything you said during that press briefing is accurate, according to the public."

Susan took a deep breath. "You're right. I'm probably overthinking this. Sorry to bother you. Thanks for being the voice of reason." Susan hung up the phone. She felt a hollow pit in her stomach.

That evening, inside the Pacific International headquarters in Los Angeles, Mr. Anderson called his chief information officer into his office.

"Yes, sir, what can I do for you?"

"During the White House press briefing today by President Turner, a reporter asked if there were any previous attempts at rescuing the pilots. Look into it. See if you can find a story. Reach out to our Ukrainian office in Kiev and our office in Moscow—they should be able to help."

"I'm on it. Anything else?"

"That's all, but make sure our friends in the media know you're looking into this story. I want the world focused on it by tomorrow morning. I think the story has legs."

Mr. Anderson walked to the window and looked down over the chaos that was Los Angeles. He poured himself a glass of Macallan eighteen-year-old single-malt scotch. Mr. Anderson rarely drank alcohol; he saved the pleasure of a good glass of scotch for special occasions. Tonight he celebrated a milestone in the Board's plan for Unified Peace. Susan Turner was indeed the perfect president. She continued to walk the United States directly into a war with the Soviet Union. In the aftermath of a war between two of the world's superpowers, the Board would be perfectly situated to implement a global leadership and take control.

31

Agent Sanders brushed the wrapper and crumbs from the top of her FBI Field Manual onto the passenger seat floorboard. She wiped the grease from her fingers. A flash of movement caught her eye. She saw Mason Adams walk down the steps of his front porch. Mason took a moment to scan the street before briskly walking away from Agent Sanders's vehicle. She watched him walk to the corner and make a right toward Meridian Hill Park.

Agent Sanders played this scenario through her mind over the past few weeks as she sat outside Mason's house monitoring his activity. The park had very little lighting at night and would be the perfect location to meet someone in secret.

She got out of her vehicle and quickly followed Mason. He entered the park and took the first path to the right. Agent Sanders stayed on the path but kept fifty yards behind Mason. She paused to catch her breath and watched Mason take a seat on a park bench. Agent Sanders slowly moved next to a clump

254

SELECTED

of bushes and took a knee. She was positioned almost directly behind Mason Adams as he sat on the bench. Mason sat alone for two minutes. He fidgeted and continuously looked toward the trail to his left.

Agent Sanders watched another man casually walk toward the bench and sit down next to Mason. The two men sat together for less than thirty seconds before Mason stood up and continued on the trail.

Five days later, President Turner, Director Redmond, and Agent Sanders met in a conference room in the FBI headquarters.

Director Redmond began the meeting. "Agent Sanders, please give the president an update on the case."

Agent Sanders looked at Susan and cleared her throat. "Madam President." Then she looked down and read directly from her notes. "I observed Mason Adams meeting with Mr. Nick Lee in Meridian Park at 11:25 p.m. They sat on a bench together for thirty seconds. Mason Adams continued his walk. I was suspicious of the meeting and stopped Mr. Lee. I discovered that Mr. Lee was delivering a prescription to Mason Adams for Cannabidiol. Mr. Lee holds a valid license to distribute medical marijuana to patients— "

"Are you telling me Mason met a drug dealer in the middle of the night at a park by his house?"

"No, Madam President. Mason is procuring medical marijuana for his mother who suffers from epilepsy. I did some research. Cannabidiol is an oil, and it doesn't produce the same effects as smoking marijuana. There are several scientific studies proving its effectiveness for treatment of patients who have epilepsy."

"Mason's getting medical marijuana for his mother?" asked Susan.

"Yes." Agent Sanders paused. "I was able to get access to the medical records for Mason's mother. She does have a history of epilepsy." Agent Sanders looked back down at her notes. "Based on my investigation, I found no evidence to support the theory that Mason Adams is leaking classified information from the White House."

Susan closed her eyes and sighed. "Thank God Mason isn't involved."

SELECTED

Director Redmond spoke up. "Agent Sanders, did you find anything else that may be helpful in the investigation?"

"Yes." She looked back down at her notes and continued. "I investigated Emily Bingham, the reporter who wrote the article. She has never married and has one child. The father of her child is Jack Anderson, CEO of Pacific International. I witnessed Mr. Anderson visiting Ms. Bingham's residence on two occasions. Pacific International holds several contracts related to the installation and maintenance of security equipment for the White House and Pentagon."

Director Redmond followed up, "President Turner, I want to be clear, we have no evidence to support any wrongdoing by Pacific International. But . . . I suggest we do a sweep of your office for electronic devices. Agent Sanders will perform the sweep."

Agent Sanders added, "The equipment fits into a briefcase and it will only take a few minutes."

Susan nodded her head. "The Secret Service does their own security checks, but I think it's a good idea to have you do an independent check. Will you two follow me back to the White House?"

Agent Sanders looked to Director Redmond for guidance.

Director Redmond replied, "Agent Sanders can handle it on her own. I attract too much attention when I leave this building. An entourage tends to follow me around. I'd rather keep this as much under the radar as possible."

Susan stood up and smiled. "Sounds good to me. Agent Sanders, are you ready?"

"Yes, Madam President."

Agent Sanders followed Susan through the doors of the Oval Office. As they walked inside, she felt an aggressive glare from the Secret Service agent standing guard. She set up the portable antenna and synced the handheld device. Susan walked toward her desk.

Agent Sanders looked up. "Madam President, could you please stand against the far wall. I don't want you to interfere with the equipment. It will just be a few moments."

Susan nodded and moved toward the wall.

Agent Sanders picked up her handheld device and methodically scanned the room. Susan's desk was the last area of the room to scan. She slowly moved the handheld scanner over each item on the desk. The Montblanc pen and wooden case Vice President Wilkes gave to Susan was on the far left corner of the desk. Agent Sanders moved the handheld screening device over the case.

Two minutes later, Agent Sanders announced to Susan, "All clean. I'll give my report to Director Redmond. Madam President, is there anything else I can do for you while I'm here?"

"Thank you, Agent Sanders. I think that will be all." Susan shook hands with Agent Sanders.

After Agent Sanders left the Oval Office, Susan sat down at her desk and looked up at the ceiling.

Over the phone, Mr. Jones explained, "It was the only option."

Mr. Anderson quickly paced across his office. "We've lost an important intelligence asset."

Mr. Jones defended his decision. "If I hadn't had the

listening device removed from the Oval Office, the FBI agent would have found it. There's no doubt in my mind."

Mr. Anderson stopped and rested his hands on his hips. "Giving the story to Emily was a mistake."

Mr. Jones rolled his eyes and thought, No kidding. Did you really think the White House wouldn't look into the reporter who broke the story?

Mr. Anderson filled the silence. "We have to assume the FBI or Secret Service knows about my relationship with Emily Bingham."

Mr. Jones finished the thought. "And going forward, under no circumstances should you contact her in any way."

Mr. Anderson ended the conversation. "Maintain surveillance on Emily Bingham. For now, she's still an asset. That will be all, Mr. Jones."

He sat down at his desk and looked at the picture of his wife, Cheryl, and their son. He closed his eyes and took a deep breath.

32

Susan's brother, Brad, walked through the front entrance of the Metropolitan Club of the City of Washington at precisely 4:45 p.m. He wore the same disguise as he did in previous interactions with Mr. Anderson. Mr. Anderson knew Brad by the name of Mr. White. Brad minimized the risk of detection by giving the persona of Mr. White a new physical appearance and demeanor with each client. He learned the best way to keep his clients from digging too deeply into his background was to give Mr. White the appearance of intelligence, mixed with a healthy dose of naivety. Clients tended to view the character of Mr. White as just another tool to accomplish their goals, rather than a threat.

The Metropolitan Club served as Mr. Anderson's preferred location for holding alternative business meetings. The club did not allow computers, cameras, cell phones, or any other electronic devices. The policy provided the ideal environment to conduct the type of business for which documentation was a liability for both parties involved.

Brad checked in at the registration desk and was discreetly escorted to the Correspondence Lounge. He sat in a dark leather chair at a small mahogany conference room table. Plush dark blue upholstered reading chairs with adjoining end tables and lamps were spaced throughout the room. The tables were just far enough apart for privacy. Large mahogany bookshelves lined the walls of the room from ceiling to floor; a ladder leaned against a bookshelf in the far corner. Brad grabbed the queen from the chess board on the table. He twirled it between his fingers while he waited for Mr. Anderson to arrive.

Mr. Anderson quickly walked into the room and closed the door behind him. They were alone. He moved with a sense of purpose. His quick and direct movements were often misinterpreted as impatience or annoyance. Under the surface of his brazen appearance, Mr. Anderson was calm, cunning, and strategic.

He sat down in the chair across from his guest with a stern grimace on his face and locked eyes with Brad. Brad quickly broke the silence. "We found Umirov, the leader of the Chechen resistance group that held the American pilots."

Mr. Anderson moved his hands to the top of the table and

loosely interlocked his fingers. The expression on his face remained the same.

Brad allowed five seconds of silence before continuing. "Umirov shared his version of the pilots' capture and release. We were able to obtain confirmation from Umirov that the Soviet government was aware of the incident from the beginning. Umirov also confirmed the failed rescue mission by the Americans. The pilots weren't released by the Chechens— they escaped during a firefight that killed Umirov's team and Umirov believes the KGB was responsible."

Mr. Anderson nodded his head. "How many others know Umirov's location?"

"To the best of my knowledge, just me. He's been in hiding since the raid."

Mr. Anderson cracked a grim smile. "Good. Keep him alive. . . . Continue."

Brad continued. "I also reached out to our contacts in Washington DC and inside the Pentagon. They were surprised at the accusation of a failed rescue mission in the media, but I wasn't able to get any helpful information. The military staff has always been loyal to their soldiers. They're a tough group."

Mr. Anderson grabbed the edge of the table with both hands, squeezed with all his strength, sat up straight, and took a deep breath.

Brad continued his sentence, "The military staff is a tough group to extract information from. Their loyalty means more to them than money."

"Do you know any details of the failed rescue mission?" asked Mr. Anderson.

"Yes, but I don't have any way to verify what Umirov told me. I know that the 'training accident' that killed seven American soldiers near the Ukrainian border was a failed rescue mission to recover the pilots. And two Soviet citizens were killed by United States soldiers during the mission."

Mr. Anderson relaxed his hands and put them back on the table. His smile was brief, and his eyes glowed with activity. Brad again broke the brief silence. "We can't go to the press without evidence. We need something more than the word of a Chechen rebel who also happens to be the same Chechen rebel who held two American pilots captive."

Mr. Anderson smiled and chuckled, mostly under his breath. "Evidence? Why do you think we need to find evidence? We'll make our own evidence."

SELECTED

Brad furrowed his brow. "I'm sorry, I don't understand."

Mr. Anderson responded, "Make the evidence."

"Do you want me to plant some U.S. military equipment at the failed rescue site? Or maybe fake a video of a Black Hawk being shot down by a surface-to-air missile?"

Mr. Anderson shook his head. "You don't understand. None of that is necessary. You know the story from Umirov, correct?"

"Yes."

"And the Soviet government clearly knew of the pilots' capture, location, and failed rescue mission?"

"Yes."

"And you know the details of the American soldiers killed in what our government called a training accident?"

Brad squinted his eyes further with each question. "Yes, I know all of those things, but we can't prove them."

Mr. Anderson's frustration showed on his face. "I just told you we don't need to prove anything. I thought I hired the best. But that's okay, I'll spell it out for you. Use the same organization that leaked hundreds of thousands of United

J. ALLEN WOLFRUM

States foreign cable correspondences five years ago. Use the same format and style of the previous leaks and create correspondence from the Soviet ambassador to President Turner."

Brad interrupted, "Understood."

"I'm not finished. The documents need to raise suspicion that every Soviet in America is a spy trying to undermine the American way of life. And they need to believe President Turner should be impeached. Use your imagination." Mr. Anderson stood up without another word and strode away from the table.

In the hallway, immediately outside the Correspondence Lounge, he came face-to-face with another guest. Mr. Anderson's mood changed abruptly. With a wide smile and a pat on the back, he exchanged animated words with the man about the conditions of the grass at Westfields Golf Club. After a chuckle, they parted ways. Mr. Anderson's face quickly hardened and he glanced back to see if Brad was still in the room.

33

Susan sat down on Tommy's bed after finishing the boys' bedroom inspections and sending them off to school. She turned her phone off in the mornings when she was with Greg and Tommy. The boys deserved her full attention. Early on in her presidency, Rose had tersely reminded her that the boys were not merely a distraction from work.

Susan turned on her cell phone and took a deep breath as she watched the spinning circle in the middle of the screen during the reboot. She let herself believe, for just a moment, there wouldn't be a crisis she needed to solve.

Her phone buzzed as it processed the incoming data and she saw three text messages from Mason Adams. The first message was all she needed to see. "Leaked foreign cables. Office ASAP." Susan took a deep breath and a few moments to refocus her energy before walking down to the Oval Office.

Susan met Mason Adams in the hallway outside the Oval

Office. The White House staff moved quickly between rooms with grim looks on their faces. Susan's pace of breathing quickened as she processed the mood of her staff. She held her questions for Mason until they walked into the Oval Office and closed the door.

"What's going on?" asked Susan.

"I'm not sure what's happening. I can only tell you what the media thinks is happening, but something seems off to me."

"What are they saying?"

"Leaked documents containing cables from U.S. State Department staff stationed in foreign countries communicating back to the United States."

Susan shrugged her shoulders. "Not the first time this has happened. I have no doubt there are some embarrassing statements but we can handle it. Why the grim faces from the staff? Was someone on the staff involved?"

"No, it doesn't have anything to do with the White House staff. At least not directly." Mason paused.

Susan raised her eyebrows and waved her hand, motioning Mason to continue speaking. Mason struggled to find the right phrase.

Susan blurted, "Say something. Don't just look at me. What is it?"

"Hmmph . . . there's over ten gigabytes of documents. We've barely scratched the surface, but the media is focused on information sent from the U.S. Embassy in Moscow which indicates the United States has a spy in President Rosinski's inner circle."

Susan shook her head. "I'm not aware of an intelligence asset in the Kremlin and certainly not one that's close to President Rosinski."

"I just confirmed with the CIA director that we do not have any active intelligence assets in the Kremlin."

"Is that what's making you nervous?" asked Susan.

"That's part of it, but not the worst part. The documents also reference a Soviet spy program, code-named Glaskov. According to the documents, the Glaskov program is a worldwide initiative by the KGB to infiltrate foreign countries. Teams of KGB undercover agents are living in America posing as American citizens with families and jobs. And it's not only America—there are at least fifteen other countries named in association with the Glaskov program."

Susan's face hardened. "You're telling me there are undercover KGB operatives living in America who work normal jobs, have families, and are pretending to be Americans?"

Mason nodded. "According to these documents. Yes. The CIA director had no knowledge of the program. The NSA and CIA are both working on verifying the documents."

"What else?" asked Susan.

"That's it so far. The documents have only been in the open for an hour."

Susan crossed her arms. "I want to talk to Ambassador Dashkov immediately."

"He's on his way, should be here in five minutes. Anything else?" asked Mason.

"As soon as possible, I want the NSA and CIA reports on the validity of the documents." Susan paused. "Is Vice President Wilkes in his office?"

"I saw him this morning, I can check his schedule."

"If he's available, I want to talk with him."

SELECTED

"I'll see if I can grab him before Ambassador Dashkov gets here."

Susan put her hand on Mason's shoulder. "Thank you, Mason. This is going to be a rough day. I appreciate your help. Keep your head up, we'll make it through this. Thank you for piecing it all together."

Mason blushed. "Thank you. I'll find Vice President Wilkes."

Thirty seconds later, Vice President Wilkes walked into the Oval Office. Susan motioned for him to sit down as she nodded her head and mumbled, "I understand," into the telephone handset before hanging up.

"I apologize for the short notice, but I want to get your thoughts on how to handle the media," said Susan.

"I'm happy to help. Do we know any more than what's being reported?"

"No, the CIA and NSA haven't had the chance to analyze the documents. At this point I don't trust the validity of the documents, but I can't confirm that suspicion. What do you think?"

Vice President Wilkes took a deep breath and crossed his

arms. "This is a tough situation. I'd try to get in front of the story as much as possible. Even if you don't have much to say, being visible during a time of crisis can help ease people's fear."

Susan nodded her head. "Good point."

Vice President Wilkes continued with his advice. "I'm sorry if this comes off as crass, but if you make a statement this early, you have plausible deniability regarding the lack of information on the incident. You could use the daily press briefing to deliver the news."

"I like that idea." Before Susan could finish her sentence, Mason Adams walked through the door to the Oval Office followed by Ambassador Dashkov.

Vice President Wilkes shook Susan's hand and graciously excused himself from the Oval Office. His mission was complete.

Before Susan could greet Ambassador Dashkov, he burst into an apology. "Madam President, I have no idea what the media is reporting. Those documents could not be further from the truth."

Susan stopped Ambassador Dashkov. "Ambassador Dashkov, please. I'm not accusing you of anything. You don't need to apologize. Let's sit down and talk."

Ambassador Dashkov tugged at his suit jacket and took a seat across from Susan. "I apologize, Madam President, how can I help?"

"I can't prove it yet, but I think the documents are fake, and I want you to hear it from me directly."

"I appreciate your candor. What can I do to help? The media is spinning the situation out of control. I'm concerned for the safety of Soviet citizens around the world," replied Ambassador Dashkov.

"If you can find a way to prove that the documents are fake, it would be of tremendous value. The NSA and CIA have the same goal. I'll have reports from both agencies by the end of the day."

"The KGB is working on the analysis as well. I'll share their findings with you as soon as I get a report."

"Thank you. I apologize but I need to prepare for the press briefing. Is there anything I can do for you?"

"No, but thank you for meeting me in person. President Rosinski will appreciate your willingness to engage in a dialog during such a stressful situation."

J. ALLEN WOLFRUM

Susan walked with Ambassador Dashkov out of the Oval Office. They shook hands in the hallway, and Ambassador Dashkov quickly walked toward the lobby and returned to the Soviet Embassy.

Susan instructed Mason Adams to notify the press corps that she would be personally delivering the daily press briefing. She returned to the Oval Office to prepare her message about the leaked documents.

The daily press briefing occurred each day at 10:30 a.m. in the James S. Brady Press Briefing room in the West Wing of the White House. The reporters in attendance were the senior Washington correspondents from their respective networks and newspapers. Depending on the mood of the reporters in the audience, it could be a tough crowd when it came to the question-and-answer period of the briefing.

Susan took the podium at precisely 10:30. Ten seconds later, in the middle of her opening sentence, an explosion knocked Susan from the podium. The room went pitch-black and plaster rained down from the ceilings. An eerie silence followed the blast. Then the screams began.

34

Susan Turner looked up through a haze of white dust and saw a group of men in black suits huddled around her body. The muffled ringing in her ears overpowered their voices. The men helped her to her feet, and they ran as a group toward the entrance of the underground tunnel. Her hearing slowly returned, screams of panic in the hallway replacing the ringing. As they ran, she recognized the men surrounding her were Secret Service agents.

Four agents surrounded Susan as they jogged through the underground tunnel together. Ten yards into the tunnel, she slowed down. In mid-stride, she took off one heel at a time and returned to the group's pace. There were no words exchanged; they moved together in focused silence. Four hundred yards down the tunnel, the group stopped at two large steel doors. The lead agent opened the doors and light from the helicopter pad above burst into the tunnel.

Before moving toward the helicopter, the agent standing

behind Susan shouted into his headset, "Checkpoint Bravo. Waiting for clearance." He nodded as the response came through his headset and relayed the message to the group: "Let's move." They ran from the tunnel into the daylight and across the tarmac to the open doors of the helicopter.

The agent sitting across from Susan handed her a communications headset. "Ma'am, are you okay? Any injuries?"

Susan wiped the sweat and dust from her face. "No, I'm fine. My family?"

"They're safe. Your children were brought to a safe location under the Pentagon, and your parents are there with them."

She nodded. "Is it over?"

He pursed his lips before responding, "I don't know. I only heard snippets of radio chatter while we were on the way to the helipad."

Susan leaned back in her seat, cupping her hands over her face and replaying the events in her mind. The group stayed in radio silence for the remainder of the brief flight. The helicopter landed at Andrews Air Force Base and the doors immediately opened. Susan and her security detail rushed across the tarmac and boarded the Boeing 747. Susan walked onto the plane in her bare feet. Jogging on concrete caused the pinky toe on her left foot to bleed. She left a trail of blood down the center aisle of Air Force One.

Immediately after takeoff, Susan went into the conference room aboard Air Force One. The monitor showed the Joint Chiefs of Staff in a conference room at the Pentagon.

Susan asked, "General Gillingham, do you have an update on the situation?"

"Madam President, we're happy to see that you made it to Air Force One safely. The situation on the ground is still active and remains fluid. Our preliminary reports indicate three attacks at three separate locations: the White House, Atlanta, and Los Angeles. All three attacks happened within one minute of each other."

Susan asked, "How many casualties?"

"As of now we have fourteen confirmed deaths and estimates of wounded are in the hundreds. We don't expect to have total numbers for another few hours."

"Sounds like the attacks were tightly coordinated. Have any groups taken responsibility?"

The Joint Chiefs of Staff all looked at each other in silence.

Susan asked again with more angst. "Has any group taken responsibility?"

General Gillingham cleared his throat. "Frankly, we don't know. But at 10:35 a.m. Eastern, five minutes after the attacks, the CNN news network was hacked. A thirty second, video was played. It was a picture of the Soviet flag with the Soviet national anthem playing in the background."

Susan gasped, "Oh my god." She regained her composure and redirected the conversation. "What details do we know about the attacks?"

"The White House attack was a car bomb. A large SUV crashed the White House, drove across the lawn, and detonated an explosive device. The Los Angeles and Atlanta attacks were similar to each other—both were also large SUVs with explosive devices. The bombs were detonated under major freeway overpasses during heavy traffic," replied General Gillingham.

"Those are the only attacks? The White House, Los Angeles, and Atlanta?"

"Yes, Madam President."

SELECTED

"I know it's early, but do we have a response plan?" asked Susan.

"We're still working on gathering intelligence. We need more information before putting together a comprehensive response."

"Understood. Any new information on the validity of the leaked documents from this morning?"

"The NSA and CIA are still working on the analysis; the attacks disrupted their work. I don't expect anything for a few days," replied General Gillingham.

Susan nodded her head. "Thank you, General. That's all I have for now. Let's talk again this evening when we have more information." Susan expressed her gratitude for their support and ended the call.

After checking in with her family who were safely resting in the Pentagon, she walked back to the main cabin and took a seat. She sat alone on the plane with the exception of the Secret Service detail. The silence gave her time to think. Susan believed the attacks and the leaked documents were tied to each other. The Soviet national anthem playing on a hacked news station five minutes after the attacks was out of place. President Rosinski would never dream of taking such direct responsibility for terror attacks on United States soil.

For Susan, finding the party responsible for the attacks was secondary to controlling the reaction from the public. The American people were already split on their feelings toward the Soviet Union, and the divide was tearing the country apart. The playing of the Soviet national anthem immediately after today's attacks would surely add to their anger and spark a lust for revenge. Once the war machine began rolling, backed by an American public thirst for revenge, there was no stopping it.

Susan turned on the television to watch the national news coverage. The blatant antagonism from the news anchors shocked her to the core. Every comment they made was intended to add fuel to the rage of the public. Susan decided her only option was to address the country on live television.

Susan got in touch with Mason Adams and he coordinated a live video feed from the Air Force One conference room. The live feed was distributed to every major news network in the world. Mason managed the logistics on the ground from his makeshift office in the Hart Senate Office Building in Washington, DC.

Susan watched the camera in front of her. When she saw the red light turn on, she began her speech to the world.

SELECTED

"Today is a tragic day in human history. I'm saddened at the loss of life and for the lives that will be forever altered due to the events unfolding today. I understand the anger and vulnerability that you feel. Although we're angry and seek revenge, we must not allow ourselves to be manipulated by the actions of our attackers. The attacks today were intended to spark fear, violence, and anger. Our attackers want our fear and our anger to be focused inward on our fellow Americans. They want us to give up our freedom in an attempt to prevent further attacks. They want America to destroy itself from the inside. I know your will is being tested, but I also know the strength of the American people. America stands as a beacon for liberty, freedom, and democracy, and we will not be manipulated into giving up those principles."

Susan continued her speech, giving her condolences to the families of those who'd lost their lives and were injured in the attacks. She reiterated that currently there was no indication that the Soviet Union was in any way responsible for the attacks. Susan ended the speech with a final promise to bring the people or entities involved with the attacks to justice.

Earl watched Susan's speech and the subsequent reaction from the media in a secure room deep underneath the

Pentagon with a dozen other government officials. Rose helped the boys with their homework in an adjacent room. She hoped to keep the boys focused on school rather than worrying about their mother.

General LeMae moved through the crowd in the room and stood next to Earl. Earl looked to his left and made eye contact with General LeMae. The two men exchanged a solemn nod; no words were required to convey the concern they both felt. They watched the television in silence as the anti-Soviet rhetoric overwhelmed the media's coverage of the attacks. The guests on the news programs quickly moved toward insisting on a military response from the United States.

Earl shook his head and spoke over the news coverage. "I sure hope cooler heads prevail."

General LeMae put his hands in his pockets. "They will. Susan knows a war with the Soviet Union would be catastrophic for everyone involved. If anyone can figure out a way to avoid a war, it's Susan."

Earl exhaled deeply. "I hope you're right. She always seems to pull through, but she's got one heck of a stubborn streak in her."

35

On the day after the attacks in America, Mr. Anderson flew from JFK International Airport to Moscow. After takeoff, he opened a secure satellite phone and dialed Mr. White. Mr. Anderson did not know his real name and he certainly did not know that Mr. White was Susan Turner's brother. Brad avoided cameras and used disguises, but during their previous meetings, several high-quality images of him were captured by Mr. Anderson's security detail. Even with access to the CIA, FBI, and Interpol databases, no information could be found on Mr. White.

Mr. Anderson dialed the emergency contact number for Mr. White from memory. The second ring was interrupted, and he heard Mr. White breathing on the other end of the line. Both men allowed the silence to continue; it was a test of patience. Mr. Anderson heard the sound of cars in the background but nothing specific enough to determine a location.

Mr. Anderson relented and broke the silence. "I was wrong to criticize your work. There are more jobs on the horizon."

After two seconds of silence the line went dead. Mr. Anderson hung up the secure satellite phone and looked out the window of the Pacific International corporate jet. Mr. White exercised far more caution than he expected. Mr. Anderson hoped to record his voice; even if he used a voice alteration algorithm, there was a chance of reverse engineering the audio. Mr. Anderson cracked a smile. He appreciated the opportunity to work with a true craftsman.

Brad ended the call and quickly removed the SIM card in the back of the phone. He crushed the SIM card in his palm and threw the phone in the garbage can.

Earl noticed Brad was no longer walking next to him. He turned around and saw Brad stopped on the sidewalk near a trash can. "Let's go, Brad. We're going to be late for the game. I want to be in our seats before they drop the puck."

Brad replied, "Sorry, Dad. Work call." He jogged to catch up with Earl.

SELECTED

Earl locked eyes with Brad. "Son. You need to talk to your mother. You two need to put the past behind you. There's no reason for me to have to sneak around just to see you. It just isn't right."

Brad sighed. "I know, Dad. I know. I want to talk to her. But it's just hard."

Earl nodded and changed the conversation. "We're going to be late for the game."

Mr. Anderson opened his briefcase and pulled out the folder titled Boris Rosinski—President, Soviet Union. He reviewed past interactions with Boris Rosinski, searching for gaps in his approach. A mistake at this stage of the plan was not an option. A successful meeting with President Rosinski was crucial to Pacific International's expansion into the Soviet Union and Eastern Europe.

Twelve hours later, Mr. Anderson walked into Cafe Pushkin in Moscow with his companion for the evening— Dominika, a tall, curvy brunette in her late twenties. Mr.

Anderson and Dominika were escorted to the third floor of the restaurant. He keenly noted that there were no other patrons on the third floor. The layout resembled a Soviet aristocrat's home more than a restaurant. The decor was dark, mahogany wood moldings, brown leather chairs, and dark red rugs. The decor dominated the dimly lit restaurant. They were guided into what appeared to be a reading room with a square four-person table in the center. Mr. Anderson sat down at the table facing the entrance. Dominika sat to his right.

Seconds later, President Rosinski's security detail entered the room. They quickly swept the room and stood guard at the entrance. Mr. Anderson and Dominika stood as he walked into the room. President Rosinski smiled and shook hands with Mr. Anderson. "Good to see you again, Jack."

"You as, well Mr. President. I'd like you to meet my friend Dominika."

"Dominika, what a beautiful name." President Rosinski kissed her hand. "Please sit down, let's enjoy our time together."

Dominika was a professional; she followed Mr. Anderson's instructions to the letter. She lightly flirted with President Rosinski throughout dinner and kept the vodka flowing at a

SELECTED

faster pace than President Rosinski was accustomed to handling. Immediately after dessert was served, Dominika excused herself from the table to meet a girlfriend at the bar downstairs. As she walked past, Mr. Anderson noted a glance of desire from President Rosinski.

Mr. Anderson brought the conversation back to his agenda. "Do you mind if we talk business over dessert?"

"Of course—I know why you're here. It isn't for my charming anecdotes and childhood stories."

Mr. Anderson smiled. "I'm glad it isn't a surprise." He wiped his mouth and put the napkin on the table. "I think Pacific International can help Gazprom get their pipeline operations in the Ukraine, Latvia, and Belarus off the ground." Mr. Anderson paused to allow the statement settle with President Rosinski. He knew the information about pipeline construction was thought to be a secret only known by upper management at Gazprom International.

Mr. Anderson closely watched President Rosinski's facial expression and proceeded with caution. "As you know, we pride ourselves on discretion. If you're concerned with the Gazprom pipeline expansion project being public information, we can use our network of subsidiary companies to hide the activity from the public. Pacific International makes discretion a priority. Financial disclosures are obscured to hide operational information from the public."

President Rosinski put down his fork. "I see. Gazprom has all the capabilities to accomplish their objectives. There is no need to add additional entities into the project. More people, more problems."

Mr. Anderson chuckled. "I like that, 'more people. more problems.' I couldn't agree more. That's why I'm proposing Pacific International handle your people problems. There is no way around the difficulties Gazprom will have with the . . . let's call them indigenous people. Not to mention the logistics of housing and feeding the Gazprom workers. Pacific International can handle the people problems and Gazprom can do what it does best."

President Rosinski paused and looked past Mr. Anderson to the far corner of the room before responding, "What can you do to help our problem with the Americans?"

"I'm not sure I understand the specific problem you're referencing."

"The American people are sure to want revenge for yesterday's terror attacks. As you know, the Soviet Union had nothing to do with the attacks. But that won't stop the Americans. Just before this meeting, I had to stop the KGB director from planning a preemptive strike on the Americans. He believes an attack from America is inevitable."

Mr. Anderson leaned forward. "I understand. Pacific International's primary mission is to secure the financial well-being and safety of our clients. I can make sure the American military leadership and the American public understand that the Soviet Union is a friend, not an enemy. And as you already know, Pacific International controls several major media outlets. We can make sure your message gets to the public."

President Rosinski took another bite of cake. "I assume you want a percentage of the pipeline profits for your work?"

Mr. Anderson smiled on the inside. "Absolutely not, we wouldn't dream of it. We want a fixed-term contract, strictly to provide security and logistical support for the Gazprom workers."

"What does Pacific International gain?"

"Another happy client and, of course, peace in Eastern Europe. The contracts will be specific to each location. If Gazprom isn't satisfied with our service at any of the job sites, they can end the relationship. No strings attached and no hard feelings."

President Rosinski nodded his head. "Where will your workers come from?"

"The entire project will be resourced out of our Moscow office. I'm meeting with our director of the Moscow office tomorrow afternoon to finalize the recruitment plan. Of course we will need to use some of our internal security personnel, but all other personnel will be workers from the Soviet Union."

President Rosinski nodded his head while tapping his fork on the dessert plate. He stared at Mr. Anderson.

Mr. Anderson broke the silence. "Think of this arrangement as risk mitigation. Gazprom will be removing the security and logistics risk. Pacific International deals with these types of problems on every project. And most importantly, the entire project will be staffed with Soviet workers."

President Rosinski looked up and stared Mr. Anderson in the eye. He held his gaze, looking for a sign of deception. He took a drink of water and contemplated the decision. "You have a partner. Have your Moscow office director meet with the Gazprom CEO next week to finalize." He picked up his glass of vodka for a toast; Mr. Anderson followed his lead. "To our continued friendship!"

SELECTED

"To friendship," replied Mr. Anderson as they touched glasses.

After a few minutes of friendly banter, President Rosinski brought the conversation back to business. "Tell me something. Why do you Americans allow your country to be governed by random peasants? How could you let that happen?"

Mr. Anderson leaned back and smiled. "Boris, do you really think we would allow the country to be governed by the people? The random selection of government officials was our way of stopping the uprising. The people believed they won. And they did win; they will be much happier now we have complete control. Democracy is an outdated concept. The masses are much better off with one strong leader, don't you agree?"

President Rosinski raised an eyebrow and nodded his head.

President Rosinski and Mr. Anderson finished their dinner with small talk. After President Rosinski excused himself for the evening, Mr. Anderson went downstairs and found Dominika at the bar. He put his arm around her shoulder and kissed her on the neck. He whispered into her ear, "Continue as planned, but be careful around his security guards."

J. ALLEN WOLFRUM

Dominika brushed him aside as if he were another unwelcome suitor clamoring for her attention. Mr. Anderson walked out of the restaurant wondering if Dominika was really as good as her reputation. If not, they were both headed for a slow and painful death.

36

Twenty-four hours after the attacks, Susan walked into the Situation Room. Every seat was taken, and the outer walls of the Situation Room were filled by leaders from various departments within the government. Susan glanced around the room before sitting down at her chair. She spotted Senator Reynolds and General LeMae standing at the back of the room next to each other. Susan took her seat. The rest of the room sat down in their chairs. Susan noted the grave looks of concern in the room.

Susan broke the silence. "I see several new faces in the meeting today. Let's start by getting everyone up to speed. General Gillingham, please give us an update on the situation?"

"Yes, Madam President." General Gillingham opened his briefing folder for reference. "As we all know, yesterday at 10:30 a.m. three car bombs exploded, one here at the White House, one on a Los Angeles freeway, and a third explosion on a freeway in Atlanta." General Gillingham looked around the room. all eyes were glued to him in anticipation.

He continued, "After the explosions, the news channel CNN was hacked and an image of the Soviet flag with the Soviet national anthem playing in the background was shown for thirty seconds. As of fifteen minutes ago, the casualty statistics included twenty-five killed and one hundred and forty-three wounded as a result of the attacks." General Gillingham paused to take a deep breath. "At each attack scene, multiple witnesses have stated they saw the vehicle carrying explosives on the road prior to the attack without a driver. We have found no evidence to indicate the vehicles were physically driven by a human."

Susan asked, "Were the vehicles operated remotely?"

"We believe so. Our forensic teams are combing through the rubble at each site trying to find evidence. They're also in the process of analyzing all communication near the attack sites for evidence. Right now, we don't have any firm leads."

Susan asked, "Do we have any information on the CNN hack?"

"Our team found that the entire station's communication infrastructure was compromised, and has likely been compromised for the past several months."

SELECTED

Susan took a breath and scanned the room. There were more men in military uniforms in the room than she expected. The presidential daily briefing was generally avoided by uniformed military personnel. Being the junior ranking military member in the room made you an easy scapegoat for any of the generals.

"General Gillingham, do you have other agenda items you want to discuss?"

"Yes, I'd like to go over our response plan. We have carefully considered all options and are recommending an immediate three-pronged response to the Soviet Union's attacks. First, we will reinforce the Ukrainian military in their fight to remain independent from the Soviet Union by removing the current regime in Crimea and returning Crimea back to the Ukraine. The second prong—"

Susan held up her hand and interrupted General Gillingham. "I'm sorry to interrupt, but aren't we jumping to conclusions?"

General Gillingham's face flushed red. "Pardon me, could you repeat the question?"

Susan put both hands on the table, sat up straight, and stared at General Gillingham. "Aren't we jumping to the conclusion that the Soviet Union is responsible for the attacks?"

"Given the content of the leaked documents of two days ago, the strategic nature of the attacks, and the Soviet national anthem being played on a national news network after the attacks . . . the Soviet Union is responsible," replied General Gillingham.

Susan sensed anger and frustration growing from the military staff in the room. This meeting was merely a formality; they had already decided on a response plan. "It certainly is not clear to me. I have yet to see an intelligence report validating the leaked documents. How do we know they're legitimate?" Susan looked around the room. Visible anger resonated from General Gillingham. The room fell silent. The awkwardness of the situation forced people to fidget and look away from Susan.

General Gillingham spoke up. "We are the United States of America. We will not let the Soviet Union get away with attacking our country. If we don't respond with force, we will lose the world's respect. If we let that happen, the world will be in grave danger."

Susan shot back at General Gillingham, "Have you reached out to the Kremlin?"

SELECTED

General Gillingham shot back, "We do not negotiate with terrorists."

Susan shook her head in disbelief. "We don't have a shred of evidence leading us to believe the Soviets were behind the attacks and you want to start a war without even talking to them? Why? Because you think your ego might be damaged? Are you insane?"

General Gillingham shot back, "What good would talking to them do? They will respond with the same denials as they always do."

Susan clenched a pen in her right hand. "That might be true, but we'll never know if we don't ask. The stakes are far too high to take that risk."

"Madam President, I am not suggesting we start a war. Our response plan is simply to help our friends in the Ukraine," replied General Gillingham.

Susan jumped out of her chair. "You cannot be that naive. What would we do if the Soviet Union decided to help Mexico retake California? Would we sit on the sidelines and watch?" Susan paused to look around the room. She was met with angry eyes.

J. ALLEN WOLFRUM

FBI Director Arianna Redmond sensed that Susan was about to lose control. She stood up from her chair to interject in the argument and immediately gained the attention of every eyeball in the room. "I've sat here and listened to your childish discussions." She looked directly at General Gillingham. "Your plan is to start a war with another nuclear power? Do you know what that means? . . . I'll tell you what it means. At a minimum, millions of Americans will die. . . . And at worst, we alter the course of human history forever. For what reason? Because your ego might get hurt? It's time for you to stop acting like a child and be a man. President Turner will find another way." Arianna Redmond turned toward Susan.

Susan immediately followed up Director Redmond's comments. "Effective immediately, I'm ordering a halt to all military actions for thirty days. General Gillingham, I want a report sent to my office every morning with the location and activities of all U.S. troops currently stationed abroad."

Susan confidently closed her briefing folder and looked around the room. "Thank you. This concludes the briefing." She walked out of the Situation Room. Mason Adams proudly followed her in silence back to the Oval Office.

Back in the Oval Office after the meeting, Susan stared out the window with her shoes off and feet on the coffee table.

SELECTED

General LeMae and Senator Reynolds interrupted her moment of contemplation. Susan stayed on the couch and turned her head toward the door.

"What are you two doing together?" Before they could answer, Susan answered her own question. "You know what, don't answer that question. I'm too upset to hear the answer."

Senator Reynolds smiled and tossed Susan a package of Reese's Cups. "Thought you might need these."

Susan chuckled out of desperation. "Might as well. If General Gillingham has his way, I won't make it to bikini season anyway. I'm going to have nightmares about Agent Schneider waking me up in the middle of the night holding the nuclear launch codes and telling me I have five minutes to decide the fate of the world."

"I don't think we're there yet," replied General LeMae.

Susan sighed. "If the Joint Chiefs have their way, we'll be there sooner than you think."

General LeMae shot a quick glance toward Senator Reynolds, who stood to his right. "Senator Reynolds and I were talking after the briefing. I'm sure you noticed some serious anger in the room. The military leadership and the American people have all decided the Soviet Union is to blame. And they want justice. I think you held them off with the halt on activity, but they aren't going to wait forever."

Susan squinted her eyes in confusion. "What are you talking about? I'm the president, the commander in chief. I dictate what the military does and, more importantly, what they do not do."

"Yes, that's true. But what I'm trying to say is, I think the situation is close to getting out of control." General LeMae took a breath before breaking the news to Susan. "I get the feeling they'll try to remove you from office. And I wouldn't discount their willingness to do it forcefully. I don't need to remind you of the horrible things done in the name of politics and peace a few years ago. The Joint Chiefs aren't scared to do it again."

Susan looked down, nodded her head, and took a deep breath.

General LeMae continued, "I'm not part of their inner circle anymore but I'm still in the Pentagon, and it doesn't take Sherlock Holmes to see that there are some very strange meetings happening. Far too many senators and congressmen have been in meetings with the Joint Chiefs. And I've seen more security contracting companies walking the halls of the Pentagon in the last week. Something is happening, and they're intentionally keeping me away from it."

Senator Reynolds added, "I've seen some unusual activity in the Senate as well. It's not as blatant as General LeMae described, but I get the feeling there are meetings happening that have been intentionally kept off my calendar and my staff is getting the cold shoulder."

Susan leaned back on the couch. "Got any more Reese's Cups?"

General LeMae brought the conversation back from the edge of desperation. "On the bright side, you bought yourself some breathing room with the freeze on military activity. Be careful—I guarantee the Joint Chiefs will try to use it against you. They tried steamrolling you into seeing things their way. It didn't work, and you can count on dirty politics as their next attempt."

"Well . . . I didn't have a choice. I sure as hell wasn't going to get bullied into starting a war. There's absolutely no reason we need an immediate response. We all need some time to think."

Susan took the last bite from her Reese's Cup and looked

down at her watch. "Greg and Tommy are still pretty shaken up from yesterday's attack and I've only seen them for a few hours since I got back. I'm going to take the afternoon off and spend it with them. I think we all need a break. If you hear anything else, let me know." Susan stood up from the couch and walked General LeMae and Senator Reynolds to the door of the Oval Office.

37

Jack and Cheryl Anderson chatted with the other owners in the paddock at Santa Anita Racetrack as they waited for their horse to be saddled. Jack wore a casual light blue suit, white collared shirt, pink tie, and brown shoes. On the surface, Cheryl made a perfect match for her husband. She was five foot seven, with shoulder-length golden-blond hair, a Southern California tan, and the muscle tone of a yoga instructor. Cheryl wore a bespoke white cady sheath dress with matching heels and derby hat. She was every bit as cunning and shrewd as her husband. After a modeling career that ended in her early thirties, she started a high-end international fashion company, rivaling the popularity of Prada and Louis Vuitton.

Cheryl hooked her arm under Jack's and squeezed his hand as their horse and jockey walked around the paddock. She waved to the horse and jockey. "Isn't he magnificent? I have a good feeling about today. I think we're going to win."

Jack looked at Cheryl and smiled. "Honey, your optimism

knows no bounds. That's why I love you." He leaned over and gave her a kiss on the cheek.

Their horse, Stylish in Black, had won his last two races and was a seven-to-one favorite in today's race. Jack and Cheryl watched their horse walk out onto the track before heading up to their suite in the Turf Club to watch the race. The Turf Club kept a strict dress code—ties and jackets for men, dresses for the ladies. The club maintained an exclusive entrance for guests that went directly to the Owners' Circle, allowing members to skip the nuisance of brushing shoulders with the general public.

Jack and Cheryl sat down in their suite as the horses loaded into the starting gate. Cheryl picked up the binoculars on the table to get a better view. She gave her own commentary as the horses entered the starting gate. "Ohhhh good, he's in the starting gate. That silly number seven horse in the gate next to him is causing problems. Uggh, why can't they just behave."

"Aanndd away they go . . . ," boomed the PA system in the Turf Club. The crowd came alive as the horses maneuvered for position into the first corner.

The race announcer kept the crowd up to date on the action. "Going into the first corner, Magic Touch leading the way, followed by Loving Handful and Stole My Art."

SELECTED

Cheryl's eyes remained buried in the binoculars following the action on the track. Jack glanced at the live video feed and took note of the crowd's growing anticipation as the horses hit the halfway point of the race.

Cheryl yelled without taking her eyes from the binoculars. "Get up there, number six, let's goooo Stylish in Black!"

The horses entered into the back stretch and shouts from the crowd rose above the ambient buzz.

"Get up there seven! Come on lucky number seven!"

"Let's go four! Run number four, run!"

The announcer took over as the horses headed into the back stretch toward the finish line. "And coming down the final stretch, Stylish in Black, picking up steam, he's two lengths behind the leader, Magic Touch. It's Magic Touch and Stylish in Black, neck and neck."

Cheryl overpowered the announcer with her screaming. She was too excited to yell anything but, "Go! Go! Go!"

The horses closed in on the finish line. Magic Touch pulled a half a neck ahead of Stylish in Black with a hundred yards left in the race. The crowd erupted in screams for both horses. Cheryl took the binoculars away from her face and jumped up and down with excitement during the last fifty yards of the race. With twenty-five yards left, Stylish in Black found a last burst of speed and moved past Magic Touch by half a length. The rest of the field followed the leaders by three lengths.

The announcer boomed over the PA system above the fever-pitched crowd. "Aaannndd the winner is, Stylish in Black by half a length, followed by Magic Touch and Forget Me Not." Shouts of joy and exasperated sighs echoed from the crowd.

Cheryl grabbed Jack by the shoulders and kissed him on the lips. "We won! We won!"

Jack smiled and hugged Cheryl. His outward reaction was noticeably muted compared to Cheryl's vivacious show of exuberance about the win. Their friends in the club quickly came over to congratulate Jack and Cheryl on the victory.

Jack interrupted the celebration. "Honey, we need to get down to the Winner's Circle." Cheryl quickly finished up her conversation with friends and they walked together to the elevator.

Cheryl and Jack were alone in the elevator. He pressed the 'L' button and the elevator smoothly moved toward the ground. She hugged Jack, then reached up and gave him a passionate kiss on the mouth and they locked eyes. "Jack Anderson . . . I love you. Who would have ever thought we'd make it this far?"

Jack smiled. "I love you too, honey. You'll always be my beautiful bride."

Later that afternoon, after dropping off Cheryl at the Chateau Marmont in Hollywood, Mr. Anderson arrived at the Pacific International Los Angeles office.

All day at the races he'd looked forward to the confirmation of two contracts that would enable the Board to achieve their goals for the year. He promised Cheryl he would leave his laptop at the office and turn off his phone during the races at Santa Anita. Not having access to his email wore on his mind all day, but time with Cheryl was more important. She was right. Work could wait.

Mr. Anderson opened his laptop. Thirty-five unread emails. He quickly found the first email from the director in the Moscow office. The email subject read, "Accepted—Proposal 34-765 Security and Human Resources for Gazprom

International." Mr. Anderson smiled as he skimmed through the executive summary section. Pacific International was now responsible for security and human resources for Gazprom's first pipeline project in the Ukraine. There would be more to come as they moved their operations into Eastern Europe.

He moved back to his inbox and found the second of piece of good news. The email subject line read "Accepted—Proposal 35-985 Office of the Department of Defense—Logistical Support—Indefinite Quantity." Mr. Anderson let out an audible sigh of relief. General Gillingham followed through on his promise. Pacific International was now the sole provider of logistics and infrastructure support to the United States government. The contract was intentionally written with broad generic language and included: raw materials, architecture, engineering services, construction, and, of course, the long-term maintenance of anything Pacific International provided or constructed for the government. More importantly to Mr. Anderson, the contract made Pacific International the primary contractor for all United States military logistics.

Former commandant of the U.S. Marine Corps, General Robert H. Barrow, once said, "Amateurs talk about tactics, but professionals study logistics." As the sole contractor for the logistical needs of the United States military, Pacific

SELECTED

International effectively became responsible for controlling the military strategy of the United States. Mr. Anderson and the Board now had more power than the President of the United States.

Mr. Anderson pushed his chair away from the desk and looked down at the picture of his son. The picture took him back to the memory of the day when two army officers arrived at his doorstep and delivered the news that his son was killed on a combat patrol in Afghanistan. That day changed his life. Until his son's death, Mr. Anderson was a loyal officer in the United States Army. After his son's death, Mr. Anderson's purpose in life changed. He never wanted another father to lose their child in a senseless war. He soon realized that even at the highest echelons of the military, control was an illusion.

Mr. Anderson resigned his commission as an officer in the army, rose through the leadership ranks of Pacific International, and found others with a common vision for peace. Eventually he was introduced to the inner circle of the Board. Within the Board, he found a home. The other members not only shared his vision for peace — as an organization, they had the power to implement their vision. For decades, the Board worked behind the scenes to create a unified world. They envisioned a world governed by a small group of leaders focused on sustainability, health, and peace. Among themselves, they referred to their plan as the Strategy for Unified Peace.

The Board understood sacrifices were required to achieve their vision of a peaceful, unified world. They believed the short-term sacrifices and struggles would lead to a better world for all of humanity. Mr. Anderson spent years creating the Board's strategy for peace. The strategy coalesced around Susan Turner. She would be the last President of the United States. Susan Turner would be labeled an incompetent leader and blamed for starting a war between the Soviet Union and the United States. History would remember her name in the same phrases as Adolf Hitler and Charles Manson. The name would carry such disdain that any attempt to resurrect the concept of national identity would be immediately stamped out by the mere mention of "Susan Turner."

Mr. Anderson pulled his chair back up to the desk. He opened his email and typed a simple message to the Board: "Milestone One—Complete."

38

Susan opened her eyes and stared at the white paint on the ceiling of her bedroom. There was no noise from the hallway; she was the first person awake in the house. She grabbed the comforter with both hands and pulled it up to her chin, without moving her head she peeked to her left at the alarm clock. It read 5:12 a.m. in bright red letters. In one quick movement, she pulled the covers completely over her head, alligator-rolled in the sheets, and closed her eyes.

Fifteen minutes later, she woke up for the second time. After a hard-fought internal battle, she convinced herself to get out of bed. Sunday mornings were the only free time she could hope to get all week. Susan walked into the bathroom, turned on the water, and squirted a glob of blue sparkly toothpaste on her toothbrush. She looked at her reflection in the mirror. Within ten seconds she found three strands of gray hair. She sighed and finished brushing her teeth. If there were any visitors in the White House this early in the morning, they would have to see the president wearing slippers, army sweatpants, and a tank top.

Susan gingerly walked downstairs in her slippers, hoping to not wake up the boys. She smelled coffee brewing in the kitchen and poured herself a cup before walking into the map room. Flipping through the television channels, she quickly found an episode of The Real Housewives of Hollywood.

She heard footsteps coming down the hallway and tried to ignore them. Earl walked into the room with the New York Times under his left arm and a cup of coffee in his right hand. Susan and her father locked eyes, nodded to each other, and Earl sat down in the chair with his feet up on the ottoman. Earl thrived on good conversation. He would talk to almost anyone, but not until he was able to drink at least half a cup of coffee in the morning.

At the commercial break, Susan shifted her body on the couch toward Earl in an attempt to gauge his willingness to talk. He was reading the paper and had moved on to page two. The front page headline faced Susan.

Susan muttered half under her breath, "I can't believe it. Son of a bitch."

Earl folded the paper down and looked at Susan with

raised eyebrows.

She jumped off the couch. "Dad, can I have the front page?" Without waiting for a response, Susan grabbed the paper from Earl and turned to the front page.

Earl broke his pre-coffee vow of silence. "What the hell is going on?"

Susan buried her head in the paper, her eyes quickly darting across the page following her index finger as she scanned the article. It took her twenty seconds before she responded to Earl. She read the headline to Earl: "President Turner Unfit for the Presidency, Rumors of Impeachment Ramp Up." Susan continued her explanation. "I can't believe they leaked this to the press. What the hell is wrong with them? They leaked the details of our security briefing. Now the entire world knows our military is sidelined for thirty days. And they want me impeached for not responding with military force against the Soviets." Susan handed the paper back to Earl.

"Hmm." Earl raised his left eyebrow.

"Exactly. And there isn't a damn thing I can do about it. What am I going to do, confiscate all their phones and try to find out who sent text messages to a reporter?"

Earl took a sip of coffee and exhaled through his nose. "Nope."

Susan sat back down on the couch and stared at the television screen with her arms crossed. Her frustration vibrated through the air. Earl sensed she was about to do something rash.

Earl folded down the paper in front of him and looked at Susan. "Princess."

She turned toward Earl.

"Take the high road. Don't let them drag you down to their level, it's exactly what they want you to do."

Susan got up from the couch and kissed Earl on the forehead. "I know. Thanks, Dad. I'll leave you alone, enjoy the rest of the paper." She turned off the television and walked upstairs to her bedroom to take a shower and think.

In the shower, Susan lost control. The stress from her day-to-day responsibilities as the president, the feeling she was failing at motherhood, the terror attacks, and her overall inability to control the situation—it all finally came crashing down on her and overwhelmed her nervous system. Susan crumpled to the floor of the shower in tears and hyperventilating. The sound of the shower drowned out her sobs.

Susan found herself on the floor of the shower curled up in the fetal position. It took a moment to regain the strength in her legs. She pulled herself up off the floor, stepped out of the shower, and wrapped a towel around her waist. Sitting on the bathroom floor, she tried to understand what just happened. She got her breathing under control, stood up, and walked over to the dresser in her bedroom.

Susan picked up the wooden music box on the dresser, cranked the gold handle, and opened the lid. The melody played and she quietly sang along.

Susan sat back down on the bed and rubbed her hands over her face. She stared at her wedding picture. She spoke to her husband out loud.

"Mike, what am I supposed to do? I've done everything I can and it isn't enough. I've never broken under the pressure. I've set clear expectations and I've given clear orders. It isn't working. I just don't know what to do anymore."

Susan slowly walked over to the picture. She put her hands on the dresser top and dropped her head in exhaustion.

J. ALLEN WOLFRUM

"I can't keep letting the Soviets take over Eastern Europe. I can't let it continue."

She dropped her arms across the dresser and rested her forehead on the wood dresser top. After two deep breaths, she stood up straight and began pacing the floor of her room.

"If I do nothing, the Joint Chiefs will start a war with the Soviets. That's pretty much a guarantee. . . . If that happens, at least it'll end the agony. We'll all be dead and it'll probably be quick."

Susan continued pacing the floor and talking to her husband. "If I don't respond with military force, there's a good chance I get lynched in the streets or at the very least thrown in Guantanamo Bay and branded as a traitor."

Susan sat back down on the bed and looked around the room. Her eyes lingered on the neatly folded American flag in her husband's shadow box. She could barely remember the funeral ceremony. It was too traumatic; her brain blocked out most of the memory. Greg cried hysterically and Tommy stared blankly at the ground throughout the entire ceremony. No child should have to bury their dad and no child should have to grow up without a father because of the greed and pettiness of a few old men in suits.

SELECTED

Susan refused to accept that imposing your will upon the enemy through force was the only means to resolve a problem. She already tried playing the good neighbor, which failed miserably and in more ways that she could comprehend.

"Mike, what can I do? I can't fight . . . I can't play nice . . . and I can't run away. What other options are there? I feel like I'm trapped in a room with a scorpion, and anytime I move, I get bit."

Susan leaned back across the bed, her feet on the floor and hands over her eyes. She counted backward from ten. At every number, she took a deep inhale, paused, and exhaled. On the tenth breath, she opened her eyes and stared at the white drywall on the ceiling.

She inhaled one more time and closed her eyes. Susan stood up, walked over to the dresser, and put her hand on their wedding picture. "I love you."

39

Mr. Jones held his daughter's hand as they walked into the ballet studio. He bent down and gave her a hug.

She put her arms around his neck. "I love you, Daddy. Can you hold my backpack?" Mr. Jones smiled, "of course honey," and watched her run into the dance studio to join a dozen other four-year-old girls.

The dance studio encouraged the parents to watch the classes from a waiting room. Mr. Jones walked into the waiting room and stood behind the group of parents gathered around the window watching the dance lesson. He noticed a television in the corner of the room turned to the evening news. The television volume was muted and he read the headlines scrolling across the bottom of the screen.

PRESIDENT TURNER ORDERS HALT TO ALL MILITARY ACTIVITY

SELECTED

PRESIDENT TURNER POTENTIALLY UNFIT FOR DUTY, RUMORS OF IMPEACHMENT

SOURCE SAYS PENTAGON IS EVALUATING INTERNMENT CAMPS FOR SOVIET-AMERICANS

Another dad standing next to Mr. Jones commented on the news headlines. "I can't believe she's letting the Soviets get away with attacking us. They oughta kick her out of office."

Mr. Jones tried to diffuse the comment. "Yeah, I don't know. It's a bad situation."

"You're right about that. I don't trust those Soviets. Locking up the ones that live here isn't a bad idea."

Mr. Jones kept his knowledge of Mr. Anderson's plan private and stayed neutral in his response. "We'll see what happens."

Inside the Pentagon, in Corridor 9, Ring C, Conference Room 3, behind blacked-out smart glass walls, General Gillingham and Mr. Anderson held their monthly program management meeting.

Mr. Anderson talked through the details. "If you flip to the executive summary page, you'll see an outline of the logistical plan. It's a lot of words but essentially those five bullet points break down the supply chain infrastructure that would be required to support and sustain U.S. troops in the Ukraine, Belarus, and Latvia." Mr. Anderson waited for General Gillingham to quickly scan the bullet points. Mr. Anderson kept quiet until General Gillingham looked up.

General Gillingham took off his glasses and rubbed his temples. "I hate reading these contracts. Just hit the high points." Mr. Anderson nodded, but before he could get a word out, General Gillingham cut him off "And Jack . . . spare me the engineering jargon. You're better than me with the numbers, you don't have to rub it in my face." General Gillingham closed the contract binder and leaned back in his chair.

Mimicking General Gillingham's mood, Mr. Anderson smiled and relaxed his posture. Before beginning the explanation, he put down his pen and closed his notebook. "You believe there is a very high probability of the need for U.S. troops in Eastern Europe within the next thirty to sixty days. Is that correct?"

SELECTED

General Gillingham nodded and put his index finger to his temple.

Mr. Anderson continued, "We have not expanded our military presence in Eastern Europe since World War II. The assets we have in the theater would be destroyed in a matter of weeks by a Soviet assault. We can quickly get ground troops in the area, but they have no logistical support—they would have water for maybe three days and food for a week. Setting up those logistical supply chains takes time. We need to start building them now."

General Gillingham frowned and seized the silence. "Tell me something I don't know. Our military strategy think tanks have been working on plans for this scenario for decades. We already have well-researched plans for a war with the Soviet Union."

"I know, I led the strategy sessions. Because of the close surveillance on both sides, we assumed that neither side could gain a strategic advantage before the war started. That assumption has already been proven false by the Soviets. They have been slowly moving troops toward the western borders for months. We've been distracted with captured pilots, internal battles with immigration, leaked documents, and now the terrorist attacks. The Soviets have clearly gained the advantage while we weren't paying attention. We can't let them keep it."

General Gillingham briefly looked away from Mr. Anderson at the blank wall of the conference room. He folded his hands on the table and exhaled deeply. "So what's your plan? If we start moving troops into Eastern Europe, we're almost certain to trigger a Soviet response and start the war before our assets are in position. And it sure as hell doesn't make sense to tiptoe into a gunfight."

"Agreed. That's why we're going to use the Ukrainian civil war and the economic hardships in Latvia and Belarus to cover our tracks. We're going to set up the supply chain for the United Nations Peacekeepers. Or at least that's what we'll make them believe. The infrastructure required for U.N. Peacekeepers and your military are virtually identical. Given the UN's track record of wasted resources in Afghanistan and Iraq, not even the KGB will ask questions about why they're building twice the logistical infrastructure required."

General Gillingham leaned back in his chair and looked up at the ceiling as he contemplated the scenario. Involving another governmental agency in a cover-up was risky. "Who would be involved from the UN?"

SELECTED

Mr. Anderson relaxed his shoulders and maintained eye contact with General Gillingham. "Pacific International already provides logistical support to the U.N. peacekeeping efforts in Eastern Europe. On paper, it looks like business as usual."

General Gillingham paused and tapped his pen on the cover of his binder. "What do you need from me to make it happen?"

"Two signatures. One on the contract, and another to classify the contract top secret. Our program manager will take care of the paperwork and coordination with the Pentagon's contracting office. You'll see the paperwork on your desk before the close of business today."

General Gillingham nodded. "All right, I'll make it happen." He looked down at his watch. "Okay, sounds like you've got a handle on the situation. I've got another meeting in five minutes. Let me walk you out."

Mr. Anderson closed his binder and followed General Gillingham into the hallway. "Plans for the weekend?"

"Nothing too exciting, probably just spend some time out on the boat." General Gillingham's head was turned back while talking to Mr. Anderson; he wasn't watching in front of him. At the intersection of Corridor 9 and Ring D of the Pentagon, he bumped into Mason Adams, almost knocking the laptop out of Mason's hand.

General Gillingham reached out to help Mason. "Oh my gosh, I'm sorry. I didn't see you there. Are you all right?"

"I'm fine. Sorry, I wasn't looking either." Mason fumbled to regain control of his laptop and briefing folders.

Susan spoke up from behind Mason. "General Gillingham, I should have let you know I was coming over to the Pentagon this afternoon. How are you?"

"Madam President, good to see you as well. Have you met Jack Anderson?"

"I don't believe I've had the pleasure, nice to meet you Mr. Anderson." Susan extended her arm and shook hands with Mr. Anderson.

Mr. Anderson replied with a smile. "Pleasure to meet you, Madam President."

Susan politely returned his smile and quickly ended the conversation. "I hate to be rude but we're late for a meeting. Good to see you, General. And nice to meet you, Mr. Anderson."

40

Susan, Mason Adams, and the Secret Service agents continued walking through the dimly lit hallways of the Pentagon. Susan's hand trembled. She concentrated on taking deep, controlled breaths to avoid dropping her daily briefing binder.

One corridor away from their destination, Susan's fear took control. The walls closed in and her sense of time rapidly accelerated. She stumbled and couldn't catch her balance. The floor moved beneath her feet. She braced herself against the wall with her left hand. A Secret Service agent grabbed her arm to hold her up. She needed time to recover. "Is there a restroom close by?"

The agents look at each other before answering, "I think the closest restroom is near the North Entrance Lobby."

Every muscle in her body screamed for her to run out of the building. She reminded herself, This is your responsibility, you CANNOT continue to let the situation escalate. "I'll stop by on the way out. I don't want to be keep them waiting." Susan pulled herself together and continued walking down the corridor.

Mason led the way around the corner to Corridor 2, Ring A, Room 22. Mason pressed the buzzer on the door while Susan and the agents waited in the hallway. Captain Arnold, a twenty-eight-year-old army intelligence officer, opened the door. Mason promptly held out his badge and identified himself.

"Mr. Adams, I've been expecting you and President Turner. Please come into the waiting area." Captain Arnold moved to the left of the doorway allowing them into the waiting area. Captain Arnold saluted and rendered the proper greeting of the day as Susan entered the room.

Susan promptly replied, "Thank you. At ease, Captain."

Captain Arnold nervously moved both hands behind his back to the parade rest position. His eyes darted around the room between Susan, Mason, and the Secret Service agents.

Susan smiled in an attempt to ease the tension. "Captain Arnold, am I the first president to visit the Direct Link Communications Office?"

SELECTED

"Yes, Mr. President." Captain Arnold's face turned ghost white and he stammered. "I'm so sorry, I mean . . . Ma— Ma— Madam President." Captain Arnold looked at the Secret Service agents as if he were expecting to get beaten with a baton for his slip of the tongue.

Susan took a step forward toward Captain Arnold, gently patted him on the shoulder, and chuckled. "Not the first time that's happened. I tend to have that effect on men. Captain Arnold, what's your first name?"

In a state of embarrassment and confusion, Captain Arnold looked around the room before answering "Umm . . . Steve . . . Madam President."

Susan extended her arm to shake his hand. "Nice to meet you, Steve. I'm Susan."

The bewildered look on Captain Arnold's face remained as he shook Susan's hand.

"Good. Now that we're all friends here, there's no reason for anyone to be nervous. I've never done this before either. I need to use the Direct Link Communication System, can you show me how it works?"

"Sure, follow me into the holding room. The security

protocol only allows the president to enter the communications room with the terminal," replied Captain Arnold.

Susan passed the palm print and retinal security checks and the metal door on the opposite side of the room opened. Susan and Captain Arnold walked through the door leaving Mason and the Secret Service agents behind. The room they entered contained a single desk with a computer terminal. The room itself was small, twelve feet by twelve feet with white walls. The computer terminal and desk were against the wall directly opposite the door.

Muscle memory took over for Captain Arnold. He launched into the training speech he practiced at the beginning of every shift. He explained to Susan that the computer terminal in this room was a dummy terminal meant for training. But the protocol to send a message was the same as the live terminal in the next room. To unlock the computer terminal, Susan needed to enter the passcode she was given in her daily briefing binder. After unlocking the terminal, she would be presented with a text box to enter her message.

The terminal provided an encrypted direct link to an identical terminal in Moscow. Any message sent through the system would immediately alert a Soviet team in Moscow, who would in turn alert the President of the Soviet Union. All messages sent and received by the system were marked "Top Secret—For the Eyes of the President Only." Each message recorded a read receipt time stamp to alert the sender when their message was received.

Susan listened silently to the instructions.

"Do you have any questions, Madam President?"

"How long should I expect before a response from the Soviet president?" asked Susan.

"We test the system daily. The operators in Moscow see the message within seconds. If their protocols are similar to ours, I'd say another five minutes before the message is delivered to the Soviet president."

Susan noted the sweat dripping from Captain Arnold's forehead. She looked at him with questioning eyes.

Captain Arnold stammered, "I know you can't tell me, but should I be concerned? My wife and daughter are at the Lincoln Memorial today."

Susan nodded and exhaled. "You don't have anything to worry about, my kids are here in the city as well. Just some friendly banter between myself and President Rosinski."

Susan passed another set of palm and retinal security protocols and walked into the room with the live terminal. Being alone gave the room a sterile and eerie feeling.

While his driver navigated DC traffic, Mr. Anderson watched the live security camera footage of Susan in the Direct Link Communications room from his phone. He watched as Susan sat down at the live computer terminal. Mr. Anderson rolled down the privacy glass between himself and the driver. "Take me back to the K Street office."

Sitting at the live terminal, Susan opened her daily briefing folder and found the page with the security code. She followed with her finger back and forth between the code and the terminal. She could only remember three characters from the code at a time; she wondered if the two IED blasts and the crash landing in Mosul were to blame. The expiration date for blaming the war had long since passed, but that didn't stop the thoughts. She entered the final character and pressed Enter.

SELECTED

The terminal screen presented a text box to enter her message to President Rosinski. Susan paused; she wondered if this was the right move. Two countries with nuclear weapons, this close to the brink of war—there was no playbook for what she had to do. Her thoughts swirled deeper into a dark hole of doubt. She closed the folder, stood up, and paced the room. On the second lap across the room, she stopped and thought to herself, This is exactly why you wrote the message in the Oval Office. Just type the words and hit Enter.

Susan sat back down at the terminal. From her daily briefing binder, she took out her message to President Rosinski and placed it to the left of the keyboard. She typed the message word for word.

To: President Boris Rosinski

From: Susan Turner, President of the United States of America

Subject: Maintaining Peace

I hope to maintain a peaceful and prosperous relationship between the United States, the Soviet Union, and the rest of the world. I believe that the diplomatic cables that were leaked to the public have been falsified. I do not believe the Soviet Union is responsible for the terror attacks against the United States.

Within our government there are many who blame the Soviet Union for these events and they are attempting to persuade the public that military intervention is necessary. I may not have the political power to stop them.

To avoid a military conflict that would inevitably alter the course of human history and destroy millions of lives on both sides, we must work together to maintain peace.

Sincerely,

Susan Turner, President of the United States of America

———

Susan pressed the Send button. She felt numb, as if nothing had changed. No alarms went off, no bells rang, there were no whistles of celebration or confetti. Susan pushed her chair away from the terminal and stood up. Out of habit, she pushed the chair back under the desk, just as she found it.

SELECTED

In the Kremlin, Boris Rosinski enjoyed dessert alone—a pastilla made with sour apples. His executive assistant walked in the room carrying a brown folder under his arm and waited patiently for President Rosinski to acknowledge his presence. After he finished dessert, President Rosinski motioned with his right hand for the folder. He quickly read Susan's letter, closed the folder, and calmly placed it back on the table.

He instructed his assistant to have Director Tremonov meet him in the Kremlin library room in an hour. The Americans had never used the secure messaging system for anything of consequence. For decades the two countries operated as if the other did not exist. The minimal amount of communication that occurred was conducted through intermediary countries or public announcements. President Rosinski saw a light at the end of the tunnel. It might be possible to finally have an open and direct relationship with the Americans.

41

Susan looked up from her desk and saw Agent Young walking into the Oval office, followed by Tommy. "Oh my gosh. Tommy, what happened to your lip?" Susan got up from behind her desk and walked toward Tommy. Tommy lowered his head. Agent Young spoke up, "Madam President, Tommy was involved in a minor altercation with a classmate."

Susan put her hands on her hips. "Tommy, look at me."

Tommy looked up with a frown. "I got in a fight at school. Mom, I didn't start it . . . I promise."

Susan exhaled heavily out of her nose.

Tommy looked down again and began softly talking. "Mom . . . they were calling you names . . . saying you were a Soviet spy and that being president was a man's job . . . I just didn't know how to make them stop. . . . I tried walking away. They just wouldn't stop."

SELECTED

Susan closed her eyes and hugged Tommy. "It's okay, honey. I'm sorry."

After Tommy and Agent Young left the Oval Office, Susan collapsed on the couch and cried. The boys had suffered enough after their father's death; they didn't deserve to be tormented at school. She knew all too well that the scars of emotional trauma never fully heal.

Inside the Kremlin, President Rosinski calmly folded his newspaper and set it on the reading table next to his bottle of Stolichnaya Red Label. Director Tremonov walked into the library. He stopped five feet from President Rosinski and nervously scanned the room.

"Please, have a seat. Vodka?" President Rosinski gestured for Director Tremonov to take the seat across from him.

Two reading lamps provided just enough light for the men to see each other. President Rosinski used the library as a place to get away from the constant interruptions in the Kremlin. Director Tremonov himself had not stepped foot in the president's library since Boris Rosinski took office.

Director Tremonov sat down in the chair across from President Rosinski. He scanned the room for movement before responding. "No thank you, I'm getting old, too much vodka late at night upsets my stomach."

President Rosinski eased his fear. "Relax Nikolai, you're going to walk out of the room." Before Director Tremonov could reply, President Rosinski raised his hand and motioned for him to stop. President Rosinski continued, "I received a message from the Americans, their president has lost control of the military. The American people and the military are blaming us for the terrorist bombings and they believe the leaked documents are true. If we don't intervene, war is imminent."

Director Tremonov sat up straight in his chair and put his hand to his chin in a nervous moment of contemplation. The men sat in silence for several seconds as the gravity of the situation permeated the room.

Director Tremonov broke the silence. "This was always a risk. We knew our expansion of the pipelines into the Ukraine, Belarus, and Latvia could spark a conflict at any moment. A war with the Americans has been brewing for decades. It's inevitable."

President Rosinski shook his head. "That might be. But the

American president wants peace. And, so do I."

Director Tremonov caught his own mistake: he'd revealed too much information to Rosinski. Tremonov spent too many years in the field as a KGB operative to believe that the Americans truly wanted to avoid a war. He remained silent in response to the president's call for peace.

President Rosinski continued, "We'll make the leaked information seem unreliable. If we can call into question the validity of the leaked documents, it will muddy the waters of public opinion."

"And our official stance after the leaked files are picked up by the press?" asked Director Tremonov.

"Silence. The world will be caught chasing their own tail, trying to figure out what information is true and what is a lie. The Americans will focus their hatred inward and we can continue building economic security for our people." President Rosinski stopped his speech to look down at his buzzing phone.

The text message read, "I'm here—Dominika."

President Rosinski looked up from his phone. "Understood?"

Director Tremonov's eyes looked upward to gather his thoughts and assess the timeline. "We can have something out to the press by tomorrow afternoon. It's just a small alteration to a response plan we have on the shelf."

"Good." President Rosinski stood up from his chair. Director Tremonov followed him to the door of the library. "Nikolai, I trust you to handle this."

Back in the United States, anti-Soviet protests continued across the country. The front page of every major newspaper focused on the same message: The Soviets planned the terrorist attacks and they needed to be stopped at all costs.

Susan picked up the telephone handset and dialed her chief of staff, Mason Adams. Ten seconds later, Mason walked into the Oval Office.

"Mason, I need to let the American people know what's going on. How soon can you set up a town-hall-style meeting? I want it to be outside the White House and open to the public."

Mason dropped his head and put his hands behind his

back. "The Secret Service informed us that they can't protect you in public. And with the riots in DC, Atlanta, LA, Detroit, and New York, I agree with them, it just isn't safe."

Susan put her hands on her hips. "So you're telling me, as the President of the United States, I'm not safe in my own country?"

Mason sighed. "Yes, Madam President, I'm sorry. I went through several scenarios with the Secret Service, it just isn't safe. Maybe in a few weeks, but not now."

Susan responded sharply, "Fine. Does the Secret Service have a problem with me giving a State of the Union address from the White House?"

"A State of the Union address? That tradition died decades ago."

"Well, I'm bringing it back—the American people deserve to know what's going on. These rumors have got to stop. Tell the media and get the live video feeds set up."

Mason tipped his head forward to acknowledge the order and turned to walk out of the Oval Office. Three steps from the door, he stopped and turned around. "Can I . . . never mind."

Before Mason could turn around, Susan stopped him. "Mason. What is it?"

Mason took a deep breath. "I know it's not my place to say. But I'm worried about the media's reaction. I know you don't watch the news, but they've been really hard on you since the terror attacks. And I'm concerned that it will . . . I don't know how to say it. I guess I'm just concerned that it will get out of hand if you don't put the blame for the attacks on the Soviet Union."

Susan looked down at her desk, then stood up and leaned forward with both of her hands on the desk of the Oval Office. "Mason, I didn't take this job because I wanted people to like me. If being an honest, caring, and compassionate leader makes me a horrible person in the eyes of the media, then so be it. Let them label me a coward in the history books. I will not be responsible for leading our country into another series of senseless wars."

Mason locked eyes with Susan. "Yes, Madam President. I'll get the video feeds set up and send out a memo to the press."

At 7:00 Eastern that evening, Susan delivered her State of the Union speech to the American people and the world.

"My fellow Americans: We are five years into our new

form of democracy. These last five years of peace were preceded by decades of continuous turmoil that unfolded with two generations of Americans fighting three long and costly wars, resulting in a vicious recession that spread across our nation and the world. It was, and still is, a hard time for many Americans.

"Just like many of you, I witnessed firsthand the horror of continuous war and economic depression. Let us never forget the pain that brought about our new form of democracy. It is our duty not to repeat the mistakes of the past. We must stand strong and not bend to the will of our enemies.

"I believe with all of my heart that the Soviet Union is not responsible for the horrible terror attacks that occurred in Washington, DC, Los Angeles, and Atlanta. If we continue to tear our country apart seeking retribution, our enemies will win. I will not allow our enemies to win. We will find those responsible for the attacks and bring them to justice, but we will not start a world war by seeking revenge."

Susan continued her speech, emphasizing the importance of community and the principles of American democracy. After addressing her dismay for the anti-Soviet violence, Susan ended her speech with a quote from Benjamin Franklin: "They who can give up essential liberty to obtain a little temporary safety deserve neither liberty nor safety."

The reaction across America to Susan's speech was neutral at best. Those who wanted retribution against the Soviet Union used her speech as more ammunition to support their cause. The media used the speech as an opportunity to question whether Susan was mentally fit to be a leader. Her history of depression and post-traumatic stress disorder were brought back by the media as leading news stories.

42

KGB Agent Larov stepped over yellow caution tape and into the foyer of the apartment. A Soviet police officer stepped in front of him and put his hand up. "This is an active crime scene."

Agent Larov pulled out his KGB Badge. "Larov, KGB. I'm here on orders from KGB Director Tremonov. What have you found so far?"

The police officer backed down. "Not much yet. It looks like he was alone. Follow me, the body is in the living room." The officer turned and headed toward the entryway to the living room and Agent Larov followed.

Larov scanned the living room and inhaled sharply. He picked up a hint of a smell that seemed out of place, but he couldn't put his finger on the source. He continued to scan the room; everything seemed neatly in order. His eyes stopped on President Rosinski's naked body lying on the floor in front of the couch. A thick brown leather belt remained cinched around his neck.

The police officer shook his head. "Asphyxiation fetish . . . took it too far. We get about two of these a month."

Agent Larov nodded but remained suspicious. "Dust the entire apartment for prints and do a thorough search for hair follicles. I don't believe he was here alone. When you're finished, send the report directly to KGB Director Tremonov."

The Soviet media reported President Rosinski's death as a heart attack. By the time President Rosinski's body was discovered, Dominika was celebrating a successful mission with a glass of champagne and a cigarette in her apartment overlooking Lake Montreux in Geneva.

After learning of President Rosinski's death, Director Tremonov immediately began making preparations. He'd witnessed several regime changes during his KGB career and knew that swift action would be his only chance to seize control. Often only a few minutes separated the winners and losers in this type of power struggle. The stakes of the game were life and death; the party who ultimately gained and held control survived, and their opponents were eliminated. It was brutal but necessary.

Susan awoke to disturbing news from two fronts: the death of President Rosinski and a swell of hatred from the media about her State of the Union speech. Throughout her presidency, Susan did her best to isolate herself from the scrutiny of the media. From time to time, she checked in on the twenty-four-hour news stations to get a pulse on the American people. It was lonely at the top.

She confided in very few people in the administration. Mason Adams, Vice President Wilkes, Senator Reynolds, and General LeMae were the exceptions. It seemed odd to Susan that Vice President Wilkes spent so much of his time outside the White House. When she casually questioned him about his minimal presence in the White House, he awkwardly confessed to her that he was writing a memoir about his time as president. She accepted the explanation as valid and encouraged him to continue the work. In her mind, anyone who did this job for two years earned the right to take some time for themselves.

Susan grew to despise the Oval Office. It felt like her own prison. Leaving the White House required enormous effort and needed to be planned out days in advance. She refused to put Mason, her staff, and the Secret Service through the extra effort simply for her to have a change of scenery.

After breakfast and her daily room inspection with Greg and Tommy, Susan met with General LeMae and Senator Reynolds in the Oval Office. Senator Reynolds cocked his head and furrowed his brow. "Hold on. So we're going to roll over and give the Soviets what they want?"

Susan raised her hand. "Your listening skills need some work." Susan raised her eyebrows. "We're going to ask them what they want. I didn't say we are going to give it to them. Tensions have been escalating far too fast without any dialogue. I am not starting a war that will alter the course of human history because of a misunderstanding."

General LeMae grabbed a glass of water from the coffee table. "I can't say I disagree. Wars have been started over less.

SELECTED

This goes against every tactic we've ever used against the Soviets, but given the circumstances, I don't see how it can hurt."

Susan smiled. "Good, I'm glad you agree. The United Nations conference in Geneva starts in four days. We'll do it there. I need both of you with me. Vice President Wilkes and Mason will be staying here to make sure I don't get impeached or put on trial for treason."

Senator Reynolds and General LeMae stared at her in shock.

"Come on. It was a joke, nobody is putting me on trial for treason. At least not yet."

General LeMae moved past the awkward moment. "If you say so. But either way, it isn't a pretty thought. Anything in particular you want us to do before the conference?"

"Not yet. I don't even know who I'm talking to."

"I just came from a Foreign Relations Committee meeting—they're in the same state of confusion," replied Senator Reynolds.

General LeMae threw in his opinion. "My money's on Tremonov. He runs the dark side of the Soviet Union—no way he's giving up that power. You don't get to be the director of the KGB by playing nice. He'll do what is necessary to take control."

Later that morning, Susan and Mason walked down the halls of the Pentagon toward the Direct Link Communication room to send another message to the Soviet Union. Mason looked down at his vibrating phone. He checked the message and abruptly stopped in the hallway. He immediately put the phone to his ear. "Find me a secure conference room in the Pentagon, I'm in Corridor 4, Ring C." Mason waited for the response, then abruptly shoved the phone in his pocket and began quickly walking forward. He led the group to a secure conference room. Susan could feel the tension in his stride; whatever had happened, it was too serious for a discussion in the hallway.

As soon as the door closed on the conference room in the Pentagon, Mason blurted, "There is another document leak. An internal memo from the British MI6 with evidence that the terrorist attacks were planned and executed by a domestic U.S.

terrorist group."

Susan sunk down in her chair and let her head roll back. She stared at the ceiling while processing the news. "I have no idea what to believe anymore."

General Gillingham walked through the door and sat down at the conference room table. He was followed by three NSA intelligence analysts.

Before General Gillingham could open his briefing folder, Susan asked, "Is the document real?"

"Madam President—"

Susan cut him off. "Stop with the 'Madam President' bullshit. I know you're not telling me everything, so now's the time to come clean."

General Gillingham cleared his throat and ignored Susan's statement. "We have no way of verifying the legitimacy of the documents. There are no immediate signs of forgery."

Susan shot back, "So you're telling me the British MI6 analysts know more than we do about who set off those bombs?"

"Those were not my words."

Susan snarled; she had no patience for banter. "Do we know who set off the bombs?" She gripped the edge of her hair with both hands to stop herself from taking a swing at General Gillingham.

"Our forensics team is still working on the evidence. Right now we don't have any strong leads."

Susan looked around the room twice before responding. Each time she locked eyes with General Gillingham, intense contempt for her radiated from his gaze. "Thank you, General, that will be all. You should leave."

Without saying another word, General Gillingham and the NSA analysts got up and walked out of the room. After they left, the Secret Service agent sitting next to Susan took a handkerchief out of his suit jacket and wiped the sweat from his forehead.

Susan took a moment to recover from the brief and tense meeting with General Gillingham and continued on her mission to send a message to the Soviet Union. She sent a repeat of her previous message, she needed to be sure the message made it to the new Soviet president.

SELECTED

To: President of the Soviet Union

From: Susan Turner, President of the United States of America

Subject: Peaceful Meeting in Geneva

I hope to maintain a peaceful and prosperous relationship between the United States, the Soviet Union, and the rest of the world. I believe that the diplomatic cables that were leaked to the public have been falsified. I do not believe the Soviet Union is responsible for the terror attacks against the United States.

Within our government there are many who blame the Soviet Union for these events and they are attempting to persuade the public that military intervention is necessary. I may not have the political power to stop them.

To avoid a military conflict that will inevitably alter the course of human history and destroy millions of lives on both sides, we must work together to maintain peace.

Please accept my invitation to discuss a peaceful resolution in Geneva during the week of the United Nations conference. The details will be arranged through Ambassador Dashkov.

Sincerely,

Susan Turner, President of the United States of America

———

Former KGB Director Nikolai Tremonov, now president of the Soviet Union, received the message from Susan. After reading the message, he unlocked the bottom left-side desk drawer and pulled out the intelligence folder labeled SUSAN TURNER, PRESIDENT OF THE UNITED STATES OF AMERICA. President Tremonov paid particular attention to Boris Rosinski's handwritten notes scribbled in the margins.

43

Greg Turner looked up at the clock from his history text book, one more minute until the recess bell. He and John exchanged glances at the risk of being caught goofing off by Mrs. Daughtry. The short soccer matches at lunch had become much more important since the girls started watching.

The recess bell rang, Greg shoved the history textbook into his backpack and headed for the door. Three steps from the doorway he heard Mrs. Daughtry's voice.

"Greg Turner, don't forget to see Nurse Freemont before you go out to recess."

Greg shouted over his shoulder, "I will."

Greg and John strategized for the game while they walked down the hallway towards the exit doors to the playground. At the corner John made a right towards the doors and Greg stopped.

"What are you doing? Let's go," said John.

"I'll be right there, I have to get my allergy shot from Nurse Freemont."

"Skip it, who cares. We need you there when we pick teams."

Greg sighed. "I can't my mom will freak out if I miss my shot. I'll be there in like two minutes."

"Alright, hurry up."

Greg turned and jogged down the hallway toward Nurse Freemont's office. He shoved open the door without knocking. "Nurse Freemont?" He heard a dragging noise from the supply closet in the back of the room. A man in work clothes and a baseball hat walked out of the supply closet. The man continued to breathe heavily as he walked towards Greg. Greg stopped, the man's behavior seemed strange for what appeared to be a maintenance worker. Greg noticed that the man's eyes were focused on him like a laser.

"Nurse Freemont isn't here today," said the man as he walked closer to Greg.

The man continued to walk towards him without speaking.

SELECTED

After hearing that Nurse Freemont wasn't in the office, his mind quickly moved back to the soccer match he was missing on the playground.

Greg shrugged, took off his backpack and held it out towards the man. "Can you hold my backpack? Tell Nurse Freemont I'll be back after recess."

The man reached out and grabbed his backpack.

Greg turned and shouted over his shoulder, "thanks," as he jogged out of the office.

Mr. Jones watched Greg Turner leave the office while holding Greg's backpack in his right hand. He slumped into a chair, closed his eyes and put his head in his hands. He did everything he could to mentally prepare for kidnapping the Turner boy. It was the backpack that threw him off. The look in the boy's eye as he handed him the backpack triggered a flashback to his own daughter. He couldn't go through with it, hurting a child was taking things too far.

Mr. Jones snapped back to reality. He needed to get out of the school and quickly. Nurse Freemont would wake up from the anesthetic in twenty minutes. He looked around the room and took a moment to clear his thoughts. The boy was gone; nothing he could do about that now. He knew the next few decisions would determine whether he would live or die.

He walked into the supply closet and scanned the room. He checked Nurse Freemont's pulse; she was out cold but she would be fine in an hour. He closed the door on the rolling tool box and pushed it out of the office. He walked down the empty hallway just like he practiced in the dry run a few months ago. He cursed himself for letting his conscience get in the way of work.

He loaded the rolling toolbox into the van and waived at the Secret Service agents as he drove out the front gate of the school. Getting out of the school was the easy part, explaining his failure to Mr. Anderson was much more dangerous.

On the drive to the warehouse where they planned to hold Greg, Mr. Jones kept repeating to himself out-loud, "Just tell him the kid didn't show up in the Nurse's office. You can come up with another plan." He repeated those two sentences to himself until he actually believed they were true.

His phone rang five minutes into the drive to the safe house . He picked it up, saw a familiar number and answered,

"This is Jones."

Mr. Anderson asked, "Do you have the boy?"

"He didn't show up for his appointment. It was too risky to attempt a snatch and grab. Too many people around."

"Alright, I'll meet you at the warehouse. We need to come up with an alternative plan."

"Sounds good see you there." Mr. Jones hung up the phone and took a deep sigh of relief.

Mr. Jones pulled up the loading dock at the back of the warehouse and walked inside.

Two men he had never seen before stood in the center of the main warehouse. Mr. Jones walked towards them, "who are you?"

The man on the right pointed toward two double doors, "Mr. Anderson is waiting for you."

Mr. Anderson leaned against a desk in the middle of the room while he waited for Mr. Jones, who was once his most trusted Lieutenant. He closely monitored the nervous look on Mr. Jones' face as he walked into the room. He gently leaned back on the desk and allowed Mr. Jones to walk toward him before asking, "Ed, how long have we known each other?"

Ed Jones' eyes darted around the room. "Must be over a decade now. There wasn't anything I could do, the kid didn't show up. The anesthetic was wearing off on the nurse. I had to get out of there. I'll figure out another way."

Mr. Anderson shook his head. "It's too late now. Timing was everything on this mission. You knew that. I don't know what to say." He raised his hands in frustration before continuing. "You lied to me. I just can't tolerate it —"

"I told you. The boy didn't show up. What was I supposed to do?"

Mr. Anderson recognized the desperation in his voice and raised his hand to stop the pathetic groveling. "Don't try to cover up for yourself. Do you really think I don't know the truth?" He looked toward the door at the back of the room. "Bring them in here."

Mr. Anderson focused on the eyes of Mr. Jones as two people were shoved into the room. He watched the vein in Mr. Jones's neck throb. The panic in Mr. Jones' eyes was replaced with the pale look of horror. Mr. Anderson glanced over at the two women. They both had their hans zip-tied behind them and black hoods over their heads.

Mr. Anderson nodded toward the two men holding the hostages and they pulled the hood's from their heads.

Mr. Anderson watched the horror turn to rage in Mr. Jones' eyes.

Before Mr. Jones could react, Mr. Anderson picked up the pistol from the desk and pointed it at Mr. Jones.

"I want you to die knowing that their death will be much more painful than yours."

Mr. Anderson paused for a moment to allow the thought to sink into the psyche of Mr. Jones before pulling the trigger twice. Mr. Jones dropped to the floor in a puddle of blood. Mr. Anderson ignored the screams of the women and focused on the stream of blood running across the floor. He looked at the two men struggling to hold Mr. Jones' wife and daughter. "Get them out of here."

44

After dinner, Susan found Greg and Tommy in the White House Map Room. Earl and Rose were helping them with their history homework. Susan hugged the boys and explained that she would be back in a few days. She promised to bring the boys Swiss Army knives and chocolate.

"Mom . . . why do you have to leave? Are you fighting the terrorists?" asked Greg.

"No honey, I don't want to fight anyone. I just want everyone to get along."

"Me, too," replied Greg.

She hugged the boys and headed for Air Force One. Senator Reynolds and General LeMae were already on the plane when she arrived.

General LeMae tapped the watch on his wrist. "You're late."

SELECTED

Susan pulled her head back and stood up straight. "Pretty sure I'm your boss now and the boss can't be late." Susan smiled and sat down in her seat.

General LeMae looked over at Senator Reynolds and raised his eyebrows. "Sure you can keep up with her?"

Senator Reynolds smiled and shrugged. "I haven't met anyone who can keep up with her yet."

Susan ended the conversation. "All right boys, settle down."

After reaching cruising altitude, they gathered in the conference room to discuss the plan.

"My best guess is that the Soviets want to build a pipeline to get natural gas and oil out of the Ukraine," said Susan.

Senator Reynolds and General LeMae nodded in agreement.

Susan continued, "And to make it happen they're going to take land in Latvia, Belarus, and the Ukraine. They'll do it by force if they have to."

General LeMae interjected, "The UN is supposed to stop situations like this from happening but they'll ignore the problem for a while. Then we'll have to step in with military force. And that is what the history books refer to as war by negligence."

Susan stopped the negativity. "Before we get too far down the rabbit hole, I need to find out what the Soviets want. And if it has to do with these pipelines, I think we can come up with a deal that makes everyone happy."

The discussion with Senator Reynolds and General LeMae continued. Afterward, Susan got on the satellite phone with Ambassador Dashkov and set up the meeting details. She would meet the new Soviet president two hours after they landed in Geneva, and she would do it alone.

While Susan was sleeping on Air Force One flying over the Atlantic Ocean, Mr. Anderson met with President Tremonov in Geneva at the Pacific International office.

Mr. Anderson attempted to ease President Tremonov's fears about the Americans. "Nikolai, I know you're concerned about the Americans. Trust me, they aren't moving any troops.

SELECTED

Pacific International is involved in every aspect of the American military supply chain. If they were moving troops, I'd know about it."

"Then why is the American president reaching out to us? I've read the intelligence files and I have no reason to trust her."

Mr. Anderson replied, "She's reaching out to you from a place of weakness. She lost control of the country. She'll be asking you what you want."

President Tremonov frowned and looked to his right.

Mr. Anderson continued, "This is your opportunity to secure the pipelines and economic prosperity for the Soviet Union. All you need to do is ask."

Tremonov locked eyes with Mr. Anderson. He'd spent his career detecting lies as a KGB operative. As strange as it felt to him, Mr. Anderson told the truth. President Tremonov inhaled sharply. "I'll deal with her."

Later that day in Geneva, Susan waited outside the

conference room before her meeting with the newly appointed President Tremonov.

General LeMae pulled Susan aside. "Are you sure about this?"

Susan gave General LeMae a confused look. "What are you talking about?"

General LeMae gently put his hand on Susan's shoulder. "I'm talking about being alone in a room with Tremonov."

"I'm fine. What's he going to do? The Secret Service will be right outside the door."

General LeMae angled his body so only Susan could see the right side of his body. He reached into his front pocket and discreetly pulled out his derringer pistol. "Here, take this. Just in case. Better to have it and not need it."

Susan grabbed General LeMae's shoulder and looked him in the eye. "Curtis, I know you're worried about me, but I'm fine."

A few minutes later, Susan sat in a conference room inside the United Nations building waiting for President Tremonov. The room was rather small—thirty feet by thirty feet square with a small conference table in the middle. Suddenly the door opened and President Tremonov walked into the room. Susan immediately got out of her chair and walked across the room to shake hands with President Tremonov. "President Tremonov, it's a pleasure to meet you."

Tremonov replied, "Madam President, it is a pleasure to meet you."

Tremonov shocked Susan with his voice. He spoke perfect English, not a trace of an accent. The combination of Tremonov's presence and his voice rattled Susan. She felt her right leg begin to tremble. The only way to regain control was to move, so she quickly took her seat across the table. President Tremonov took his seat on the other side of the table.

President Tremonov's presence in the room created a threat of violence. Susan had spent her military career with high-ranking officers and government officials; Tremonov brought with him a much more ominous presence. There was not an ounce of nervousness or apprehension in his demeanor.

Susan began speaking out of fear; the silence was more than she could handle. "I'm very sad to hear about President Rosinski's death. He was a great man. My deepest apologies."

"Thank you," replied President Tremonov.

Silence filled the room again. Susan hoped for a bit more depth in the response from President Tremonov. She let the silence linger for as long as possible. "As I said in my message to you, I want there to be peace between our countries. What can I do to help maintain our peaceful relationship?"

President Tremonov smiled on the inside. Mr. Anderson was right: the Americans were groveling. He calmly folded his hands on top of the table before responding.

"A Soviet-owned company, Gazprom, is in the process of purchasing the rights to build a pipeline for natural gas and oil from the Ukraine, through Belarus and Latvia. We would like this process to be peaceful. It is an important project that will provide future economic prosperity for our country."

Susan leaned slightly forward. "Would you be willing to discuss the project with the leaders of the Ukraine, Latvia, and Belarus? I believe we can come to a peaceful solution that will bring prosperity for everyone involved."

President Tremonov showed his first signs of emotion with a smile. "I welcome the opportunity to have an open dialogue."

It was not the menacing smile that Susan expected, but a warm, genuine smile of appreciation. Again Susan was thrown off by Tremonov's behavior. She couldn't get a read on his true mood or intention. "I'll make the arrangements for the meeting. Is there anything else you want to discuss?"

"No, that's all. Thank you for taking the time to meet." President Tremonov stood up. Susan pushed back her chair and walked around the corner of the table. She shook hands with President Tremonov and kindly patted his shoulder with her left hand.

He turned and walked toward the exit. Just before reaching the door, he spun around toward Susan and met her eyes. "I want you to know that we did not have anything to do with the terror attacks." Before Susan could respond, he opened the door and left the room.

Immediately afterward, Susan explained the brief and awkward meeting with General LeMae and Senator Reynolds.

"It was surreal. He said maybe three sentences and the meeting lasted less than five minutes," explained Susan.

"It seems like he's onboard. This could be the beginning of something great," replied Senator Reynolds.

General LeMae nodded. "All first dates are awkward. And you're the first president to meet a Soviet president, face-to-face and alone. Nobody has ever done it."

Susan exhaled through her mouth. "Well, it happened. I think we're in a good place. This is going to work." She felt a tremendous amount of stress taken off her shoulders. The plan was coming together.

In his office, Mr. Anderson dialed his chief operations officer. "Pat, how's it going? It's Jack Anderson. Go ahead and get Project Goliath started."

On the other line, Pat Weller responded, "Did we finally get the go-ahead from the Pentagon?"

"Yeah, they finally saw the light," replied Mr. Anderson.

"Fantastic news! Good work, Jack."

"I know we've been over the details a hundred times but don't forget that last set of changes. For the first two weeks, we're going to be using three times the trucks, and every convoy needs a security detail riding with them. We want to make sure the routes are safe."

"Got it, boss. Convoys headed toward the Ukraine, Belarus, and Latvia work sites will start in the morning."

45

The morning after her meeting with President Tremonov, Susan woke up with a mind-numbing hangover. The combination of jet lag and one too many glasses of chardonnay made her nauseous. She staggered to the bathroom and poured herself a glass of water. She caught a glimpse of herself in the mirror and hung her head in disgust. Throughout her life, she'd fought against the bottle. It went in cycles; she could control it for a while, but it always snuck back at the worst possible time.

Susan washed her face in the sink and took a long drink of water. She fought off the urge to throw up and refilled her glass of water. She found a bottle of hydration tablets in the outside pouch of her suitcase and thumbed one into her glass of water. They were marketed as a quick way for endurance athletes to rehydrate after a workout, but they were even better at easing the pain of a hangover.

Susan heard a knock on her door. She looked through the peephole and saw a Secret Service agent. She unhooked the chain and opened the door halfway. "What is it?"

"President Tremonov is requesting to see you immediately. He's waiting in a conference room downstairs. I counted twenty-three heavily armed security guards with him, and he has the briefcase containing the Soviet nuclear launch codes."

Susan closed her eyes and put her hands over her eyes. "What? I just talked with him yesterday."

"Madam President, I'm not sure what's going on. The only information I have is that President Tremonov has requested your presence downstairs immediately."

Susan took a big gulp from her glass of water mixed with the magical hangover cure. "I'll be right down. I need five minutes to get ready."

"When you're ready, our team will escort you to the conference room."

Susan walked back in the room. She still needed to throw up but calling in sick wasn't an option. She walked into her closet and grabbed a pantsuit from the hanger. She used a quick makeup trick to hide the hangover: a light concealer, eye shadow, and lipstick. She pulled her hair up into a bun and left the room.

SELECTED

A team of Secret Service agents met Susan in the hallway and escorted her to a conference room on the second floor of the hotel. In the hallway outside the conference room, Susan counted twelve men in black suits with earpieces, all carrying short-barreled AK-47s slung inside their sport jackets.

One of the Soviet security officers approached Susan with his hands in plain sight. He stopped six feet in front of Susan and her Secret Service agents. He asked with a thick Soviet accent, "Madam President, would you be willing to join President Tremonov in the conference room? He would like to speak with you."

Susan took a step forward and the Secret Service agents immediately tightened their circle around her. An agent leaned closer to her and half-whispered, "Madam President, at least take one of us with you. If you go in there alone we can't protect you."

"He wouldn't dare try anything," replied Susan. She smiled and gently tapped the shoulder of the agent directly in front of her. "Excuse me, gentlemen, I'll be back in a minute."

Susan emerged from the circle of her Secret Service agents with a smile on her face and terror in her stomach. The Soviet security agent returned her smile. "Madam President, please follow me."

President Tremonov stood just inside the door at the edge of the conference room table. Susan entered the room. Before she could speak, Tremonov pointed to a stack of pictures spread across the table. "Explain these photos."

Susan didn't immediately respond to Tremonov's statement. She calmly locked eyes with him, then looked down at the photos and picked one up. Susan quickly scanned the picture. It was an aerial photograph of what appeared to be a troop convoy. She scanned a half dozen more of the photos and placed them back on the table.

"What am I looking at?" asked Susan.

Tremonov replied with hatred in his eyes. "You're looking at your last mistake."

"Then why are we talking?"

President Tremonov replied, "I want to know why you're mobilizing troops and moving toward the Soviet border."

"I don't know what you think is happening, I haven't ordered any troop movements and I certainly haven't ordered any troops to move toward the Soviet border." Susan paused to let her message sink in. "And that image I just looked at . . .

that isn't a military convoy. It's a supply chain convoy with scout vehicles that make it look like a military convoy. I've spent more time than I care to remember in the cockpit of a Black Hawk staring down at military convoys. And that is not a military convoy."

Without missing a beat, Tremonov replied, "Then why was I woken up by Kremlin security with a message that we are at DEFCON 1 and the United States is beginning an invasion?"

Susan put the photos down on the table. "I have no idea. After the terror attacks, I gave an order to the United States military to stand down for thirty days. There is not currently and there will be no future movement from our military. And whatever is happening in these aerial photographs, I'm stopping it as soon as I leave this room."

President Tremonov tightened his jaw, jammed his hands in his pants pockets, and exhaled deeply. "Fine. The Soviet Union is remaining at DEFCON 1. You've lost control of your military." President Tremonov pointed his finger at Susan. "I will not hesitate to launch an attack if there's another sign of aggression. You can leave now."

President Tremonov stopped her before she left. "One more thing you should know."

Susan turned around. "Yes."

"You're the only reason I didn't launch our nuclear arsenal. I trust you. You have the integrity of a true soldier."

Susan didn't know how to interpret President Tremonov's explanation. She turned and left the room without responding.

Susan instructed the Secret Service agents to take her to General LeMae's suite. He was reading the London Times when Susan arrived.

"What's going on?" asked General LeMae.

Susan nodded to the lead Secret Service agent in the room. "Would you mind waiting outside?" When the agents left the room, she debriefed General LeMae on her meeting with President Tremonov.

"We need to get General Gillingham on the phone. I don't know what's happening but something's wrong. If there are convoys moving around in that area, he'll know about it. Especially after you pressed him for the daily updates on troop movements."

General LeMae grabbed his cell phone and dialed General Gillingham. Susan grabbed his arm to stop him. "Wait, do you think he's involved?"

"I don't know. I'll keep the questions vague, we'll find out what he knows."

General Gillingham picked up the call. "General Gillingham speaking."

"Tom, it's Curtis LeMae, and I've got President Turner sitting next to me. We have a few questions that you might be able to answer."

"Fire away," replied General Gillingham.

"Do you know anything about the logistics convoys moving near the Soviet border?"

"I know there's a plan on the table to deliver humanitarian aid and build shelters in that area. But that isn't supposed to start for a few months."

"Okay, do you happen to know the contractor's name?" asked General LeMae.

"It's through Jack Anderson and Pacific International."

Susan and General LeMae exchanged concerned looks.

Susan leaned toward the phone. "General Gillingham, listen to me. You have got to stop those convoys. I just met with President Tremonov—the Soviet Union just went to

DEFCON 1 because he thinks the convoys were American troops invading the Soviet Union."

General Gillingham replied, "I don't even know who's responsible for the—"

Susan cut him off before he could backpedal any more. "Then you need to find out. Tremonov is walking around with a team of heavily armed guards and the nuclear launch codes. You need to stop those convoys."

The gravity of the situation hit home for General Gillingham. He felt a hollow pit of despair in his stomach and the blood left his face. He tried to cover up for whatever role he might have played in the situation. "It must have been an administrative error. I'll find out what's going on and stop the convoys—"

Susan snapped, "I'm not done. You need to get on the phone with the commanding officer of Landstuhl Air Base in Germany and alert them of the situation. If the Soviets are at DEFCON 1, they are going to increase their air patrols near the border. We need to keep our distance. Do not engage. And do not give them a reason to engage with us. Ground all of our routine security flights."

"Yes, Madam President. I'll update you ASAP on the

progress."

General LeMae sensed something was wrong and jumped into the conversation. "Tom. I don't know what Jack Anderson has dragged you into . . . but you need to put a stop to it."

General Gillingham wasn't sure what to make of the situation. He stayed neutral and noncommittal. "Understood."

Susan hung up the phone and put her head in her hands. "We're an inch away from starting a nuclear war and he's worried about covering his ass and blaming it on a clerical error."

"Yeah, he's always been a coward. Makes him a great politician. And you know who's behind this, right?" asked General LeMae.

Susan responded, "I'm getting the feeling that Pacific International isn't just a coincidental player. Does this have anything to do with what you have on that flash drive?"

"I'm not sure, but I think so. I don't have all the pieces yet. That snake-in-the-grass, son-of-a-bitch Jack Anderson has been spending way too much time at the Pentagon lately. That can't be a coincidence," said General LeMae.

Susan asked, "How do you know Jack Anderson?"

General LeMae frowned. "Long and sad story. We were roommates at West Point. He was a hell of a soldier. After his son died—" General LeMae looked down. "Well, let's just say he changed." General LeMae shook his head and looked Susan in the eye. "But we've got bigger problems."

Susan nodded her head. "We need a plan but first I need a shower. I have a feeling it's going to be a long day. Meet back here in forty-five minutes?"

"All right, I'll do some more digging on what Pacific International has been up to lately."

46

Susan walked back into her room and collapsed on the couch. The hangover was nowhere near being gone and she needed food. Senator Reynolds knocked on the door. His smile turned cold after seeing the look in Susan's eyes.

Susan invited him into her room and quickly rehashed the morning's events. "Meet me in General LeMae's room in about forty minutes."

Senator Reynolds nodded. "All right, sounds good."

After Senator Reynolds left, Susan ordered room service, took a hot shower, and got dressed. She sat on the couch with a few minutes to spare before she needed to be back in General LeMae's room.

She grabbed her cell phone and scrolled through her email inbox. She clicked on an email with the subject line "Device #287642—Silence Removed—Automated Recording Transmission" and played the attached audio clip. Susan could barely hear the audio. She turned up the volume and held the speaker to her ear. She listened to the entire ten-minute recording of President Tremonov's conversations after he left their meeting the day before.

Before leaving Washington, Susan acquired a stealth listening device from FBI Director Arianna Redmond. The device was designed to stick in the fabric of a suit jacket and disintegrate within two hours. The person wearing the device would never know it was there and it left behind no evidence. Susan didn't tell anyone about the listening device; there was already too much scrutiny of her meeting with the Soviet president. She didn't need the additional concern about getting caught placing a bug on him.

The recording confirmed Susan's fear about Tremonov's intentions. Based on the audio recordings, Susan learned that Tremonov planned to use the trade agreement with Belarus, Latvia, and the Ukraine as a springboard for the Soviet Union's takeover of those countries. He saw it as reclaiming territory that the Soviet Union already owned. President Tremonov wanted to use the proposed trade agreements as a cover for moving Soviet troops closer to the borders with Europe.

Susan flipped her phone to the other end of the couch in frustration. All the progress she made to stop a war with the

SELECTED

Soviet Union was lost. President Tremonov's violation of the trade agreements would certainly be the next spark to start a world war. Susan laid down on the couch in defeat. She leaned her head against the armrest and hugged the pillow.

Susan heard her husband's voice shouting in her head, Don't even think about quitting! You survived a hell of a lot worse than this. You've been training your whole life for this. This is the moment you've been waiting for. Get off that couch, right now. He was right. This was her time to rise above; she had to, there was too much at stake. Susan wiped the tears from her face and took a deep breath to regain her composure.

Susan walked into General LeMae's suite. Senator Reynolds and General LeMae sat at the coffee table, flipping through satellite images.

"It looks like the convoys turned around. I had the Pentagon send me live drone images," explained General LeMae.

Susan replied, "Good, I just got an email from General Gillingham saying the same thing. Can you send those images to me? I need to get them to Ambassador Dashkov. Pretty sure Tremonov isn't going to take my word for it this time."

"Yeah, no problem. We need to give Tremonov an excuse to come down from DEFCON 1. At that level, even he doesn't have full control over the military. All it will take is one Soviet general with an itchy trigger finger and we'll all be dead."

Susan pulled up a chair next to the coffee table. She took off her suit jacket and laid it over the back of her chair.

"Getting the Soviets out of DEFCON 1 is the immediate problem. I have . . . ahh . . . kind of a confession to make," said Susan.

General LeMae and Senator Reynolds both stopped moving and turned their heads toward Susan. Neither said a word; they just stared at her.

"Before you get upset, let me remind both of you that it all worked out fine."

"Go on," said Senator Reynolds.

Susan gave them both an executive summary of the recording from the bug she planted on President Tremonov.

Senator Reynolds leaned back in his chair. "Sooo that seems bad."

Without verbally responding, General LeMae stood up and

put both hands in his pants pockets. He stared at Susan for a moment before walking over to the desk. He reached into the drawer and came out with a cigarette and lighter. He lit the cigarette with a gold Zippo and cracked open the window.

General LeMae muttered as he took a drag from his cigarette, "Goddamn smoke detectors."

Susan and Senator Reynolds were mesmerized by the show; it was like watching Clint Eastwood in real life. General LeMae took another drag, blew the smoke out the window, and turned back toward Susan.

Susan spoke up before General LeMae could start a lecture. "Listen, I know it was risky, but I had to know what he was thinking. I didn't see another option."

"Where'd you get the listening device?" asked General LeMae.

Susan slightly shrugged her shoulders. "A friend."

General LeMae saw Senator Reynolds was getting ready to admonish Susan for being so brazen. He cut in before Senator Reynolds could say something he would regret. "Never mind. It doesn't matter how you got it. It was worth the risk. If you didn't find out what he was thinking, we would have walked right into World War III." General LeMae paused, then asked, "So what's your plan?"

Senator Reynolds keenly read the situation and held his tongue.

Susan raised her eyebrows. "I don't have one."

Senator Reynolds and General LeMae began trading ideas and pontificating on the pros and cons of collaborating with the Soviets.

Susan lost interest in the conversation and focused her attention on a painting of the world map on the wall. It was an older painting; the countries and borders represented the world as it looked before the First World War. She moved closer to get a better look and studied the Soviet Union's borders, waterways, and natural trade routes. The map reminded her of playing Risk with her family at their cabin in Idaho.

Susan interrupted the conversation between Senator Reynolds and General LeMae. "We need to get the Chinese involved in the trade talks."

They both gave her a skeptical look.

Susan explained further, "The Soviets aren't going to take a trade deal seriously unless they feel their security is at risk, and the United States can't do it alone. Yes, we're a threat, but Tremonov doesn't think the US or the United Nations will follow through on any threats we make."

Senator Reynolds jumped in. "And for the Soviets, breaking a trade deal with the US and the Chinese could mean fighting a two-front war. And doing it with their trade routes cut off in the east and the west. Not such a pleasant thought."

General LeMae nodded and crossed his arms. "Makes sense, except we're not exactly friends with the Chinese."

Susan held up her hand. "One problem at a time."

"Well, I did go to boarding school with the Chinese finance minister," said Senator Reynolds.

Susan and General LeMae exchanged looks of surprise.

General LeMae spoke up. "I still talk to a Chinese general who went to the War College with me."

Susan nodded. "Good. Now we need a plan, a plan that benefits the Chinese."

Senator Reynolds sighed. "And the Soviets . . . and the US . . . and Eastern Europe."

Susan stopped the negativity. "Save the sarcasm. The real

reason the Soviets want the Ukraine, Belarus, and Latvia is because they want to ship natural resources."

General LeMae replied, "Sure, among other things, but that seems to be their main goal."

Susan replied, "So let's start there. The Soviets have two huge oil fields in the southeast, near the Chinese border. And right now, they ship that oil over twenty-two hundred miles west via rail to the Caspian Sea. What if they had a route to ship their oil south, directly to Beijing?"

Senator Reynolds interjected, "It would cut their transportation costs by at least fifty percent."

"And they would have a chance to gain a powerful ally in the East," said General LeMae.

"Exactly," replied Susan.

"But I don't see what's in it for the Chinese?" said General LeMae.

"Two things. They're going to get a cheaper and more reliable source of oil to fuel their economic growth, and we're going to decrease their import tariffs to America," replied Susan.

SELECTED

"What leverage are we holding over them?" asked General LeMae.

Susan replied, "That's where it's going to get dicey. We don't have any."

General LeMae took the last drag from his cigarette and added, "Tremonov is no fool. He won't risk a war on two fronts. But there's a chance he'll back away completely."

Senator Reynolds interjected, "I don't think so. The Soviets are desperate—they're on the brink of economic collapse. They've been playing it off for the last few years, but they're desperate. That's why they're making such a strong play for the pipeline through Eastern Europe. If he backs away from this deal, he's taking a big risk that the country could fall into chaos. If that happens, he'll end up like Gaddafi, lynched in the streets."

Susan replied, "I can't force them to work out a deal. But if we can get the Chinese president to attend the Eastern European trade meeting tomorrow morning, I think they'll both see the benefits of a trade agreement. I don't know how, but I think it'll work."

General LeMae stamped out his cigarette in the ashtray and turned toward Senator Reynolds. "Let's get to work. We've got some old friendships to rekindle."

Mr. Anderson picked up the phone in his office. "Tom, how are you doing?"

General Gillingham spoke rapidly. "What the hell did you get me into? Why is the president accusing me of attempting to start World War III?"

"Slow down. I have no idea what you're talking about."

"We had a deal. I get you government contracts for Pacific International and when I retire, Pacific International hires me as a consultant. I don't know what you're doing but I will not be the scapegoat."

Mr. Anderson attempted to neutralize the situation. "Tom, you're clearly upset. Why don't we talk this over in person. I'll be back in Washington later this week."

General Gillingham snapped back, "Whatever you've got me involved in, I want out. This is not what I agreed to." He hung up the phone.

Mr. Anderson slammed down the office phone. He

grabbed his personal cell phone and dialed.

"Yes, sir."

He quickly gave his orders. "You need to find General Gillingham. He's somewhere in Washington, DC—try the Exchange Saloon on G Street. Keep an eye on him. I'll be in touch with further instructions."

"Got it, boss. I'm on it."

47

Susan walked through the lobby of the hotel on her way to dinner. A Secret Service agent rushed toward her security detail with a briefcase. He reached into the briefcase and handed Susan a sealed plain manila folder marked Top Secret—For the President's Eyes Only. She immediately ordered her security detail to take her back to her room. Susan needed to know what was in the top secret folder before any negotiations. The stakes were too high to make a careless mistake due to lack of information. She hoped the folder contained confirmation of the Soviets returning to the normal alert status of DEFCON 5.

As soon as the room to her door closed, she opened the envelope and stared at the cover document. The subject line was all she needed to see: "President Susan Turner Impeachment Proceedings—Summons to Testify." She tossed the folder down on the coffee table and ran both hands through her hair. She had trouble believing her eyes. She picked up the document and read it again.

SELECTED

Every time she closed her eyes, she saw a white flash card with the definition of "failure" playing in an infinite loop in her mind.

Failure

1. Lack of success

2. The omission of expected or required action.

Each time, the flash card was followed by a string of memories played as a highlight reel of failures throughout her life. They flowed in chronological order, and every time she closed her eyes it would pick up where it left off.

How could she let it get this far out of control? No president had ever been impeached; all the others had resigned before their impeachment trial. If the human race survived, her impeachment was going to be remembered in the history books as the trigger for World War III.

Susan physically shook herself out of her downward spiral. She wiped her sweaty hands on the couch and scanned the remaining documents in the folder. She was summoned to testify in Washington, DC, in fourteen hours. The documents also contained an itinerary. Air Force One was scheduled to depart in less than two hours back to Washington, DC.

Susan picked up the phone and called Vice President Wilkes's office.

"Vice President Wilkes speaking."

"This is President Turner, what's going on? I just opened a court summons for my impeachment trial."

"I don't know any more than you, I got one as well," replied Vice President Wilkes.

"Can you stall them? I'm in the middle of some important trade negotiations, I can't just leave."

"I'll do what I can. How are the negotiations going?" asked Vice President Wilkes.

"Too early to say, but it looks promising, I think we're finally going to make progress on a friendship with the Chinese. . . ." Susan heard an echo in the background. "Am I on speaker phone?"

Without missing a beat, Vice President Wilkes eased Susan's concern with a chuckle. "I'm afraid you caught me slacking off, I was in the middle of practicing my putting game in the office. Now that I have some free time, there's no excuse to let my golf game slip."

Susan felt something wasn't right but kept going. "Anyway, yeah, I've got a lot of things to get wrapped up here before I can make it back. See what you can do about getting my testimony pushed back."

"I'll do my best. Good luck—anything else I can help out with?" asked Vice President Wilkes.

"No, that's it." Susan hung up the phone.

Vice President Wilkes picked up the handset and put it back down to end the call.

Mr. Anderson stood up and put on his jacket and quietly walked out of Vice President Wilkes's office. His work for the day was done.

Susan's next call was to General LeMae. "I just got served a summons to testify in my own impeachment trial."

"Me, too. I just got a summons to testify."

Susan's tone hardened. "I'm not abandoning these trade talks. We're close to a peaceful resolution, I can feel it."

"I know, but things stateside are getting worse and this impeachment trial isn't going to help."

"I just called Wilkes to see if he could help push back the hearing date. I got a weird vibe from the tone in his voice. Something isn't right," said Susan.

General LeMae snapped, "I don't trust him."

Susan sighed out of frustration. "If I go back and testify without having a peaceful relationship with the Soviets, they're going to kick me out and we're going to end up in World War III on a whim."

"And if you don't go back for the trial, they're going to suspend your authority and put Vice President Wilkes in charge. God only knows what he'll do . . . well, God probably doesn't know, either," replied General LeMae.

"I'm not going back until we get this deal made."

General LeMae unconsciously breathed heavily into the phone while he ran through potential scenarios. "Just hold out as long as you can before leaving for Air Force One. I'll talk to Senator Reynolds. We'll keep working on getting the meeting set up for tomorrow morning. Got it?"

"Roger that. Curtis, please don't do anything that's going

to get you in trouble."

General LeMae hung up the phone without responding. He answered a knock on his door; his security detail briefed him on a change to their itinerary. They were heading back to Washington, wheels up on Air Force One in two hours. He quickly packed his bags.

General LeMae had already talked with his Chinese military friend from War College—the word was going up the Chinese military chain of command. His friend promised an update later in the evening.

An hour later, Senator Reynolds stepped onboard Air Force One. He was early and General LeMae was the only other person in the main cabin. Senator Reynolds talked through an exhaustive list of the problems their early departure would cause. He wasn't yet aware of Susan's impeachment trial. General LeMae calmly nodded his head in agreement and tuned out the frantic rambling from Senator Reynolds.

After a few minutes of ignoring Senator Reynolds's complaints and theories about why their itinerary was changed, he looked down at his watch. Thirty-five minutes until wheels up. He reached into his briefcase and pulled out his portable humidor. Senator Reynolds kept talking. General LeMae opened the humidor and offered a cigar to Senator Reynolds.

"What are you doing? You can't smoke on a plane."

General LeMae ignored his comment and pulled out a silver Zippo lighter with the 1st Air Cavalry Division insignia and "OIF 2003–2007" engraved on the side. Senator Reynolds stared at him with a confused look on his face. Two puffs after getting his Montecristo properly lit, two dings rang from the Air Force One sound system.

Senator Reynolds looked at General LeMae and rolled his eyes. "I told you."

Over the loudspeaker, the pilot informed the passengers that there were mechanical complications in the safety check procedures. The part required for repairs wasn't available on-site; they would have to wait for it to be flown in from Landstuhl Air Base in Germany. He apologized for the inconvenience and instructed the passengers to deplane.

General LeMac puffed on his cigar as he walked down the steps from Air Force One onto the tarmac. He saw Susan walking toward Air Force One surrounded by her security detail. She was hiding her concern behind a smile, they shook hands and she leaned closer.

SELECTED

She whispered in his ear, "I'm sorry. I held out as long as I could."

General LeMae responded loudly, "I'm not sure what's wrong but they just told us to deplane. I guess some kind of mechanical failure; they're waiting on a part from Landstuhl. We aren't taking off until tomorrow afternoon."

An Air Force One crew member standing near General LeMae confirmed the information.

"Okay if we ride back to the hotel with you?" asked General LeMae.

Susan nodded. "Good idea."

Susan, General LeMae, and Senator Reynolds climbed into the armored Mercedes limousine. As soon as the door closed and they were alone, Susan and Senator Reynolds stared at General LeMae, waiting for an explanation.

General LeMae shrugged his shoulders, cracked the window, and continued to puff on his cigar. "What can you do? Murphy's Law."

Frustrated with the lack of an answer, Senator Reynolds turned toward Susan, hoping for an explanation. His hope was met by indifferent silence. Susan's phone rang, but she didn't recognize the number. "This is President Turner." Susan looked up toward the roof of the limousine and nodded her head. Then she smiled. "Good. I look forward to meeting you this evening." Susan ended the call and continued her smile. "The Chinese president will be joining the Eastern European trade meeting. He wants to discuss strategy this evening."

Susan walked into President Qing's suite, her Secret Service security detail remaining in the hallway. President Qing greeted Susan, "Madam President, it's an honor to meet you."

Susan smiled. "The honor is all mine."

President Qing skipped pleasantries and went straight to business. "I've heard from my finance minister and my military advisors that you want to meet. What is so urgent?"

Susan took a calm breath. "The Soviet Union is on the brink of starting a war in Eastern Europe. And I think you can help stop it."

President Qing's face hardened. "What does a war in Eastern Europe have to do with China? And why would I help you?"

SELECTED

Susan nodded. "I'm not asking you to help me. I'm asking you to help the world and help China." Susan paused. President Qing remained silent. She continued, "A war in Eastern Europe is bad for everyone. Global trade will come to an abrupt halt. Everybody loses."

President Qing frowned and remained silent.

Susan continued, "I organized a trade summit with the leaders of Ukraine, Belarus, Latvia, and the Soviet Union to discuss the oil and gas pipeline being constructed in their countries. I want you to be a part of that agreement. The United States can offer you a ten percent reduction in tariffs for your participation."

President Qing crossed his arms. "What do you want in return?"

"In return, I'm asking you to come up with a way for China and the Soviet Union to become economic partners. It's the only way President Tremonov will adhere to a peaceful relationship with the other Eastern European countries."

President Qing stroked his chin. "It has become difficult for us to obtain the natural gas and oil required to support the recent population growth in Beijing. The Soviet Union has an oil and natural gas reserve near the area. I have reached out to them on several occasions to discuss a rail system. They have ignored my communication on the topic."

Susan nodded. "How long since you last reached out to them?"

President Qing raised his eyebrow. "I'm not sure, maybe three years ago. But the Soviets are in a desperate economic situation. I don't see how they could pass up the opportunity."

Susan leaned forward. "Would you be willing to propose the idea again at tomorrow's meeting?"

President Qing responded, "What assurance do I have that the Soviets will keep their word?"

Susan took a deep breath. "Every country will vote on whether to continue the partnership on a quarterly basis. If the Soviets break their agreement with China, the United States will dissolve the partnership. President Tremonov will gain two powerful enemies: the United States and China. Tremonov is no fool. He won't risk fighting a two-front war against the United States and China."

President Qing nodded in agreement. "I'll propose the idea. But that is all I can do. I have no control over President Tremonov."

SELECTED

Susan stood up and shook hands with President Qing. "I understand. I'll have a representative from our trade office meet with your finance minister to talk details. President Tremonov doesn't know you're attending the meeting tomorrow. Please keep this information secret."

President Qing responded, "You have my word. I'm glad we had the chance to meet in person. I look forward to strengthening the relationship between our countries."

48

The Eastern European trade meeting included four nations: the Soviet Union, Ukraine, Belarus, and Latvia. Susan waited until the other leaders arrived in the conference room to inform them that the Chinese president would be joining the meeting.

She requested that the Chinese leader, President Qing, arrive five minutes late in order to give Susan an opportunity to inform the other leaders of his attendance. By keeping the Chinese involvement a secret, Susan led President Tremonov to believe that he still had the upper hand in the negotiations.

As the leaders entered the room, Susan warmly greeted each of them and kindly asked them to place all electronic devices at the far end of the table. It was overly cautious but she couldn't take the chance of an information leak.

Fresh flowers were placed on a table at the entrance to the conference room. In front of each chair was an eloquent black

SELECTED

placard with a name printed in gold letters, accompanied by a small centerpiece of flowers and a pitcher of fresh water. Coffee, tea, and assorted pastries were at the far end of the conference room table. Susan's nameplate was at the head of the conference room table, with President Tremonov to her right and President Qing to her left.

The leaders of Belarus, Latvia, and the Ukraine arrived just before 9:00 a.m. Susan graciously greeted them and explained that the Chinese president was invited at her request. She gave her word that the Chinese involvement would be beneficial to all of Eastern Europe. She casually looked down at her watch: 9:06 and President Qing had yet to arrive. She felt a bead of sweat begin to form on her lower back. Susan moved toward the door of the conference room with the intention of ducking quickly outside to check if President Qing had arrived. She was three strides from the door when it was quickly flung open. President Qing walked through the door accompanied by two security guards in black suits, white shirts, and black ties. They wore similar clothes to the American Secret Service agents but their presence was much more ominous. They looked more like Triad hit men than presidential security guards.

After exchanging brief pleasantries with Susan, President Qing scanned the room. All other conversations ceased after he entered the room; the other leaders stared at Susan and President Qing. Susan immediately recognized the awkwardness of the situation and began the introductions.

"President Qing, allow me to introduce you to the rest of the group." Susan stepped in front of President Qing and walked across the room.

President Qing cautiously followed Susan. After the formal introductions, the president of Belarus made a joke about the pastries and his wife complaining about his weight. President Qing laughed, and the ice was broken.

President Qing relaxed and mingled with the rest of the group. Susan's anxiety doubled with every minute that passed. President Tremonov was a no-show. The conversation between the leaders began to die down. Susan looked at her watch—it read 9:15. Susan dragged out the conversation with stories about Greg and Tommy.

At 9:18, President Tremonov walked into the room with the look of a king standing above his peasants. He scanned the room and his posture went rigid. Susan quickly pounced on President Tremonov and greeted him with a smile and a handshake. Before Tremonov could completely process the situation, Susan stepped behind him and closed and locked the conference room door. She didn't get to see the look of shock on Tremonov's face, but the other leaders had a front row seat.

Immediately after she locked the door, Susan disarmed Tremonov. "You missed out on tea and crumpets." Tremonov's face was blank; he muttered under his breath in Russian. Susan walked to her chair at the head of the table. The rest of the leaders also sat down at the conference room table.

President Qing broke the awkwardness. "President Tremonov, please have a seat, we're all very interested in working with you."

Tremonov's pride wouldn't allow him to leave the room. He silently walked over to the seat with his name placard and sat down. Susan's trap had worked—not exactly as planned, but it worked. Tremonov and Qing were at the table together. What happened at the table was up to them.

Susan opened up the speaking by formally thanking everyone for their attendance and commitment to peace in the region. "This morning, I want to discuss the framework for a unilateral trade agreement between our countries. As a starting point for the agreement, the United States will reduce all tariffs on goods imported to the United States from China by ten percent." Susan paused to let the message sink in. "And we will eliminate tariffs on all goods imported to the United States from the Ukraine, Belarus, and Latvia."

Susan scanned the room and settled her eyes on President Tremonov. "The United States will also reduce tariffs on goods imported from the Soviet Union by ten percent."

Susan briefly scanned the room again. She held her gaze on President Qing. "Are there any objections?"

Susan waited. Then she smiled. "Fantastic, point one of the Eastern European and Chinese Trade Agreement is settled."

President Tremonov sharply interrupted, "I didn't agree to anything."

Susan replied, "Is a five percent reduction in tariffs better for you?" Her quick wit got a chuckle from the other leaders.

Tremonov's face turned a dark pink with anger. "Stop the charade. What do you want in return?"

"It's not about what I want, President Tremonov. It's about what we—"

Tremonov's anger got the best of him and he interrupted before Susan could finish. "Who do you mean by we?"

Susan replied, "The leaders of the world. The 'we' includes

you."

President Tremonov moved his cold stare to President Qing, who nodded his head in agreement with Susan. Susan noted the slight weakening of Tremonov's posture and jumped into the conversation. "As the leaders of the world, we want peace and prosperity for all of humanity." Everyone at the table nodded in agreement.

"Agreed," grunted Tremonov.

"Fantastic," replied Susan.

The president of the Ukraine jumped into the conversation. "I speak on behalf of Ukraine, Belarus, and Latvia." He nodded his head toward each country's leader as he spoke. "In the spirit of peace and prosperity, we are proposing that the workforce used to build and maintain the Soviet pipeline through our countries be staffed with seventy-five percent local workers, who will be managed by the government. We will not ask for a percentage of the profits from the oil and natural gas flowing through the pipelines, only a portion of the construction and maintenance work for our people."

President Tremonov stiffened in his chair. The knuckles on his right hand turned white and he increased the pressure of his grip on the edge of the table.

President Qing interrupted before Tremonov could respond. "President Tremonov, I believe this arrangement will leave you with idle workers. I have a proposal to employ those workers that will benefit us all."

Tremonov furrowed his brow and stared at President Qing.

President Qing continued, "I would like to begin the construction of a pipeline between your largest oil fields in the southeastern region of the Soviet Union directly into Beijing. And eventually a railroad line following the same routes. I'm open to your thoughts on how to collaborate on such a project."

President Tremonov cleared his throat and scanned the room. He was wary of the offer from the Chinese. "What are your terms for purchasing oil and natural gas from the Soviet Union?"

President Qing replied, "We will agree to the same terms as your European customers. I hope that this is a first step in our countries becoming business partners."

The focus of the room went back to President Tremonov.

SELECTED

"Over half of the pipeline will be within the Chinese border. What capital investment are you willing to make?"

President Qing smiled. "Our engineers estimate the project will cost a total of fifteen billion dollars. As a part of the agreement, both of our countries will contribute five billion dollars to the project as an up-front capital investment. It will keep us both honest."

Tremonov looked around the room. He took a moment to consider the offer. "The details need to be worked out. In principle, I agree."

President Qing stood up and in good faith extended his hand across the table toward Tremonov. Tremonov stood up, looked President Qing in the eye, and shook his hand.

President Tremonov sat back down in his chair with a sense of accomplishment. In his mind, he had gained an alliance with the Chinese and lost nothing in the relationship with Eastern Europe. Trade negotiations were notoriously difficult to enforce and he had no intention of honoring any agreements made with his Eastern European neighbors.

Susan looked around the room. "Now that we're all friends and economic partners, let's make sure we stay friends. As part of this agreement, we will hold a quarterly conference. At that conference, each country will vote whether or not the agreement should continue. If more than one country votes against the agreement, all tariffs and agreements between countries will be reset to their present state as of today." She paused to let the information sink in.

Susan focused on Tremonov. He curled his front lip and shot her a hard stare.

Susan looked around the room. "Do we all agree?"

President Tremonov looked down at the table. He couldn't deny the agreement had the potential to pull the Soviet Union out of a depression. If he violated the agreement with the Eastern European countries, they would surely vote to end the agreement. The Chinese would block the port of Vladivostok in retaliation. At that point, the Soviet Union would face the threat of fighting a two-front war against China and the NATO coalition. Tremonov cursed himself for allowing the American, a woman, to back him into a corner.

One by one, each leader verbally replied, "Yes."

President Tremonov was the last. He stared at Susan with cold eyes. He finally relented. "Yes."

After Tremonov's commitment to the agreement, Susan

stood up. "Gentlemen, the world is a better place when we are peaceful allies and economic partners. Today we made great strides in a positive direction for humanity."

President Qing stood up and started the celebration by clapping. The other leaders followed.

49

Susan collapsed into her seat on Air Force One, the effects of sleep deprivation hitting her hard. Before asking her any questions, General LeMae handed her a Miller Lite and Senator Reynolds tossed her a package of Reese's Cups King Size. Susan cracked open the beer and took a long swallow.

Senator Reynolds couldn't hold back his curiosity. "So what happened?"

Susan raised her eyebrows and shrugged her shoulders. "Tremonov agreed to the railway between his oil fields and Beijing. I really didn't have any control over what was happening. It was up to Tremonov and Qing. They made it happen."

Senator Reynolds shook his head in disbelief. "Wow, I didn't think they would ever agree to work together."

Susan took another long swallow of Miller Lite. "Tremonov had no choice. The Soviet Union has some real economic problems."

General LeMae kept a serious look on his face before asking, "You think Tremonov will hold to the agreement?"

"I think so. If he doesn't, the Chinese are going to be awfully upset. He won't risk agitating powerful enemies to the east and west," said Susan.

General LeMae nodded his head. "He's no fool. He won't risk starting a two-front war."

Susan slouched in her seat. "Don't celebrate yet. If I get impeached, I won't be able to follow through on our end of the deal."

Senator Reynolds sighed. "I've got some bad news on that front."

Susan opened the package of Reese's Cups. "Can't be any tougher than what I just went through."

"Vice President Wilkes has been the person drumming up support for your impeachment. Through the grapevine, my staff found out he's been meeting with senators and congressmen and pushing them to consider your lack of action against the Soviet Union as an act of treason."

"Since when did it become treason to be cautious about starting a war with another nuclear power?" replied Susan.

"My staff just started to put the pieces together this week. Of course, there's no tangible evidence, it's all hearsay. Wilkes did a good job covering his tracks."

General LeMae jumped in. "I knew it. I should have cut that son of a bitch off at the knees when I had the chance," he grumbled under his breath before changing topics. "I got word from General Gillingham that the NSA analysts don't believe the terror attacks were tied to the Soviets. They think it was a domestic terrorist. Sophisticated, but domestic. No suspects at this point and it doesn't look promising. Whoever did it, they were a pro. Likely trained by one of our intelligence groups."

Susan turned to General LeMae. "Can you get General Gillingham to make that statement publicly?"

General LeMae nodded and smiled. "I don't think it'll be a problem."

The engines came to life as Air Force One picked up speed on the tarmac. Susan finished her beer, closed her eyes, and fell asleep before they reached cruising altitude.

She was homesick and missed the boys. Talking over Skype

in the evenings was better than nothing but it just wasn't the same as being there in person. Her heart sank every time she ended a Skype call with the boys.

While Susan crossed the Atlantic Ocean back to Washington, DC, President Tremonov and President Qing both made public statements in Geneva praising the newly agreed upon trade agreement. Photos of the two leaders shaking hands and smiling found their way into the twenty-four-hour news cycle. President Tremonov released a press statement to the Pravda newspaper in the Soviet Union stating that effective immediately, the security threat level would be officially reduced to the normal peacetime level of DEFCON 5.

Vice President Wilkes walked out of his attorney's office with his wife. They stood on the street corner. She turned to him and asked, "Honey, I know I've been pestering you for years to update our will. But why did we have to do it in such a rush today?"

Vice President Wilkes looked his wife in the eye and smiled warmly. "I love you, dear. I've been planning this for a long time. I don't know why I held off for so long. I just wanted to get it over with, while it was on my mind." He kissed her on the cheek. "I need to be at the Senate session this evening. I'll be late for dinner." Vice President Wilkes gave his wife one last hug and walked slowly to the Senate building.

At 8:00 that evening, the Senate met to vote on whether to proceed with impeachment hearings for President Turner. The Senate hearing occurred after the results of the Eastern European Trade Agreement were made public and after the statements of peace were made by President Tremonov and President Qing.

The Senate floor rocked with chatter. Vice President Wilkes confidently walked through the chaos up to the podium and struck the gavel three times. The Senate floor quickly silenced. All eyes in the room went to Vice President Wilkes.

Vice President Wilkes cleared his throat and began, "Friends and colleagues, in recent months many of you have listened to me point out the flaws of President Turner. I'm ashamed to say, my motivation for criticizing President Turner was not for the good of the country. Although I led you to believe President Turner was leading the country down a destructive path, it was I who was leading the country down a destructive path. I allowed myself to be blinded for selfish gain. Instead of admitting my own faults, I chose to lash out at

SELECTED

President Turner. And in doing so, I put the country at risk, and I put the lives of Americans at risk." Vice President Wilkes paused and looked down at the podium.

He continued, "I'm here to say I'm sorry. I apologize for misrepresenting President Turner's actions and pushing for her impeachment trial. President Turner is a shining example of what we all should strive for as leaders. The effectiveness of her leadership was proven this week by the instrumental role she played creating the Eastern European Trade Agreement. As we saw earlier today by the statements from President Tremonov and President Qing, the trade agreement will serve as the foundation for a peaceful partnership between the United States, the Soviet Union, and China. I ask not for your forgiveness but for your action. President Turner should be praised for her leadership in such turbulent times, not admonished. Please follow me and vote to dismiss the impeachment trial against President Turner. Thank you."

Vice President Wilkes left the podium. A small group of senators stood and clapped. They were quickly followed by the entire Senate floor. The Senate voted unanimously, 50–0, in favor of ending the impeachment trial of President Turner. Vice President Wilkes left the Senate building to meet his fate.

50

Susan walked into the White House dining room. Greg and Tommy both jumped up from the breakfast table and came running at her with open arms. Earl and Rose listened closely as Susan answered an onslaught of questions from Greg and Tommy about her trip. The aim of their questions moved from her trip to whether she was getting fired, and, subsequently, whether that meant they were moving back to Idaho.

Susan felt the stares of Earl and Rose pressing on her as she answered Greg and Tommy's questions about her impeachment. She explained that the Senate voted to stop the hearings and they weren't moving back to Idaho.

After breakfast, Susan rode with the boys to school and then headed to the White House. On the ride back to the White House, Susan called Mason Adams and arranged a press briefing on the White House lawn. The major news outlets had already started to run with bits and pieces of information about the trade agreement, the potential bombing suspects, and the dismissal of her impeachment trial.

Susan took the podium on the White House lawn just after 2:00 p.m. It was seventy-five degrees with 80 percent humidity. There was no escaping the inevitable stream of sweat that would be pouring down her forehead. The crowd gathered on the White House lawn was silent as she delivered her prepared remarks. Her prepared remarks addressed three main points:

The trade deal would be beneficial to all countries and deescalate the tension that had built up in the region.

She reiterated General Gillingham's previous statement. The Soviet Union had been ruled out as an entity that supported the bombings in Washington, DC, Atlanta, and Los Angeles.

She concluded by highlighting the peaceful resolution to the tensions in Eastern Europe.

After finishing her prepared remarks, Susan opened up to questions from the press. She fielded several softball questions about her impeachment trial and evidence gathered about the bombings. Susan relaxed at the podium and answered the questions from the press with a warm smile. She felt the press finally accepted her as the president and was on her side.

Susan confidently joked, "All right, one last question, then I need to get back in the air conditioning before I sweat through this dress." A young female reporter caught Susan's attention with an enthusiastic wave and a smile. Susan gave her the last question of the briefing.

"Madam President, several sources inside your administration have alleged that your lack of a response to the Soviet Union's aggression has caused our enemies to lose respect for the United States and that loss of respect will result in future terror attacks on American soil."

Susan took a deep breath and looked down at the podium for inspiration before responding. She picked her head up and looked out into the crowd. She saw reporters exchanging nervous glances. Susan felt her own heartbeat and the heartbeat of the crowd accelerate like a freight train.

"I have no control over what will happen in the future. I can't control the actions of our allies or our enemies. But I can control how we respond." Susan took a breath. "For those who believe that war is the answer: think long and hard about the impact of your words. Unlike many who are quick to espouse the virtues of war . . . I've seen firsthand the horrors of war. I've seen the horrors of war from the battlefield and as a grieving widow. I understand their long-lasting impact. For the rest of my life, I'll live with those memories. I promise you . . . I will go to the ends of the earth to find a peaceful solution before resorting to war."

Susan paused again to let her response resonate with the audience.

"The last few months have been difficult. It's easy to get caught up in ideology and hatred. When you talk to your friends, your neighbors, your coworkers, your family, and strangers on the street, give everyone the same amount of respect. We all have different opinions; don't allow those differences of opinion be the basis for hatred. Hatred and violence have no place in our society. A genuine respect for each other and thoughtful discourse will illuminate the road to a peaceful and prosperous future.

"We live in America, the greatest democracy in the history of the world. This is a country where we embrace healthy discourse. After we have a healthy conversation, we may still disagree with our neighbor, but afterward we can sit down together and share a soda as friends. Every single person should be treated with respect, no matter their race, color, religion, gender, sexual orientation, or age. We are all Americans. That's the America I know. And that's the America we fight every day to keep."

J. ALLEN WOLFRUM

Susan stepped down from the podium to a standing ovation from the audience. For Americans, Susan's words triggered a realization of how close they had come to being involved in a tragic, needless, life-changing war against the Soviet Union. Across the country, Americans awoke with a renewed sense of community

.

51

Susan found her father in the map room of the White House. He was sitting alone and reading the newspaper. She sat down across the table from him.

Earl lowered the newspaper and said, "You don't look happy."

"You know what? I don't feel happy."

Earl folded the paper and put it on the table. "What's on your mind?"

"Lots . . . When I first accepted the selection, I thought I had things under control. Then it kept spiraling out of control. I felt like I was always one step behind. I just don't know if I can keep going at this pace."

Earl took a breath and fidgeted with the paper. "If you ask me; you've done a hell of a job keeping this country afloat. I know it's impossible, but you can't let what gets printed in the newspaper impact how you feel about the decisions you —"

"I don't care about the newspaper articles saying that I

compromised our national security by entering into a trade agreement with China. They're just plain wrong and I'm over it. They'll never know everything that happened behind the scenes. I did the right thing, that's enough for me. I'm concerned about the impact on Greg and Tommy. Tommy already got into a fight at school because of me."

Earl exhaled. "Have you explained it to the boys?"

"No, not yet."

"I think they're old enough to understand. If you give them some context around the rumors, it'll be a lot easier for them to process."

Susan nodded. "You're right, I need to have a talk with them. I've been trying to keep them as far away from all this nonsense as possible. But they need to know the truth."

"It's a good life lesson for the boys."

"Oh yeah, what's the lesson? Never trust the media?"

"No . . . Trust your heart and do the right thing, no matter what people might think afterwards."

Susan stood up, hugged her father and gave him a kiss on the forehead. "Dad, you're always right."

Epilogue

Mr. Anderson confidently walked over to the office window and looked down on Los Angeles. He reflected on his failed attempt to lure the United States into a war with the Soviet Union. The cell phone in his pocket vibrated and he answered the call. "This is Mr. Anderson."

Mr. Anderson continued to stare out the window as he listened to the voice on the other end. He responded, "I understand your concern. I assure you, we remain on schedule. The Board's objectives are not in jeopardy. This is a minor setback. The timeline for Unified Peace remains unchanged. I will provide a detailed debriefing and update on the path forward at the next Board meeting."

Mr. Anderson ended the call and put the phone back into his pocket. He stared out the window for a moment and calmly went back to work at his desk.

ABOUT THE AUTHOR

J. Allen Wolfrum is a fiction author and former Marine. He served four years as a Marine Corps Infantryman in the most decorated Regiment in Marine Corps history. During Operation Iraqi Freedom he led an infantry squad on missions spanning from the oil fields of Southern Iraq to the streets of Baghdad.

After the Marine Corps, he spent the next fifteen years exploring life from several perspectives: press operator in a plastics factory, warehouse stocker, confused college student, Certified Public Accountant, bearded graduate student, management consultant, and data analyst.

J. Allen Wolfrum's writing career began in 2017 with his debut novel, Selected. He uses the unique combination of his Marine Corps, professional and life experience to create a realistic perspective on the political thriller genre. He lives in Southern California with his beautiful wife and two cats.

He publishes a weekly column about reading, writing and life on his website www.jallenwolfrum.com.

90124358R00255

Made in the USA
Columbia, SC
26 February 2018